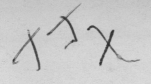
"Get the hell out, while you got a chance, Morton, " Landry shouted. "I've got a posse that will be looking for me."

"Maybe. Maybe not," Rattlesnake Morton called. "We will be watching for you and for them, if they exist. And if they do—we just might give them a Morton welcome." The outlaw rider laughed. "Now let's get serious. The only water around here is in the old town up above. Course, we don't plan on letting you get to it. So you do the only other thing. You go into the desert. There's water in three days, maybe." He laughed heartily. "So we'll follow you, and we'll find you. And if you are still alive, we'll put you out of your misery. You might welcome that, Landry. You ever see a man swell up in the heat, his tongue big and black till it chokes him?" Morton chuckled loudly, then changed his tone. "You can't get away, Landry. Nowhere you run. Nowhere you turn."

Heartsick, Landry lay back. Now he was in the desert with no horse, no food, and no water. . . .

*Also by Kenn Sherwood Roe:*

MOONBLOOD

# DUST
# DEVIL

## Kenn Sherwood Roe

FAWCETT GOLD MEDAL · NEW YORK

A Fawcett Gold Medal Book
Published by Ballantine Books
Copyright © 1992 by Kenn Sherwood Roe

All rights reserved under International and Pan-American Copyright Conventions. Published in the United States by Ballantine Books, a division of Random House, Inc., New York, and simultaneously in Canada by Random House of Canada Limited, Toronto.

Library of Congress Catalog Card Number: 91-93158

ISBN 0-449-14778-9

Manufactured in the United States of America

First Edition: May 1992

To my parents,
who
gave so much love,
assistance, and support

# (1)

Anxious and a little heavy of heart, U.S. Marshal Dirk Landry watched the lumbering mule ahead carrying the hunched figure of Billy Temple, an old friend and known prospector in the bleak stretches of southwestern Nevada. A shotgun crossed in his arms, the old man led a pack mule heaped with provisions for the boy and girl in the ghost town ahead. Behind came Deputy Dale Thomas on a black gelding; although only twenty-two, in his three months as a lawman he had proven himself dedicated and capable. His boyish face belied an ingrained toughness inherited from his father—a longtime associate of the marshal, a respected man who had been back-shot, the murderer never found.

Several days earlier Temple had sought the assistance of Landry. His partner, Noah Crawford, had left working their mountain mine on a sudden and unexplained trip to Silverpoint, a small town to the north. Normally a round-trip took some five days. But when ten had crawled by, Crawford's two children became concerned and fearful of foul play. It was unlike Crawford to leave Vallee and Seth without any explanation other than to take care of personal business that had demanded immediate attention. Realizing he could wait no longer, Temple had set out to Silverpoint, reluctantly leaving the two alone, but when he could find no one who recalled seeing his partner, he had headed after the marshal, north again to Limbo City.

Far below, at the foot of the mountain, sweeping around them, stretched the yellow-gray of stark desert, punctuated by barren hills and separated by alkali sinks. The three men

1

had come south paralleling a high snow-flecked range that
afforded adequate water holes. The major route, although
roundabout, ran in marshy land between the White Mountains and the high central plateau of wilderness desert. Deliberately, they had avoided a direct line across the latter, a
blazing wasteland. For all his years patrolling, Landry had
always feared the shimmering vastness, knowing that for all
its lonely beauty, it could kill cruelly those who did not respect it.

Now at nearly eight thousand feet, the yellow-green of
juniper mingled newly with the rounded blue of pinyon, all
young growth, but quickly thickening. Years earlier the
mountain, a strikingly blunt rise out of the flatland, had been
stripped of trees to supply wood for the mines, and coal for
the smelters in Desert Roost, a town long dead but where
Temple and Crawford had taken up their mining.

Ahead through the trees the rise of mountain opened, revealing windowless buildings and hoisting works, inter-
locked by ghostly head frames and crumbling tramways. As
they approached, the ruins became evident: broken flumes,
a leaning water tower, the stretches between slag piles snaked
with braided steel cable and strewn with cylinders, drums,
giant spools, pulleys, flywheels, and pipes—the legacy of a
once prosperous town. A rising wind played mournfully
through the frames.

Where the remains of the old road ended, Temple edged
his mule toward the best-looking building; once the superintendent's cabin, it linked to an elongated structure that connected to the main mine drift above. Desert Roost, with a
peak population of three thousand, had been a producer of
both gold and silver more than a decade earlier; but the rich
veins had petered out quickly, shattering the dreams of a
bonanza. And with depressed silver prices, the town had
quickly emptied; the Wells Fargo office, the banks, the news-
paper folding almost overnight. Only the saloons and gam-
bling palaces had hung on for a time to satisfy the last patrons.

Landry, a big man with broad shoulders and a lanky frame,
sat high on his horse. His face was narrow, with a wide

forehead and a generous mouth that mocked more than smiled. His strong-angled nose had been broken, revealing a brawling youth. The quiet gray eyes moved constantly, observing, assessing, recording. There was purpose in his every move, an overbearing presence that made strangers aware of him and a little uneasy—they sensed he could be dangerous if provoked.

As they approached, Landry shifted in the saddle with discomfort; he favored his left leg, holding it out to ease the pain that still wracked his shattered hip. The old wound, which had left him permanently disabled, had come after the trial. The Osmand boys had ambushed him, splattering him with buckshot, because their old man had been sentenced to hang. After a painful recovery, Landry had hunted them down one by one.

They could hear the dog, Mono, barking. Billy Temple swung slowly in the saddle, directing his words at Landry. He had been carefully studying the sage-covered terraces. "Usually have grouse around here. Been lookin' for an hour now. One or two would make good fixin's for the kids." As they broke into full view of the town, the prospector changed his concern. "Don't see no sign of Crawford's horse. He barns it in that tin shack up yonder. He still ain't returned." Landry nodded soberly. A chunky man, Temple's chest had sunk around his midsection with age. Under the flop of a wide-brimmed hat, his ponderous features were lost in wiry gray whiskers. He had wise blue eyes set deep in leathery skin, sinewed and cross-hatched by countless seasons in the desert.

The bullet whacked over their heads, snapping a pinyon branch. The buckskin skewed in fear, tossed, and came down to dance sideways. Quickly the men kneed their animals into cover. A dog barked from the building. Clearly the bullet had been meant as a warning. The old man cupped his hands around his mouth: "Vallee, Seth—it's me, Temple."

There was a long, anxious silence. "That you, Billy?" came a high voice.

"Me and Marshal Landry and a deputy."

"Sounds like you, Billy, but let's see you."

"Smart girl." Billy motioned toward Landry and led the way out, both letting the animals saunter in a natural way.

The open door widened and a girl emerged carrying a Winchester rifle. "Thank God," she said. "Oh, thank God. I thought something for sure had happened to you." A rangy yellow dog with short hair emerged after her, to wag vigorously and sniff at the animals.

"Did my best, kids." Temple dismounted and hugged the girl.

She squeezed him in delight, her eyes shut. Then she regarded Landry with relief. "I'm glad to see you, Marshal." Landry tipped his hat. Her eyes hesitated with interest on Deputy Thomas, then she looked away quickly.

Landry blinked, disbelieving. He had not seen Vallee Crawford for several seasons. He guessed her seventeen now, a full bodied young woman with soft white skin—dressed in a long gray dress, slightly scooped at the neck, with the sleeves trimmed at the elbows to give her freedom. She had a pleasantly statuesque appearance, especially with her long brown hair pulled back with a ribbon to reveal a shapely neck and head. Her blue eyes had dilated and her cheeks had pinkened from fright. The flushed exhilaration gave her a robust vitality.

From behind her, smiling, Seth Crawford emerged jerkily on a makeshift crutch; he appeared frail, smaller than his twelve years. There had been two children between Vallee and Seth, both dying before their first year. The mother had succumbed from complications after giving birth to Seth. He had been born with a club foot, but had learned to handle the disability with quiet acceptance.

"Ain't like you, Vallee, to shoot at people. Something spook you?" Temple challenged. Both the girl and her brother blurted words and stopped, looking at one another. "You, Vallee, you tell me first."

"Mono, here, he started growling mid-afternoon yesterday, and kept it up until it got light this morning. We couldn't sleep," Vallee answered.

"Yeah, and we heard something movin' out here—all around us," Seth added, wide-eyed.

"Did you see anything?" Temple pursued. "It's almost a full moon."

Vallee shook her head decisively. "No, not a thing. At first we thought it might be a mountain lion." She turned toward the marshal and added, "We've had them up here before."

"Why at first?" Temple asked.

"Because we could hear it crunching around now and then. And a mountain lion don't make those sounds. And Mono." She pointed at the dog, its soleful eyes and floppy ears humorous. "He acted different than when it's an animal on the prowl."

"Appears like you had a human visitor snooping around," Landry interjected. "A bear would be bulky enough to crash around, but I never saw signs of one in this part of the country. Too much open desert around the mountain."

"Me neither," said Temple. "I shouldn't of left you two alone here."

"But we wanted to stay," Seth protested.

"Ornery brats, they was," said Temple, looking at Landry as if to explain. "Besides, their pappy didn't leave no horses, and I didn't want them to walk, not in this godforsaken country."

"Awful glad you're all here," said Vallee.

"Any sign of your father?" Landry asked.

"Nothing," said Vallee. "Not a thing. It's been near two weeks now."

"We even said some prayers for Pop," Seth added. They both stood sadly.

Temple looked tenderly at the young people. "I'm sorry. Real sorry." He turned to the marshal. "He shouldn't have been gone more than five or six days, at the most."

"We was gettin' low on everything," said Seth.

"Well, we brung you some goods," said Temple, untying the packload. Landry moved to assist him. Deputy Thomas dismounted, his eyes on the girl. "Got you kids something special." Temple removed a tarpaulin and dug into a leather pouch, producing a handful of stringed licorice and hard rock candy. Gleefully, Seth reached out and clutched some. Daintily, Vallee selected a few pieces. "Ain't through with you, girl. Here, for that skin of yours."

Vallee squealed when she saw him produce a blue bonnet with white trim. "Oh, Billy, I wouldn't have expected this of you." She squeezed his big arm. "And then again, I guess I would." Immediately she fitted it on, primping and tucking curls out of the way. She looked at the men, her blue eyes dancing under the frame of the hat. "I'm going to look at myself," she said, moving swiftly toward the building.

Grinning, Seth crunched noisily into a mint candy. "It would taste even better if Pop was here."

The three men began unloading the mule, carrying goods into the home. It was a clean and simple building with three rooms. The main one was large, with rough-hewn furniture on one side and a stove on the other, backed by a wall with shelves of cooking utensils and dried goods. In the adjoining room, which Crawford and his son shared, they could see bunk beds. There, Vallee was swaying and posing before a small round mirror on a wall.

Landry smiled, laughing to himself. "That was nice of you," he said to Temple when they were out of the girl's hearing.

"I've grown kind of fond of them kids," he said. "Too bad about their pappy. I don't understand. It's not like Noah to go off and not say a thing to me or especially to his kids. And what did you make of someone prowling about?"

"Doesn't sound good," said Landry. "After we've settled things in, we best look around. Might find something out there that'll clue us in on what's going on."

"I'll show you the operation, too." Temple grunted, placing a cask of flour down. They packed in basic staples of bacon, salt, sugar, beans, and coffee. Vallee, who had emerged to watch, clasped her hands in glee as she saw cans of tomatoes, and corn, and a plump sack of dried apples.

"Oooh, now maybe I can feed my family with something

imaginative," she bubbled. But Landry could see through her brave pretense that she was worried for her father and his whereabouts.

"You make that sled?" Landry asked her, motioning to a crude flat of boards nailed crosswise by several two-by-fours with a loop of rope at one end.

"Me and Seth—yes."

"By God," Temple exclaimed, "I didn't see that. Vallee, you was preparin' to pull Seth out of here. Pull him down the mountain, wasn't you?"

"Me and Seth, we had to do something eventually, if you didn't come back. And Papa. God only knows what's happened to Papa." Her voice caught with emotion.

"But after you got down the mountain, you couldn't have pulled that thing across the desert. You'd have died out there."

"I didn't plan on pulling him. With his crutch or even a cane, Seth can do real well. In fact, he gets around tolerably good without anything. I would have pulled goods—especially water—on the sled. I remembered when Papa brought us here. I remember the road along the big mountains to the north, water holes all green and pretty under them. We would have gone that way. Somebody out there would have come across us, I figured. Got us to a camp or town someplace. If you didn't come back, Billy, we'd have had to leave, with no more food or provisions. Or if an early snow came. You know how it can be up here."

Disarmed, Temple smiled warmly, sweetly. "God bless you, child, you got courage. And you was thinkin'. You was thinkin' good."

Vallee looked imploringly at Landry. "Do you have any idea about Papa? You knew him. Do you think you can track him somehow? I'm awful scared, Mr. Marshal." The girl bit her lower lip and crossed her hands over her chest. Touched by her concern, Seth limped up beside her, leaning on his crutch for support.

"I can't promise anything, Vallee," Landry said gently. "But that's why I'm here, to find out what I can."

Vallee smiled. "You can't imagine how much we all appreciate that, Marshal. Now, I'm gonna fix a good supper tonight. And I'll start right now."

"I'll make the biscuits," said Temple. "You know me and my biscuits. You get the fire going and I'll knead the dough."

"You wash up good, then. I don't want no desert grits in my food."

"Seth, you take care of my mule, and the deputy's black, and Mr. Landry's buckskin here," Temple told the boy. "Feed 'em oats. We'll curry 'em down after supper."

"You had a beautiful big chestnut, last I remember," said the boy to Landry.

Landry smiled. "This is my desert horse. I call him my camel."

Although Landry preferred his chestnut gelding, he had chosen the buckskin, a favorite for desert treks. The deep-chested mustang, with its black mane and tail, had been born in the south central desert, somewhere in the Kawich Range, where it had run in a wild herd before capture. It had an amazing tolerance for heat and for the dry wastes, with a minimal need for water.

The three men and the dog walked out back, where the afternoon sun arrowed long shadows up the talus slope from the myriad hoists and headframes. Landry's hitching stride kept an easy pace with the others. Some two hundred feet behind the house, not far from a wooden tramway that had once brought ore to a steam crusher, lay a shallow pit with fresh tailings.

Temple pointed above it to where a mighty slab of mountain had slid away. "I come up here two springs ago for fresh water and to get away from the summer heat. I thought the old town was all worked out, but it ain't. Apparently there must have been an earthquake, or maybe just the weight of the winter snows. But a part of that mountainside up there fell away some seasons back. And lo and behold, it opened up a whole pocket of rich gold." He walked to where they had been gouging the ground with pick and shovel and kicked away a nipple of quartz, picked it up and handed it to Landry. In the pearly white stone the lawman could see flecks of high grade metal. "Some of them samples we dug are nearly half gold."

Thomas took the rock from Landry's hand and studied it, his eyes widening. Temple continued, his voice lilting with the remembrance. "I went to Limbo City and staked a claim. That's when I looked up Crawford for a grubstake. But he wanted to see it with his own eyes. So I brung him back here. When he seen such rich ore, we become partners, with him in charge, 'cause it's his money carrying us."

"Looks like you finally hit it," said Landry, pleased for Temple.

"Come on," the old man said, beckoning them to the long wooden tramway. "This building connects to where Crawford and his family live, what used to be the superintendent's place. We been keeping our take in here, and much of it— what we've crushed by hand—in the storage shed back of his place." Temple opened the door. Several dozen sacks of ore lay piled along one side. "Soon we plan to buy a train of mules and pack all this out to the state mint before winter."

"Shortly, you can afford clean sheets, catered meals, and a rocker before the fireplace," said Landry jovially.

"Maybe, but I ain't quite ready for that yet."

"At first there were rumors in town," Landry said. "Everyone wondered why Crawford had sold his store and cleared out. Then we learned he was mining. Now I see why he did what he did. Never dreamed you two had anything like this."

"He wants to give his kids a good life, a chance. He loves them more than anything," Temple said seriously, wagging his head. "That's why him taking off just don't make sense."

Landry swayed his head in agreement. Raising the children, especially the girl, had been hard for Crawford, but he had managed with household help. Now, the gold pocket promised the security that he sought.

"Mighty strange, when you think how many people must

have walked over this pocket," said Temple. "Day after day, over some of the richest ore in town, right under their nose."

"Of course, this may be all that's left," Landry reminded. "It may not lead to any more."

"Of course. We know that. But it's plenty enough for us, or at least for me."

"Well, as I said, I'm glad for you and Crawford. Now if we can just find him, he might enjoy all his efforts here." The three men ventured through the old town, took a climb to gray outcrops above the cabin. For nearly an hour they looked about, finding nothing other than the natural growth of sage and rabbit bush blooming profusely amongst the mining paraphernalia and crumbling ruins.

As early evening shadows darkened the slope, Billy Temple turned back toward the cabin, a slow rheumatic hitch in his stride. "Got to get back and scrub up. Promised Vallee, you know, that I'd make them biscuits."

Cutting downslope, they crossed a narrow flat, jumbled with broken boulders. "Look, there," Thomas remarked. All three froze. The crusted droppings of a horse were spread in a protected enclosure, the earth around it softly patterned by hoofprints, older manure nearby. Quickly the men moved in to examine the site. "One animal, here less than a day ago," said Thomas, looking up at Landry. "Whoever Vallee and Seth heard left his horse here."

"I see that," said Landry, hitching his gun belt and glancing about expectantly. "Let's look around; with the summer dust, his footprints are going to be around somewhere. Best we spread out. I don't hanker on being in somebody's gun sight."

Temple stroked his beard. "Good idea. Whoever's prowlin' around probably ain't gone too far. Damn good water on this mountain, and nothing down there in that desert."

With guns drawn, their eyes scanning the landscape, they moved along the rocky slope. Then Landry found scuff marks and a half indented print, not from the angled heel of a riding boot, but flat and wide—a working shoe like farmers or lumbermen wore. For nearly an hour they scoured the area, but found nothing more.

A desert wind brought a refreshing cool, swaying the pinyon and juniper. After supper the men cut extra chunks of firewood for Vallee. Efficiently, she had fixed a hearty supper. By early dark they relaxed to the crackling fire in the old wood stove as water heated in a kettle for dishes. Dale Thomas had rolled up his sleeves and pitched in to help Vallee pump the water and lift the heavy container to the stove. The water hot, Thomas removed it to the sink as Vallee cooled it and began methodically washing. Although tin plates were for the normal daily use, Vallee had set her mother's china for the occasion. Thomas began drying each scrubbed plate with diligent care. Vallee laughed, eyeing him appreciatively. Landry, Temple, and Seth watched, expecting the worst.

"If you drop one of those, and break it, you'll have to shoot your way out," said Landry. "And don't look to me for sympathy."

"Don't remind me," said Thomas, piling some dried saucers with the utmost care.

"If me and your pappy make it on this mine, we'll buy you all the china you fancy," said Temple to the girl.

"Except it won't be Mama's," she replied simply. Thomas smiled at her with understanding. Temple saw them eye each other, and winked knowingly at Landry.

"This mine—this your richest find?" Landry asked.

"Richest I ever found, certainly, but not the richest I ever looked for. For fifteen years now I've searched for the Lost Breyfogle Mine. 'Course, so has everybody else."

Seth's eyes grew big. "I hear tell about that—richest in all the West."

Temple nodded slowly in agreement; the flames in the stove flickered warmly over his earnest features. "I seen one of the Breyfogle's nuggets once—long ago. It was on display in the Palace Saloon up in Austin. Seen Breyfogle once, too. A bear of a man, with wild black hair and a beard down to his belly. His eyes had a crazy look. Don't think he ever fully recovered from them days wandering in the desert, out of his head. The desert does things to a man. Ain't a good place to be lost in.''

Thomas dumped the dishwater outside, and he and the girl settled down for a spell. She set a basket of dried clothes in front of her and began folding them. The hound, Mono, stretched out before the warmth, his eyes shut, his ears flopped, one forward, one back.

"What all happened to Breyfogle?" asked Seth.

Temple needed little encouragement. He laced his fingers around a freshly filled pipe and sucked deeply. "There's different accounts as to exactly what happened, because Breyfogle was out of his mind for how long, nobody knows." Temple then retold the familiar story of how in June of 1862 a man named Jacob Breyfogle and his two partners, a McLeod and an O'Bannion, set out from Los Angeles for the Reese River silver strike in central Nevada. Unwittingly, they crossed the most desolate, forbidding desert region in America: the unearthly basin of Death Valley and the Funeral Range. Somewhere on the northeastern side they came upon an old Indian trail and a rock pile pointing to a water seep. The partners rolled out their blankets to sleep. For some reason, Breyfogle bedded downslope from his friends. "Don't know why, except maybe it was cooler since night air settles in the valley floor. That decision was to save his life," Temple explained.

Everyone waited, listening to a man who knew the desert and the world of which he spoke. From the darkness an owl hooted, and farther out a coyote yapped, its voice lifting in a tremulous wail. The fire in the stove crackled softly. Temple spoke with animation. He related how Breyfogle had been awakened by a scream and agonized moans. From the guttural shouts, he knew his comrades were being murdered by Indians. Crazed by fear, he grabbed his boots, leaving his rifle, food, even the canteen of water, to run barefooted through thornbush and across jagged lava. "He was scared them Injuns might track him down," said Temple. "He hid during the day and walked by night. His feet was so cut and swelled, he couldn't put his boots on, but he kept carrying them. Somehow he found water, a little geyser—an alkaline spring, probably. He drunk from it and filled both shoes with more of it, but the water from the spring made him sick. And apparently under the hot sun, he drunk the contents of them boots, but that salty water made him even thirstier.'' Temple paced himself, his eyes roving over the listeners as he elaborated.

''How far he trudged ain't certain. But he kept headin' northeast toward Austin, probably came through the desert below us somewhere, the heat and the thirst preyin' on his mind and body.'' Temple paused dramatically to watch his audience. Satisfied, he proceeded with his narrative. ''Along the way, he seen a big green mesquite bush on a hill that he thought marked a spring. About halfway to it, he noticed some float in a wash along a ridge; the rocks had that look that only a prospector understands. Breyfogle picked some up. They was gold nuggets. He put the richest pieces in a bandanna. But before he had walked much further, he seen the vein itself—pink feldspar, solid along the base of an overhang in an embankment, or at least that's how he remembered. Bad off as he was, he still had enough common sense to break out some chunks. He threw away the float because he knew the pink nuggets was richer than anything he had ever dreamed of.''

Thoughtfully, Temple drew on his pipe and let the smoke out slowly. Seth leaned forward from his bench to hang on to each word. Vallee folded laundered clothes while listening. Thomas sat watching Vallee. Landry slouched back in a chair, his eyes studying a water-stained ceiling. He had heard the story often, the various versions, although Temple's account was the most popular, and certainly the most accepted.

The prospector continued. ''Knowing he had found the discovery of the century, he headed toward that green spot that he took to be a spring. It was just a grove of mesquite, full of green beans which he gorged on.'' Temple told how

Breyfogle, disappointed at not finding water and weary from the hellfire desert, collapsed. Delirious, he lost his mind. He wandered after that. The experiences he endured for days remained a blank for the rest of his life. Without doubt he found water somehow, somewhere, to survive, but the man did not remember. Of what he ate, he did not know. Something had driven him on with boundless determination toward the Reese River strike. He traveled northeast two hundred and fifty miles until he was discovered by a rancher named Wilson, the first human being he had seen since the murder of his partners.

Wilson's first impression was indelible. A swarthy Bavarian, Breyfogle was big-chested and heavy-boned. He had bow legs and enormous feet that left wide impressions in the sand. He was nearly naked when Wilson chanced upon him, his pants and shirt in tatters, his hair and beard long and matted. He was still carrying his boots. Wilson took the man home, where he and his wife nursed him back to health. When Breyfogle showed Wilson the nuggets in his bandanna, the rancher was stirred to great excitement.

"But what of the mine, he never found it again?" Seth interrupted.

"He sure as hell tried," Temple answered. "Once he recovered, and after the weather cooled, he organized a party. But they were turned back by Injuns. So he gathered a bigger force. And he had no trouble gettin' volunteers. Them pink nuggets he had was all he needed. His story went over the country like wildfire across a dry prairie. Meanwhile, officials learning about Breyfogle's partners sent a search party up from Los Angeles, and they found the remains of them poor fellows, just as Breyfogle had described it. Well, him and his followers found that geyser of alkali water where he had filled his shoes. Without any difficulty he located them Indian rocks where he spent the night after his partners got killed. He knew then that he had gone by the spot of discovery, so they retraced their steps. You see, he was lookin' in reverse of how he had found the mine. Well, there was mesquite bushes all over, but none looked like the grove that he remembered. He found a group of dead bushes that he claimed is where he had gorged himself and fainted. But he wasn't sure.''

Temple told how the men had searched frantically but found nothing. Breyfogle had wavered then. Eventually some followers jeered him; some cursed him before they came home to Austin in failure. Breyfogle returned to search numerous times, but he found no sign, nothing. What he had thought would be a simple find, was to become a frustrating mystery that haunted him.

Temple looked seriously around the room at each person. "You know his big mistake?"

"What?" asked Thomas, interested.

"He never really made an effort to repeat his original journey from Death Valley north. Him and his followers always just wandered around the region, and that wasn't smart. You got to get your bearings as they happened.''

Breyfogle eventually disappeared. Some thought he may have perished in the desert. But his name became forever linked with the fabulous wealth, a lost treasure that sparked the imagination of untold adventurers and fortune seekers. Many, themselves, disappeared in the forbidden wasteland—in search of the legend.

"You think anybody will ever find it?" Seth inquired.

"Someday," Temple said immediately, his eyes aglow. "I seen that nugget on display in Austin and I ain't ever forgotten it. Whoever finds it will be richer than a king.''

Thomas nosed forward. "You think you ever come close?"

Temple lowered his head. "No way of knowin'. But I figure that Breyfogle found that gold somewhere in this area, not down in Death Valley like most think.''

"How do you figure that?" Landry asked.

"I seen pink feldspar in this region, much like what is in that sample nugget.'' Temple's eyes narrowed thoughtfully, the lantern light accentuating his facial creases. "Breyfogle had passed out of Death Valley. He had headed maybe a hundred miles north before he lost his mind. He himself had admitted that. That would place his find, if I'm right, somewhere in the desert below here, somewhere out there.'' He pointed north down the mountainside.

"Lot of space out there," said Thomas. "Lots of empty space.''

"But somebody, someplace, somewhere, is going to stumble on it," said Temple confidently. He looked into the darkness of a window. "It's out there—just waiting.''

"Why couldn't nobody ever find it?" the boy pursued.

Temple shifted and rested on an arm of his chair. He spoke with conviction. "I figure while Breyfogle was waitin' for cooler weather, a cloudburst come, swept down the slope and covered it up; or maybe a sandstorm poured over it. Them dust devils can move a lot of earth.'' The old man punched a forefinger at the listeners. "Remember, that gold he found was in a wash. What the sands and the water cover, they also uncover—some day.''

A rising wind pelted the siding. A horse nickered outside, then another. The men sat alert. Mono rolled to his belly, a growl reverberating from deep within. Again the horses sounded in a nervous, skittish manner. Temple's mule made a baritone protest. "The light," said Landry. "Turn down the light. Somebody or something is out there.''

# (2)

Mono was before the door, wanting out, alternating barks and growls. "Quiet him," Landry ordered. Both Seth and Vallee cautioned the animal and together held him, but he kept jerking with fitful yelps.

"We should let the dog out," Thomas whispered. "He'll find whoever it is."

"No," said Landry, "whoever or whatever it is might be scared away, or he might kill the dog. I want whoever it is." With the light in the cabin out, Landry and Thomas moved through a back door, into the adjoining storage shed where the gold was stacked. They slipped out the side door, which squeaked. "Damn," Landry uttered.

Together they lifted it on its hinges, slightly, to swing it wide. They then stole into the darkness, moving some thirty feet before dropping next to the rusted and broken remains of a hoist. The ghostly form slanted at an angle in the moonlight. They moved around the hoist and took refuge in a rut of torn earth. In front of them, a short growth of juniper whipped back and forth in the wind.

"Best we wait," Landry whispered. "Too dangerous to go on." The scattered equipment, the pulleys and snaked cable, the broken wood and shattered iron, the hanging flumes and teetering headshafts, were deadly menaces in the dark, despite the moon's brightness. They waited. Nothing moved or sounded, save the restless stirrings of the wind. "Go back in," said Landry. "Have them turn on the lanterns, but have them stay out of the full light."

"Won't that peril them in there?"

"If whoever's out here thinks the scare is over, he might move in. With the cabin lights back on, he could think everything's back to normal; I just might spot him."

"I understand." Thomas slipped away. Landry could hear the soft tread of his boots. He disappeared.

Soon the lights came on, one from a lantern on the table, and one from a bedroom. The wan rays lit the front and side yard in an eerie orange glow which contrasted with the pearly rays of the moon. Landry waited, watched, but he heard nothing. The tethered animals emitted no more alarms. Thomas returned. Then he and Landry, wrapped in blankets, took turns guarding throughout the long night and into the chill of morning. They had kept Mono on a rope beside them, added protection should someone spot them and attempt harm. Frequently throughout the hours, the dog peered into the dark and growled, indicating that something was still around.

With the light of dawn, Thomas again joined Landry, who had taken the last watch. The deputy's handsome face looked tired from the intermittent hours of restless naps. Both men scanned the harsh land that tumbled below them, slashed with trees and rugged outcrops. The first light touched the peaks behind with a rose tint. From below, a jay squawked and was answered by another nearby. The two lawmen sat higher; they heard movement, like the muffled steps of a hoofed animal; then, distinctly, a rattling, the blowing of a horse.

Landry gestured for Thomas to follow him. Stealthily they moved out of their hideaway, keeping the trees before them as a concealing buffer. Fifty feet down, they crouched beside each other. An eighth of a mile away they glimpsed the spotty movement of a horse. Once, briefly through field glasses, they saw the rider, hunched over his mount; from back of his flat-rimmed hat flopped a strand of long black hair.

"An Indian," exclaimed Thomas.

"Or a half-breed. Come on, get the horses," Landry snapped.

Well before dawn, in anticipation, they had saddled their

mounts. With long strides they climbed back to lead the animals from the makeshift stalls. Thomas could not conceal his admiration in the climbing ease of the crippled lawman.

"What's happening?" Temple asked, peering from the front door.

"There was a stranger. He's heading out and we're going after him," Landry announced. "You watch the kids, and keep the dog with you. And keep your shotgun handy. Don't know what's happening, but there may be more of 'em around somewhere."

"Me and my big gun have been ready for hours. Thought I might pick up a couple of grouse for supper. They come to feed around the springs."

"Well, be prepared for more than grouse."

Temple saluted. "Be careful."

Thomas and Landry mounted. The suspect was descending an ancient Indian trail, later used by travelers who dared cross the treacherous desert from the east. Landry preceded his deputy in a steady drop; twice they saw the rider emerge from cover and cross a sage-covered flat. His horse, a scraggly sorrel, twisted back and forth attempting to pick its way through difficult footing. "I don't think we can catch him," Thomas said, raising his rifle. "But I can drop his horse from here."

"No," said Landry. "I want to know more."

For half a mile they shadowed the rider, seeing him stop often to look, standing once in his stirrups as if expecting someone. "Don't think it's us he suspects," said Thomas, pulling up beside the marshal.

"No, but he's worried about something or somebody. Come on, let's find out." From back on the mountain they heard the resounding impact of a shotgun. The blast echoed for a time. The two lawmen looked at one another and then at the stranger, who pivoted in his saddle to glance curiously back. Spooked, he spurred his sorrel toward the desert flats.

"You think Temple's got trouble?" Thomas asked anxiously, reining up.

"Wait." Landry pulled his buckskin up and cocked his

head, listening. Silently they sat their restless mounts. But no more bombardment followed.

A growing uneasiness setting in, Thomas said, "Maybe one of us should go back."

Landry chewed his lips. "Only one blast. Temple was looking for sage grouse, remember? But it concerns me."

"Yes, why now? He knows that shot would probably draw us back."

" 'Course, you don't know Billy," Landry said with fondness. "He does what he does when he wants." The marshal shifted in the saddle to ease his leg and looked at the peaks. "But it might be smart if one of us checks. I want you to go back, Dale."

"Go back now?"

"Yes." Landry saw the young man recoil. "There's something stirring out here. I can feel it. That's why you must go back and give Billy support." His words were firm, insistent. "He's tough, but he's old. I don't want nothing to happen to the Crawford kids. I know, and you know, there could be others lurking around up there, all in cahoots with whoever this fellow is."

"What about you? Ain't too good to go it alone."

"No worry. I want to scout this fellow a little longer. See if I can piece anything together. It may be best if we take the kids out of here; doesn't look like their father's coming back. You best prepare them for that."

"I been thinkin' the same thing, but Temple won't go with all that gold layin' there."

"He would if we take his share out on the pack mule. Besides, he thinks the world of those kids. He'll go if he thinks they're in danger."

"They'll have to be out before winter anyway. Gets brutal in this high country sometimes."

"And it's storm season coming on. I didn't like what we saw out there yesterday. Those dust devils." Landry was referring to the smoky signs of dust storms in the distance, the willowy spirals of dirt and air whipped by the restless winds, a coming time of wind blasts, twisting and blinding and destructive.

"Okay," said Thomas dutifully, backing his horse away. "But take care. Don't want to see you ride into a trap. How long before I can expect you?"

"Give me a couple hours. If all goes right, I'll be back before high sun." Landry narrowed his eyes as he studied the slope where the rider had momentarily vanished. "Just maybe I can find out what our visitor wants."

Thomas tipped his hat. "Don't like leavin' you, but you're the boss. And maybe Temple does have problems up there."

"Doubt if there's trouble, but Temple's not the man he once was; proud still, but aging. I'd feel better if you were up there with them. And Dale . . ." Landry's face had a serious intensity that froze Thomas in the saddle. "If the worst did happen—if I don't get back, you know, by nightfall, maybe give me to morning—get them all out fast as you can. There is something happening here that I don't like, and those kids would be in danger. Hear me?"

Thomas, his jaw set, waved an assurance and turned his horse toward Desert Roost.

Grimly, Landry urged the buckskin on in a sliding descent where the trail dipped steeply. With great care he continued, holding to the thickest cover available and halting always behind a boulder or rocky extension for surveillance. Far below, the mysterious rider appeared, riding more with care than hurry. The sun warmed. Little puffs of dust rose under the buckskin's hooves. The opening land grew tangy with sage. As they reached the desert basin, the rider galloped his horse straight ahead through a cleft in a wall of black lava that formed the base of two rocky spires. Not willing to chance an ambush, Landry swung left, skirting the wall where it curved east. He advanced with care, his eyes sharp for trouble, as the sun was blinding in the east, seeming to center on him. The cloudless sky stretched empty, except for a distant hawk that wheeled on the updrafts.

Landry hugged the rocky base, riding with as much speed as he judged safe. He heard what sounded like shouts. Then he heard shots, and saw dust ahead, rising beyond an incline. He rolled forward and swung from the buckskin with his rifle, to take refuge behind a tilted rupture of lava. His horse turned about and came up behind him, to wait, tossing its head nervously. Landry saw the mysterious rider racing across a flat; another crackle of shots sent his little sorrel down to twist and turn in a shriek of death. The rider pitched headlong to hit hard, roll in the dust and come up with a gun in hand as a swarm of riders surrounded him. Four men dismounted and rushed the fallen man to kick his gun away and wrestle him down, while a fifth remained in the saddle, barking orders. The four pinned their victim, working feverishly over him, then standing back like cowpokes after bull-dogging a heifer.

The man in the saddle was pointing and shouting. Landry dropped back to the buckskin, removed his field glasses, and returned to sprawl on his belly. Through the glasses he saw one of the four, a bulky bear of a man, move to the prisoner and crouch with a knife thrust to the victim's neck. The fallen man lay on his back, his arms outstretched, bound to wooden pegs now. Landry adjusted the glasses on the mounted rider, a hefty, broad-shouldered man in a shirt and vest. Under the low-pulled Stetson, appeared long black hair and a dish-faced profile with a droopy mustache.

"Leander Morton. Rattlesnake Morton!" Landry uttered the name like a curse. Morton was the most wanted outlaw east of the Sierras—a one-man plague. Morton and his gang had ravaged the territory for a decade, robbing, pillaging, terrorizing. Years past, Landry had brought Morton to justice. But following a lengthy sentence in state prison, Morton had led a sensational break with enough fellow prisoners to make national headlines. Lawmen, military personnel, and armed citizens had banned together in a desperate attempt to protect the citizenry and to capture the escapees, a dangerous mixture of cutthroats, murderers, bandits, and horse thieves. Ultimately, those not killed had been captured, all except Morton, who made good his escape.

Landry crawled forward to see better, keeping the broken

land between himself and the outlaws. He glanced to be certain his mustang still waited. The animal watched impatiently, the reins on the ground to hold it. Landry never liked to stray too far from his mount, for a man could be easily stranded and left nearly helpless in the desert if a horse were spooked; but he wanted to get closer to Morton. Landry ran low, circled slightly above the gang members and emerged between two clusters of peeling lava. He heard the victim scream as the bulky, bear-of-a-man worked him over with a knife. Then Morton ordered the men away and looked at the sky, where the sun was arching higher. Landry thought he heard the leader say something about the victim making good buzzard bait.

The outlaws came back to their horses, and all discussed the situation while watching the helpless man writhe. Eventually he would bake and shrivel under the merciless sun. Unaware that anyone observed, they were taking their time, apparently enjoying his suffering as they waited. They could be punishing him for some reason, or just being their ruthless selves. But Landry judged that they wanted something from the Indian. Then he noticed two packhorses in a rocky hollow where the outlaws had apparently waited in ambush. In addition to the canvas-covered goods, they both carried water packs. Morton and his men had come prepared. As Landry assessed the situation, the bulky fellow walked over and kicked the helpless man in the ribs. He screamed and cried out, "No. No, don't know where it is."

"You went back and took it," Morton roared.

"No. No, swear I didn't." The victim's voice went shrill.

"The hell you didn't," Morton bellowed. "You snuck back and took it. And God damn it, you worthless bastard, you're going to tell us where you hid it." The big man placed his heel to the prisoner's throat. Landry recognized the hapless man, a roustabout half-breed—a desert guide and petty thief named Shoshone Joe.

"It wasn't there."

"Then you did go back!"

"But it wasn't there. I swear it wasn't."

"We hid it too well for anyone to find it." As if emphasizing his leader's words, the bulky man again sank a sharptoed boot into Shoshone Joe's ribs. The victim lapsed into moans. Morton sauntered his horse up beside the helpless man. "You moved it, didn't you?"

"Yes. Yes," the half-breed gasped, "but when I go back it gone."

Landry readied his rifle and loosened the Colt in its holster. To attempt to take in five desperadoes, the likes of Morton's gang, was bordering on suicide, he knew. Through the glasses he recognized Lee Van Liddicoat, an expert marksman who had been with Morton for many years. And there was Jenson, a mousy, nondescript little fellow used mostly as a spy or liaison in the past by Morton. Jenson had recently been released from prison. Landry did not recognize the burly man, or the slight man, possibly in his teens, with curly blond sideburns below a flat-brimmed hat.

Landry considered dropping Liddicoat and the burly one first, and any others he could take. To bring Morton and anybody else who survived back, roped and handcuffed, would be as satisfying as any feat he had ever accomplished. But Morton was their leader, a resolute, magnetic individual who could rally his men under the worst of duress. Without Morton the others might lose their composure, might fall into confusion and disarray, making temporary but easy targets. Those surviving would probably flee for their lives. Landry raised the Winchester, sighted between Morton's shoulder blades and swayed the sights to the rhythm of the man's prancing horse. But Landry's ego and pride held sway for the moment. Deputy Dale Thomas and Billy Temple were not that far away and could assist, if he arrested the gang and herded them in at gunpoint. "What a feather in our cap that would be," he said under his breath. The thought gnawed at him.

Landry hesitated. A side of him knew that he should drop them all as fast as possible; a side of him persisted, desiring the heady feat of bringing them to justice. He had done it before; he could do it again. With cool deliberation he sent a bullet smashing into the ground in front of Morton. It ripped dust up and sang away. The horses tossed and shrilled. Three of the dismounted men, their hands wrapped in their reins, were jerked off balance but managed to draw sidearms. Startled, the burly man dropped heavily to the ground, while Morton whirled around in the saddle and pulled his rifle from a scabbard.

"Halt," Landry bellowed, "All of you—you're all under arrest. Move, any of you, and I'll kill you." The men, trying to control their horses, gawked around in a desperate attempt to locate the caller. "Now, all of you holding a gun—drop it," Landry snarled. "Drop it, now!"

They did—intimidated by the authority in his voice. Morton, with a flip of the wrist, sent his rifle away.

"Now raise your hands. Slowly. Damn slowly," Landry ordered.

The burly man came to his knees, his hands high, as his revolver rolled from his thick fingers into the dust. The others, still holding reins, obliged.

Morton steadied his horse, a dapple gray, and cupped his hands up, slowly, shoulder high. "By God, is that you, Landry?" He squinted in the direction. "Sounds like you."

"You—all of you—drop your gun belts now, I want them all off," Landry said evenly, effectively. "You first, Morton. And very slowly. Very slowly; that's right. Lower your hands. Just easy. Just like that." Morton, still groping for the whereabouts of the voice, maneuvered his hands, ever so slowly, to unbuckle his heavy belt and let it thud on the dry earth. "Now, put your hands back up." With great satisfaction Landry watched Morton do exactly as he was told.

Still flat on his stomach, protected in the vee between two rocks, he held the rifle directly at Morton's middle as the outlaw fanned his hands and fingers wide, but his eyes encompassed the others as well. "Now the rest of you, do the same." In unison the outlaws followed his command. "Now all of you, step back three paces and keep your backs to me. Get down Morton, and do the same as the rest." Again the men obeyed his word.

Morton swung his leg over the saddle with deliberate ease

and came to the ground; he was squat, muscled, with slightly bowed legs. "You'll never get us in, Landry. Why not just back off while you're still alive? Clear out and we'll call it even for now."

"Shut up," Landry snapped. "You, the big one. What's your name?"

"They call me Wasatch." The outlaw's eyes roved over the rocky rise where Landry hid.

"You listen to me and you listen good. All of you." Landry's brittle words stiffened the big man so that he licked his fat lips and waited. "You got a knife?"

"Yeah."

"Cut that man free."

"We're not through with him," said Morton.

"He won't do you any good where you're going. Now cut him free. Then toss that knife back with the guns." Wasatch turned around and grunted, moving forward. He removed a big-bladed knife from his sheath and severed the bonds, then tossed the knife back on top of his sidearm. The half-breed sat up, rubbed his wrists, and came to his feet with uncertainty to grasp his throat and left ear with both hands; blood spread across his neck and over the shirt collar, tinting it. He moved toward Landry, stumbling, not yet in control. Landry noted that he wore big, flat farmer's boots.

"Now if any of the rest of you have some knives, dump them, too." Landry came steadily to his feet. Instantaneously he saw a man moving to his right. Rattlesnake Morton, ever alert, ever cautious, ever prepared, had left a backup man in the rocks behind. Landry pivoted and fired from the hip; his bullet caught the man in the midsection with a splatting sound, stiffening him so that his revolver went wide of the mark, the discharge loud. Landry levered a second shot that smashed the man high in the chest, spinning him into a boulder where he leaned helplessly, two red spots growing in the dirty white shirt between the vest flaps. Gradually he sank to a sitting position, and there, seemed to blend into the knotted rock. He hung momentarily and pitched over.

From the rocks behind, his horse shrieked and thundered away.

As the half-breed managed to flounder forward and tumble behind low rocks, the outlaws scattered. Landry swung his rifle back at them, but not before the young blond made a graceful dive into some guns. He came up with a Colt which he stretched out in front of him in both hands, splaying bullets at Landry, who threw himself backward into a shallow wash as lead twanged and spiraled about him. The blond grabbed a gun belt with a second revolver and rolled away, firing all the time at the marshal. The outlaws Liddicoat and Jenson found weapons and disappeared, the latter with surprising speed despite his saggy paunch. Wasatch, crawling like a squat bear, managed to grasp his gun and knife. He pushed himself up and lurched into some protective rocks. Landry fired and heard the man howl.

Morton caught one of the outlaw's horses, whipped it with the reins, and as it bolted, hooked one leg over the saddle, the other cramped in the left stirrup, his right hand grasping the pommel. Deftly, he used the animal as a shield. Landry snapshot at the horse; it screamed and went down, rolling, hooves up and over. Spinning, Morton rolled clear, the force carrying him into a swale of mesquite, where he disappeared. The remaining horses fled in terror.

Quiet settled. The half-breed lay hunkered like some wounded animal, his eyes feverish as he watched the lawman. Landry scanned the sparse shrubbery, the rimrock, the bouldered slope behind them. Except for Morton, most of the outlaws had their sidearms again. But the saddle horses were gone with the rifles. Morton doubtless had survived the fall. And worse, Landry was separated from the buckskin, if it was still there. The outlaw leader had disappeared in that direction. He motioned to the half-breed to follow him, leveling his palm down to indicate the need to remain low. Carefully they retreated to higher ground to retrieve his horse. Could he trust the half-breed to oversee what remained of the arsenal if he provided him with a gun? Landry wondered.

Morton's voice came clear and taunting in the warm desert

air. "Nice buckskin you got here. Big and strong. Nice saddle too, with water and grub and plenty of bullets, I see. Maybe we'll just leave you here. You got guns; we got guns. It's a standoff, Landry. But we got your horse, and Evans's horse here, the man you killed, and the packhorses still with water . . . and we'll round the others up out there. Now you won't have no horse, no water. Oh, we got a good game goin'. You agree?"

"Get the hell out, while you got a chance, Morton," Landry shouted. "I've got a posse out there that will be looking for me."

"Maybe. Maybe not," Morton called. "We'll be watching for you and for them, if they exist. And if they do—we just might give them a Morton welcome." The outlaw leader could not suppress a raucous laugh. "Now let's get serious. The only water around is in the old town up above. You know that. 'Course, we don't plan on letting you get to it. So you do the only other thing. You go into the desert. There is water in three days, maybe, if you can make it across all that salt and sand." He laughed heartily. "By God, Landry, you keep Shoshone Joe alive for us. We got to talk to him some more. So we'll follow you, after the sun softens you up. We will find you. No way can you escape us." His shrill laughter carried in the dry air. "If you're still alive, we'll put you two out of your misery, that I promise. You might welcome dying at our hands. You ever see a man swell up in the heat, his tongue black and big until it chokes him? You ever see that, Landry? For old time's sake, I might even bury your worthless carcass, so the coyotes and the buzzards don't get you for a while." He chuckled loudly, then changed his tone. "Come on, men. We go now, but not far; we'll be waiting and watching." Morton bellowed again, "Hear me, Landry? You can't get away. Nowhere you run. Nowhere you turn."

Heartsick, Landry lay back, suddenly aware that the heat would be sweltering by afternoon. "Damned arrogant fool, I was," Landry mumbled bitterly, wishing he would have back-shot Morton when he had him in his sights. He would rue his actions, he knew. Now he was without a horse, food, and water. And in the desert without water? He had guns, a rifle, bullets, and an injured half-breed. But Morton's men were short of horses for a time. And, of course, most of their rifles were on those scattered animals. That would limit the gang's range of fire. The half-breed lay sprawled on his side, blood streaking the caked dirt on his neck where Wasatch had gouged. The lobe of his left ear had been severed. From the dark, impassive face, the flint-black eyes regarded the lawman with restrained approval.

"They call you Shoshone Joe," Landry said. "You used to ride off and on with Morton."

"Only when he need me. I track for him, maybe guide him a couple times to water holes." The man's voice was low and raspy. "Why you save me?"

"Let's say I don't hanker seein' a man spread-eagled in the desert sun, whether he deserves it or not. And I'd like to know why you been prowlin' around Desert Roost, scaring those two kids to death. And I'd like to know what Morton wants out of you." As he spoke, the marshal studied the rimrock and the rocky draw before him, the gradual rise that he had descended. The bulk of the mountain was in bright sunlight now—the remains of Desert Roost lost in the upper crags. The wheeling hawk had winged on, and the sky had turned milky with the increasing heat.

The half-breed offered no explanation. After a time of silence, Landry looked at him. "If I'm going to get your hide and mine out of here alive, I've got to know what I'm up against. You best level with me, mister." The black eyes ignored him. With a no-nonsense move, Landry grasped the black tail of hair and twisted it, forcing the head to the side. Shoshone Joe grimaced. The bloodied tendrils of flesh in his neck where the knife had probed were darkening. They continued to ooze slightly. "I asked you," Landry said through gritted teeth. "I got no time to play games."

The half-breed gasped, coughed, and chokingly replied, "A couple months ago, we hide up in Desert Roost what we take from a bank. Now he think I go back and take it."

"Why?"

" 'Cause he couldn't find it when him and his men went lookin' for it.''

"Did you take it?''

"No.''

"Then why in the hell you been snoopin' around up there?'' Landry grasped the man's head again. His eyes squinting, his mouth contorting, Shoshone managed, "I wasn't.''

"The hell you weren't. You took the loot, didn't you? Hid it on your own.'' Landry punched a finger into the half-breed's chest.

The man pushed his neckerchief up against the bleeding ear. He said tightly in pain, "Yes, yes. I go back and get it and hide it in another tunnel.''

"Then why you been hanging around up there for so long?''

"When I go back for it, I can't find it. It is gone again.''

"How much was it worth?''

"Twenty-five thousand, I hear someone say.''

Landry whistled.

"Morton pay me a measly fifty bucks to find a shortcut— then he hide all that money himself.''

"And you think somebody else found it?''

"Must of. There are miners up there with a girl and a boy I seen, but I hide the money in a tunnel far away from them, higher even than the first time.''

"Maybe you went to the wrong tunnel. Maybe you got confused.''

"I know where I bury it.''

"Then Morton figured what happened and laid for you.''

The half-breed trembled. "I don't know. I never seen hide nor hair of him or any of the others while I was up there.''

"Well, he sure as hell knew about you. That's Morton. He was probably waiting for you to come off the mountain so he could take you alive out of sight and sound of anybody up there. Why did you leave in such a hurry?''

"I seen you come in with your badge and all,'' the half-breed confessed, his dark eyes flashing with sudden emotion.

"Thought maybe you was on to us, that you was lookin' for the money. I was tryin' to find out what you was up to last night."

"You would have been smart to have led your horse and your hide out the moment you saw me." Landry sighed. "But Morton would have found you sooner or later."

The half-breed sat up stiffly and swayed as if he were going to pitch forward. Landry pulled him out of the sun and back into a shaded overhang. The injured man clutched him and groaned in pain.

When they were settled, Landry's eyes, clouded with concern, strayed toward the mountaintop. Thomas and Temple would not suspect that Morton and his gang were present, that the members could sneak up and surround the superintendent's cabin once they secured their guns and horses. Even though they would be on guard, Temple and Thomas would be unsuspecting and vulnerable. Morton could kill them from ambush and easily overpower the girl and her brother. Landry's granite features hardened even more with the thought of Vallee in Morton's hands. But Morton had sworn to see Landry dead and to take the hapless half-breed alive if possible. That commitment would draw the gang away from the old town into the desert for the time being. Landry shuddered at the thought of facing a pack of killers with the burden of a wounded man, with no food or water, and on foot. But he had his guns and plenty of ammunition. He was a crack shot with a rifle—second maybe to Lee Van Liddicoat—and in the open desert he would make most of them pay dearly. His jaw firmed with determination, "We can't do anything now, until dark."

# (3)

Above, on their bellies, the five outlaws lay watching the flat where Landry had held down on them. They could make out the remaining gun belts and the knives in the dust. The young blond rested his .45 on a boulder in front of him. Morton held the second one, which the youth had secured as he fled. He scrutinized the area where Landry and the half-breed apparently hid. "If it hadn't been for Landry, we'd have got what we wanted by now out of that bastard half-breed. But in ways, I'm glad. I like it, because he'll pay. I'll see to it that he pays. I got a chance at Landry at last, a real chance this time. Out there in that desert—with no water, no horse, just sun and sand. We'll get both of them. It's only a matter of time now." Morton licked his dry lips with mean satisfaction.

"How the hell did he find us?" asked Liddicoat—a slender man with a hatchet-thin face. He had long been Morton's most faithful cohort.

"He was probably tracking that half-breed for some reason," Morton replied, looking at the blond named Tunin. "You, I want you to go back, get as close as you can to Landry. And Jenson and Liddicoat, you watch from up here. I'll get your horses, and maybe the rifles shortly." He settled the revolver into his holster.

"But he's got a rifle. I only got this handgun," the youth protested. He had smooth, boyish features, but his narrow blue eyes had a cruel gleam.

"I didn't say to duel with him. You're small and young.

You could get in close without being seen. And with luck, you just might get him, that's with a lot of luck.''

"I ain't going to be no good to you,'' Wasatch whimpered. He had ponderous features in an uneven face, the left side more bunched than the right, which gave him a constant, disoriented look. His fat lower lip protruded from pain. Wasatch was nursing himself with a wet neckerchief, his trousers down. Landry's bullet had grazed the right cheek of his buttocks, to draw slow blood.

A rare smile split Morton's face. Wasatch looked absurd: the tentlike trousers around his boots, a redness coloring his gray longjohns. "Soak it good with water first. I got that whiskey bottle in my saddlebags on the gray. When I round the Cayuse up, you can pour some of that on. 'Course, with the size of your tail, you'll need the whole bottle. So maybe I should just keep it.'' The men laughed as Wasatch glowered at them. "Now I'm going to take the marshal's horse and go after the others.'' Morton rose, hunching low. "They can't have gone too far. Evans's horse is just back a ways. And I have an extra .45 in my bags on the gray. Until we get all our rifles, we're at a disadvantage to Landry.''

"Marshal shot my horse,'' said Jenson. "Damn good saddle on that animal. And my rifle's with it.''

"You can use Evans's horse. He won't have no more use for anything now.''

"What about Evans?'' Liddicoat asked.

"The coyotes and buzzards will have to take care of him. I ain't going down there with Landry waiting, not to bury no deadman.'' Morton chewed his thick lips. "Before anything, we got to get them stray animals. I can see the packhorses are still back in the draw there. And the others, they couldn't have run too far.'' He rose and moved swiftly toward the nervous buckskin.

Liddicoat's thin face took on a grave seriousness. "When we go after Landry? Tonight?''

"Before dawn. I want to be able to see him and not walk into a bullet. If they run for it, they'll leave tracks. And with Shoshone Joe hurtin', and both on foot, they won't be movin' fast; so we ain't gonna rush 'em; we'll just push 'em out into the desert to burn.''

"And what about the posse he mentioned?''

Morton wagged his head. "There might be a posse. But Landry usually works alone. He brings a posse in when he needs a backup. I'll wager he's bluffing.''

"He ain't stupid enough to go into the desert," said Jenson, scowling.

"But we're going to make sure he don't run through us. We're going to spread out, cut him off from getting back up the mountain.''

"You don't think he can sneak through?''

"Not with Shoshone Joe, not with him groanin' and sloppin' around. And Landry can't carry him.'' Morton warbled his words confidently. "In a desert night, him tryin' to climb a rock mountain—if they don't break their damned necks first, we'll hear every rock he knocks away.''

"Maybe Landry will just leave Shoshone Joe and try it on his own,'' Jenson pursued.

"No, not Landry.'' Morton crunched a twig between his teeth and dug at them. "He's too decent and proud, and that's his weakness. See, he rescued the half-breed. And by God, hell or highwater, he'll try to save him now.''

"So what choice has he got?''

"No choice but to head into the desert. Him and Shoshone Joe will try it by night when it cools and there's a near full moon. But come daylight, it's mighty bare country to hide in. Three days on horseback and they might make it, but on foot without water, it will take four or five, and with that half-breed as he is, it'll do them in.''

"But that Landry fellow is smart and smart is always dangerous, no matter what,'' said Liddicoat. "Think if the wind covers their tracks?''

Morton smirked. "Like I said, in this open country, there ain't greasewood big enough to hide a jackrabbit.''

"You want him bad, don't you?'' Jenson asked.

"Most I want the bank take that Shoshone Joe double-crossed us on. That's what I want. And I'm going to get it.''

"That ain't what you want most," Liddicoat said, his steely eyes narrow, filling with a rare light. "You still want Landry. I seen it in you a thousand times."

Morton's mouth twisted and his teeth gritted in a strange, venomous way. "I want to be around when he kicks in. I want to see him crawl and squirm." Morton clenched and unclenched his hands. "And I'd like to send the bullet that does him in." The outlaw tensed, then relaxed his taut features. "But I still want answers from Shoshone Joe first."

Liddicoat puckered his mouth in acceptance and squinted uncomfortably in the warming sun as he studied the land below. "Could that miner and that old prospector have found it?"

"Remains to be seen. But I don't think so, not after the way we buried it—in that mine shaft, way up above 'em. They didn't know we was there. And they had no cause to go explorin'."

"Well, somebody sure as hell dug it up. We know that."

Morton shrugged in resignation, then sat up confidently. "But for sure, it wasn't one of us. 'Cause we all been together since that day. Now Shoshone Joe, that worthless bastard, not only knew where it was, he's been out of our sight since then. I got this gut feeling about it. And that feeling has kept me alive more years than than you'll ever know."

Jenson rubbed his twisted mouth; his eyes narrowed. "Then why the hell did that half-breed hang around until we discovered him? Why the hell didn't he take the haul and run?"

Morton looked squarely at Jenson. "That's why him and me are going to have one more little talk before we bury him. Before we bury *them*." Morton slipped a derringer from inside his vest pocket and checked it.

"That and your Colt ain't going to stand up to a rifle," Jenson said sharply.

"Don't worry, I'll be back shortly." Morton began leading the buckskin out the back way.

"But what if you can't find all the horses?"

"Then we pay a visit to them miners and that pretty little

girl up in the ghost town. They got a couple animals, and they must have guns." He looked back, grinning with yellow gappy teeth. "Besides, like Liddicoat said, maybe they do know something about that loot. But first things first."

The afternoon came in a sweltering intensity. The high sun beat down on the bland hills, dulling colors and driving any life far into recessions or underground. The heat wavered across the land, distorting all forms. Shoshone Joe lay languidly, hardly breathing, his mouth slightly ajar, the pained eyes watching Landry, who lay back using his coat as a cushion, a rifle across his lap. The Morton gang was lying low. But he knew they were watching, waiting.

"You got a posse up there?" Shoshone Joe asked suddenly. His neck wounds were painfully raw, and what was left of his ear seemed to have shriveled. "If they save our necks, you turnin' me in?"

Landry considered his words. "All I'm thinking about right now is getting out alive. You help me—you cooperate—and I just might work on a pardon for you."

"There a posse comin'?"

"Some partners. But they won't miss me just yet."

The half-breed turned his head aside, aware now of their grave situation. "Ain't no use tryin' to get through Morton and back up the mountain then, not on foot anyway."

"No, it wouldn't be smart," said Landry seriously. "They'd hear us, probably see us in a full moon if we didn't break our necks first. We don't have much choice. We're forced to head out tonight, north into the desert, which Morton expects, so he'll try to follow us. But if we travel in the moonlight and hide by day, we might have a chance. On horseback it's about three and a half days to Silverpoint—more, of course, on foot. It's a rugged desert plateau, I understand. But I've never had to be in that part of the desert, thank God."

"I know the country."

"If you know it, that helps. But you've got to be able to make it. I'll help you best I can."

The half-breed looked at him skeptically. "I try."

"There's a constable in Silverpoint named Dunlap."

"Bull Dunlap." There was fear and hatred in the half-breed's eyes.

"I see you've met him," said Landry. "Unfortunately, he's not much of a lawman. Used to be a sheriff in a county east of here, until he lost his office for some questionable doings; but for a crack at Morton, I think he'd join me with some of his men. He needs good press. There's some politicians and plenty of lawmen around that would put him out to pasture if they could. He's an embarrassment. But I can't be choosy, if we can only make it that far without water."

The half-breed was lost in thought, his dark eyes staring afar. "You would turn me over to Dunlap?"

"Not if I can help it. Not if you cooperate. You claim you know this plateau country."

"Yes."

"Lots of canyons and desert mountains, I hear." Landry had heard stories of the terrifying immensity of fault blocks and purple gorges and high battlements—a sepulcher of infinite space and death.

"You try to lose Morton in there?"

"It's our only chance. Trouble is, Morton will expect us to go that way, deadly as it is. What I'd like to try is go north, hope to cover our tracks; then cut west where we could swing back to Desert Roost. Problem is, between the plateau and Desert Roost is all open flat country."

"No chance out there. Morton, he'd hunt us, gun us down in no time," said Shoshone Joe, his dark face twisted with resignation.

"If we move at night, hide by day, maybe not—lots of wind out there to blow away footprints. Don't forget, I can still shoot. And Morton and his men in broad daylight, in the open, will be choice targets, and they'll be constantly thinking about that."

"You not give me a gun."

"Not unless I need you against Morton."

The half-breed nodded in acceptance.

"Now try to rest, we got lots of walkin' tonight."

"Out in the flatlands he will kill us, but there is another way." The half-breed's words seemed to crackle in the desert air. "There is water out there. Water not known to white man."

Landry sat up. "What the devil you talking about? Out in that desert?"

"One day's long travel is a spring. 'Bout twenty miles northwest of here."

"A spring northwest of here? In that plateau country? There's nothing out there but alkali and rocks. You're lying," Landry scoffed. "If there was, I'd have learned about it. And certainly I'd have heard of it."

"There is—not much, but there's water, and we need water." Already the half-breed's mouth was loose-hanging. He talked with difficulty.

"Where exactly?" Landry probed with disbelief.

"Out there in the plateau, beyond them first mountains there, is a half circle of hills. In a curve on the far side is the spring, it called Pah-hah by the Shoshones. That means stones, because the water comes slow out of many busted rocks, spouting a little."

"Like a geyser?"

"Yes, but now it come slow. It is not pure water. But it can be drunk."

"Alkali."

"Some."

"If there is, that would give us a real option, either to go on to Silverpoint or swing back to Desert Roost." Landry smiled heartily, uplifted for an instant. "Morton will expect us to take as direct a route as possible toward Silverpoint. If we can hide our tracks, and if there are some good winds, Morton won't realize that we're traveling west of where he'll be looking."

"Yes."

Landry grew disbelieving again. "Why isn't it on a map? Or why haven't I heard about it? Any water is damn precious in this country. Even if it's a muddy hole, people know about it, especially pocket miners.''

''As I tell you, it's only a trickle, nothin' to water a team, but enough to save a man.''

Landry looked skeptically at the half-breed. In a career that entailed years of professional work in the territory, he had never heard any mention of such a seep. Certainly prospectors who combed the desolate land would have learned of it, although the region's horrendous reputation discouraged all but the most foolhardy. The fact remained, however, that the whereabouts of life-saving water was the most important knowledge that a man could take with him into the wilderness. And yet the Shoshones—Indians in general, for that matter—had a secretive bond amongst them, a cultural suspicion of strangers, and especially of white men, a learned necessity for survival. Too often the red man had been betrayed by those he had helped. Landry wanted to believe the Shoshone. There was no reason to lie, for he had little choice. Injured and alone, he had no chance against Morton and his men, who would surely find him, and kill him once they had extracted what they wanted. The half-breed's only hope lay in Landry's success in crossing the desert. ''And do you think you can find this Pah-hah?''

''Yes.''

''How many times you been there?''

''Once, with an uncle on my mother's side, a shaman of the Shoshones.''

''And how long ago was that?''

''Some years ago.''

''It might have dried up. The land shifts, avalanches fall, rainstorms wash rocks out. Anything could have happened.''

Shoshone Joe shook his head. ''Pah-hah been there since my Indian fathers walked this land.''

If at all possible, Landry wanted to get back to the ghost town, to Temple and to the youths. Would Thomas leave them to come after him? Landry suspected he would. And that worried him. Thomas could wander into a Morton trap. The deputy was no fool, but he was young and inexperienced, and worse, alone. If something happened to him, Vallee, Seth, and even Temple were in danger. Surely Morton would eventually visit the old town in search of the loot, whether he got information from Shoshone Joe or not. But then again if the injured half-breed could guide them north to Silverpoint through a plateau that apparently offered nooks and crannies to hide, then ultimately there would be lawmen and citizens. He could gather a posse, a force big enough to contend with Morton. If the seep didn't exist, they would be no worse off and would at least be moving west of where Morton figured. And if the water existed, they had everything to gain. "At dark—you'll take me to Pah-hah," Landry said.

The cool of the mountain was refreshing as Deputy Dale Thomas rode his black through the thin gnarls of sagebrush and juniper. Ahead, above the pinyon he could see the wood skeletons of the hoists and the headframes come into view. Smoke curled invitingly from the chimney of the cookstove in the superintendent building. A zing of exhilaration surged through him. Vallee would be there doing her home chores. In a way, he was glad that Landry had sent him back, although he questioned how wise it was for the marshal to proceed alone. But after all, Landry had survived many years on the frontier. He knew what he was doing, and he could take care of himself.

Billy Temple emerged from the building, a double-barrel shotgun embraced in his arms and Mono at his feet. "Where's the marshal? And what happened? What did you learn?" Seth limped out behind him, carrying a small Winchester. And Vallee emerged from behind Seth. She was wiping her hands on an apron. A smudge of flour flecked her right cheek. Her hair was tousled in a beguiling but unpretentious way. "Landry sent me back, he wants you folks to be prepared to move out if necessary."

"When and why?" Temple looked disgruntled.

"Probably early morning. And I can't tell you why, really,

just a gut hunch on Landry's part," Thomas explained. "Did you see anyone else around?"

"No."

"We heard your shotgun. Thought maybe you was in trouble."

"I bagged a couple of sage hens ground feedin' around one of the springs."

"Christ." Thomas sucked in his breath. "You realize that maybe I didn't have to come back here? I could have stayed with Landry."

Temple looked upset. "Sorry, Deputy. Figured if I went about business as usual, I wouldn't bother whoever was out there. That it might give you men a better chance to nab him. So I didn't worry about blasting away." He stroked his whiskers. "Did you find our visitor?"

Thomas dismounted and checked the cinch on his saddle. "Yes, Landry's tailing him. He's an Indian or a half-breed. I don't think he ever suspected us. But he kept acting strange, like he was expecting someone, almost like he was fearing someone would back-shoot him. I think that's what made Landry figure there may be more going on than meets the eye. Landry should know shortly. Said he'd be back by high noon."

"But everything we have is here. We just can't leave it all," Vallee protested. A spark of disobedience lit her eyes.

"I'm sure Landry don't mean that. He wants you to pack whatever you and Seth need to hold you for however many days you might be gone, that's all."

"But my father, what of him? How can Seth and me leave without knowing? And when he comes back and we're not here, what then?"

They all filed inside the superintendent's building as Thomas attempted to console her. "I would expect you to leave a message. I'm sure your father would rather know you're safe in the hands of the law."

"And what about the mine?" Temple asked. "We got a lot of crude gold for the taking. Hate to just leave that."

"Couldn't you pack much of it out on that second mule, or can you hide it somewhere here? Lock it up someplace?"

"Might."

Seth spoke up. "There's a spring door in the floor under that rug." He pointed to a space near the far wall.

"Yes," said Vallee. "Whenever I clean the place, Papa makes sure I cover it up again."

"Well, I'll be damned." Temple puckered his mouth.

"I seen Pop put things down there," Seth offered.

Thomas slid the heavy oblong rug aside—a worn Persian, doubtless imported around the Horn in a wealthier, more opulent period—its design crawling around, making loops and sworls. Underneath, a rectangular hatch with hinges and a cupped handle lay hidden. He lifted it. A rush of damp, musty air engulfed them.

"Ugh," Vallee exclaimed. Thomas lit a match and let the weak glow flicker down a crude ladder, created out of seven-foot poles and bound with cross links. The feeble light played over walls barricaded with planks. Miscellaneous mining equipment lay abandoned: picks, shovels, candles, cables and such. The back of the pit extended into the black depths of a tunnel.

"It's a manway," said Temple, peering over Thomas's shoulder. "Must have been used as an emergency passageway. The superintendent and his engineer probably used it as a shortcut to the main drift."

"You could hide your gold down here," said Thomas. "Ain't no one gonna find it for a time."

"Guess I could. I seen a lot of windows along the tramways, but I never explored 'em or knew that they connected to this. And Crawford never told me."

Thomas waved out the match. "I'll help you get the sacks down there." He turned to Vallee. "And I'll help you ma'am, with whatever you need, but don't pack much."

Vallee compressed her full lips and spread her hands with a despairing shrug. "I don't know where to start."

"Take just basics. It may not be for long, if the marshal follows through with his order. Some changes of clothes for you and the boy, a warm coat for the night, something to cover your head and face in case we get hit by a sandstorm, and, of course, food for a couple of days.''

"I've lived all my life in the desert," said Vallee, amused. "I know pretty much what's expected."

In the next hour, Thomas helped Billy Temple lower the sacks of crude ore into the manway. The sacks, although only partially full because of the weight, were awkward and unwieldly, so that the men struggled with effort. Temple, although doubtless in his fifties, maybe sixties, was a bull of a man, with arms strong and sturdy like oak limbs. The young Thomas was impressed. As he worked he noticed a busy Vallee observing him off and on. A professional, he did not mix personal feelings with work. But admittedly he found the girl disturbingly attractive. The almond-shaped eyes, the wide forehead, the heart-shaped face, a woman in full, youthful bloom. He intensified his efforts at packing the gold.

Later, as Vallee set to preparing a meal, Thomas found himself peering down the trail. A growing uneasiness made him want to follow up on Landry. If the marshal did not arrive within another hour, he would go searching, he decided, although he was inviting Landry's wrath if something happened to his charges. After all, he had been given orders.

Seth hobbled up to the open hatch and looked down as Thomas lowered a final sack to Temple. "Good place to hide money," the boy said.

"Sure as hell hope so," Temple commented crustily.

"Pop figured it was a good place."

Both men stopped work. "What do you mean, boy?" Temple queried.

"Yeah, what do you mean?"

"Nothing. Except Pop figured it'd be a good place."

By early afternoon the heat from the lower desert rose steadily, baking the land and forcing wildlife into hiding. A few bees hummed in the yellow rabbit bush; the sage and pinyon, wilting slightly, perfumed the air. Seth took refuge under a corrugated roof of a collapsing shed where he industriously carved a wooden whistle, until Vallee scolded him thoroughly and quickly engaged him in assisting her. She worked steadily, efficiently, packing what she believed necessary for a forced exit. Temple and Thomas fed and watered the animals in preparation of leaving. The girl uttered only one remark to Thomas. "Where's the marshal?"

The deputy blanched slightly. "I wish I knew." He said the words low and softly.

Temple combined his simple belongings in a masterful arrangement of compactness: a pick and shovel, some assay equipment, a vessel for beans, a coffeepot, a frying pan, a pan to mix bread in. He looked earnestly at Deputy Thomas. "Ain't my business. You and Landry made your plans," he opened, with an undertone of emotion. "But shouldn't our big friend be along soon?"

Thomas felt terribly young and inexperienced at that moment; whatever happened now was his decision. And yet before him was a wise old owl of the desert, a man who could find his way across a wasteland as stark as Hades and not only survive, but prevail. "Been thinkin' about him all the time these last hours," Thomas admitted. "Think I best go lookin', but he'd skin me alive if I left you folks and somethin' happened."

"If anybody can take care of himself, it's Landry," Temple said easily, picking his teeth with a splinter. "But it worries me still. And I'd feel partial blame too, if something happened. Now, you don't need no concern about Seth and Vallee. Me and my double-barrel, we got lots of say. If you want to traipse down the mountain a ways and look, that might be good. No tellin' what the marshal might have run into. Things have been mighty spooky around here these last days."

Thomas anguished for a time, then announced to Temple that he had to find Landry. "I just gotta. You understand?"

"I'm with you, son, and proud of you."

"Well, Landry will run me out of the territory and out of my job if something happens to you or Seth and Vallee."

"I shore understand. But me and the kids, we been takin' care of each other for some time now."

"I know. That's why I'm trusting you."

"I feel responsible for this—bringing you away, to leave Landry with no backup, so now you got to go out again, all 'cause I shot them grouse."

"All part of my job."

"You be careful, lad," Temple said.

"I will." His young face hard-lined, Thomas checked his rifle and his Colt; then he went inside the house. "I'm going looking for the marshal," he told Vallee.

"You're worried, aren't you?" She addressed him with big, soulful eyes.

"Yes."

Her next words came like a fist. "What if you can't find him?"

Thomas rocked back slightly. "I'll face that if or when I have to."

"Would you still take us out?"

"That's what the marshal thought best."

"But my papa—it bothers me so to leave without knowing."

Thomas licked dry lips. "It could be weeks, months until we find out about your pop, if ever."

Vallee looked down quickly; her eyes smarted with tears. "I'm sorry."

"It's all right."

"I know this is your home, but don't you ever miss people your own age? It must get awful lonely on this mountain here." Thomas noticed how the flow of hair hooked behind the small, flat lobe of her left ear.

She looked up at him, her pupils dilated and lustrous. "It has been lonely. Terribly lonely at times. And for Seth, too. But Papa needed us." She paused. "He needs us now, maybe more than ever when he returns. I just feel it." Her voice caught with emotion. "I feel deep inside that Papa is fine. Just delayed somewhere for some reason. He'll come back, and he'll explain it all."

As she spoke, her eyes looked over the great drop of mountain plunging in waves of domes and rents. Far out, the yellow desert was mysterious and moody, with the lesser mountains bare and foreboding beyond. She had come to love the spicy tang and the dreamy silence, the stone-walled heights with their green, choked niches, and the far-flung distances.

Thomas nodded and smiled with assurance. "I'll be back."

As he turned, Vallee touched his arm, her slender fingers warm and firm. "Be awful careful." She gazed at him beseechingly. "If something has happened to Marshal Landry—then there's something terrible out there." Her soft face was so acutely pinched white with fear that Thomas found himself cupping both her hands in his.

Without words he checked his outfit on the big black and swung into the saddle. He turned the horse and threw a salute to Temple, who watched sullenly, the double-barrel shotgun hung over his right arm.

"We'll be waitin'," Seth called.

Vallee watched Thomas turn once and wave. She remained standing forlornly long after he had disappeared into the trees, her fingers interlaced and pressed against her breasts, the yellow dog close beside her.

# (4)

Deputy Thomas set a steady pace down the ancient Indian trail, giving his horse free rein to judge the steep descent. The sage and juniper filled the warming air with their perfume. The shifting winds could grow stronger with evening until they would blow harshly, possibly whipping a pall of stinging dust that spiraled across the wastes in what locals called dust devils. He didn't relish leading the girl and her brother into the lowlands. For ease and safety, they would avoid the hostile desert by skirting the western edge on a main road between a cirque of mountains and the central plateau. The way offered a few oases. Then, of course, he would have Temple, a veteran of survival. The old man gave Thomas a sense of security.

But what concerned him now was the whereabouts of Landry. The marshal was too wily, too experienced to do anything foolish. But he might have ridden into an ambush. The most cautious tracker could fall into that trap. A man concealed in a cleft of rocks or in a glade of brush, especially with the sun at his back, was nearly impossible to detect. The Indian had been expecting someone. Could that someone have gunned Landry?

Thomas reined the black up frequently to study the rocky breaks below where the trees began thinning. Gradually he could see the loaflike rises of rock where the Indian was heading when Landry had given the order to return to Desert Roost. A silence hung over the mountainside; the desert beyond stretched yellow and shimmering. The horse nickered and swished from side to side in control against the steep-

ness, its hooves clicking on the rocky path. Then Thomas
spied several horses standing patiently in a notch of boulders.
"Whoa, boy," he commanded quietly. He looked around
nervously, a chill of suspicion running through him. He removed the rifle from its scabbard and proceeded slowly, taking care to keep along a line of frail juniper. Ahead, behind
a breach of rock, he would leave his horse and advance on
foot, he decided. Suddenly, below, he saw a man spying
through field glasses.

It is said that one never hears the bullet that takes you. But
Thomas heard the thunderous peal of a rifle, then felt the jolt
of smacking lead that shattered his right elbow, sliced up his
arm, and flattened against his shoulder blade before carom-
ing away. The horse pivoted and squealed, pulling instinctively into cover, the sudden movement almost toppling
Thomas, but he hung on somehow, and kneed the animal
away, uphill. The lawman's ears rang, and the landscape
hazed before his eyes. A slippery warmth of crimson slid
down his arm and messed his vest and shirt. He swayed and
thought vaguely that he was going to pitch from the saddle.

Down the mountain, the rifleman called Liddicoat pulled
his long-barreled Winchester back and cursed when his target
was not snatched from the saddle. "You hit him. You got
him, but he's gone, still ridin'," Morton roared, taking down
the field glasses. "He looked like a law dog. I can smell 'em
from here."

"Think there's others, like the marshal said?" Jenson
shouted in alarm.

Morton considered the question. "Don't seem likely. It
ain't the way I ever seen a posse ride, to send one man
ahead." Morton smiled slowly with satisfaction, not succumbing to any hint of apprehension. "I suspected Landry
was lying to throw us off. That means it's just him and that
thievin' half-breed."

"You want me to go up there after that tin star?" Liddicoat
asked, cocking his rifle with a disgusted snap. "Wounded,
he shouldn't be too hard to stop." He stared at the upper trail
with smoldering eyes. "Don't like leavin' a job undone."

"No. No, he won't bother us none. Let him bleed to death."

Landry heard the shot. Instinctively he lifted his Winchester and squinted into the desert glare. Nothing moved that he could see.

Sluggishly, the half-breed raised himself on one elbow. "A rifle," he said with effort. "That is a rifle shot."

Landry frowned and said gravely, "Thomas. I wonder if he's looking for me?"

"Thomas?"

"My deputy. God, I hope they didn't hurt him." Frustrated, the marshal looked at the pale sky. "Damn long time until dark." They had glimpsed Morton once, on the desert, retrieving one of the fleeing horses. And Landry suspected that in the intervening time, the outlaw had rounded up others, if not all of them. Anxiously, Landry waited, listening. He swallowed hard. Already a dryness clutched his throat. No more gunshots sounded.

"Morton, he's got a man with a rifle, that ain't just a rifleman."

"I know, Lee Van Liddicoat."

The half-breed turned his head stiffly to look with burning eyes at the marshal. "He don't often miss. One shot, that's all he needs."

"I know, he's as deadly a shot as I've ever come across."

As if reading thoughts, Shoshone Joe said dryly, "Wish we was almost to Pah-hah now."

"Well, we're not."

"Morton, he's laughin' probably. He's like the coyote waitin' for the mouse to come out. That's us and he knows it." The half-breed jawed his words. He moved a brown hand exploratively across his ragged throat and froze upon contact, his eyes expanding.

"He doesn't have us yet," Landry said defiantly. He rolled the half-breed to his knees. "Come on, let's get over there." He pointed. The overhead sun had shrunk the shade; but thirty feet or more east, a boulder with a granite brow made a narrow band of protective dark. From it they could see the heights and the accesses where the gang hid. Moving low, the two men ran, Landry guiding the wounded one until they grunted down in the shadow. With effort the half-breed lay back, closed his eyes and worked his mouth. The throat cuts had pinched together, but he was still suffering much. Afar, on the desert, Landry could see the spiraling swirl of dust. Toward evening the wind could whip menacing clouds, stinging and blinding, possibly forcing them to seek safety. But that same blow would batter Morton and his men too, although they would have an advantage with horses. But shifting sands would cover tracks, and that would be a blessing.

Suddenly Landry saw movement and recognized the outlaw Tunin a hundred feet out. He poked his head up from a vee of rocks. He was looking at the place they had just left. Landry eased his .45 out, but then thought it best to use the rifle for accuracy. But before he could aim, the young outlaw dropped from sight. Landry waited.

"What you see?" The half-breed asked anxiously.

"One of them that looks like a blond weasel." Then for an instant Landry caught sight of the little weasel crawling away. Because the outlaw had not seen them, the marshal judged it best not to expose their new hideaway, as a shot would surely do.

Dale Thomas swayed in the saddle from shock and from the steady drain of blood. He had wrapped his neckerchief around the elbow and part of the upper arm, but it helped little; he knew his effectiveness was over. If only he could get back to Desert Roost, he thought, to warn Billy Temple and to protect Vallee and Seth in whatever way he could. He spurred the horse into a choppy, sometimes struggling climb. Who were the men he had come upon? And how many? He hadn't even seen the one who had shot him. Doubtless all were somehow connected with the half-breed who had been hiding about. But how? Landry had been right. There were more of them. And would they now pursue him back to Desert Roost to endanger those he had been charged to protect?

Or had he simply stumbled upon them, and now would they be satisfied to have driven him off? Had the man with the glasses been able to see his badge? And Landry—what of Landry? Was he trapped or surrounded down there somewhere? Was he lying out in the sun, wounded or dead? Thomas's mind fuzzed. He tried to see ahead, then behind, but his eyes commenced watering and he felt faint. He managed to open a canteen with his left hand.

The cooling water revived him some, so that he didn't lurch as much. But by the time the ruined remains of the town came into view, he was so exhausted that he hung forward over the pommel, to sink gradually, his head bobbing. The horse, sensing arrival, began trotting. Thomas heard Mono bark excitedly. Tilting his head slightly, the deputy glimpsed the girl through swimming eyes as she rushed out the doorway; he heard her scream as he slid helplessly from the saddle.

The desert night brought relieving cool as a full red moon sailed high, washing the crusted land with a shadowy light. Shoshone Joe plodded ahead toward the promised seep. He moved unsteadily, using the dead splinter of a mesquite as a walking stick, probing ahead for slithery creatures. A few paces behind, a limping Landry carried a broomlike creosote bush in an attempt to sweep away any deep foot imprints that would be telling signs to Morton when he followed, as Landry expected. Fortunately, a brisk wind had risen by evening to send streamers of dirt and sand across the wasteland, particles that stung and worked into one's clothing to cling miserably. But at the same time, the wind gradually covered their route, providing a hope that Morton and his men could not track effectively—a desperate wish perhaps, but a possibility, especially since they were moving at an off angle toward the promised water, a direction Morton would not anticipate.

They traversed the first miles easily, for they felt relieved and invigorated to be moving and not caged by the rocky recesses or to be vulnerable in the bright daylight. But after they skirted an alkali playa, where their boots sank in crunchy white earth, slowing them, Landry ordered the half-breed to higher ground. The man plodded toward some low hills, rounded and weathered, the beginning of the central plateau, a chaotic ruptured terrain where the going became harder. The earth held heat still, but Landry welcomed the irregular landscape, for it gave protection from searching eyes. He kept looking behind him, expecting to see the Morton gang riding after them, even though he knew they would not expose themselves in the moonlight. Around them rose ghostly stands of Joshua, their prickly arms uplifted, like gaunt worshipers reaching imploringly to heaven. Their shadows crisscrossed in weird patterns, changing gradually with the flowing moon.

The long, sultry day had taken its toll. A dryness of mouth, a constricting of throat, the sense of body shrinkage that might be more in the mind than real had already made them fearful with imaginings. And it would grow worse. The half-breed seemed humped in the light, his head bowed and his shoulders rounded. How far could he make it? Around the puffy throat where blood caked and the tendrils of flesh had darkened, a redness streaked his veins, a festering setting in that could not be dismissed. Once, the man had tried spitting dryly on his hands to press saliva into the wound, but the sweat and caked dirt on him had muddied with coagulated blood, and the sensitive nerves had responded, making him jerk and cry out.

"Best we rest for a spell," Landry called. Gratefully, Shoshone Joe dropped into the dust to rock back and forth from the agony of his wound. "I sure as hell hope you know where that so-called spring is," Landry said tersely. The half-breed did not reply, but Landry could see him nod, the moonlight shining in the obsidian black eyes. For some time they sat in silence, both aware that random conversation could drain precious energy. In the pale light, Landry picked out a handful of pebbles and handed half to Shoshone Joe who popped them into his mouth and worked them around methodically. Both knew that the gesture was more detracting from the want of water than practical. But the men sat, wallowing the particles about, then spitting out the little stones as they continued their trek.

Twice more they rested as the moon diminished over high clouds, but the light remained sufficient. Once, near a cavernous recession in the lee side of a rock mound, they heard the clackety warning of a rattler that ceased only after they moved on. A strong wind buffeted them before dawn, swirling a pelting dust that forced them to wrap their mouths and nostrils with neckerchiefs and pull their hats low and tilted over their eyes. The half-breed's blood-dried neckerchief was of little use. "Pull up your coat," Landry called. The man tugged the collar up, past the sensitive ear, and leaned into the westerly. They trudged on. The temperature dropped dramatically, making them shiver.

Gradually they reached the rise of the second range of hills, toward an elbow of cliffs that Shoshone Joe claimed contained Pah-hah, the lost spring. They climbed the hump, taking great care not to stumble or fall, for the low hills held sinks of stone and loose rocks that made travel precarious, especially in the silver light. Once the half-breed, growing tired, turned an ankle and cried out as he fell heavily. Landry reached him immediately, and without words hoisted him up.

In the fading light, Landry left the half-breed sitting on a flat rock and entered a grove of mesquite; he snapped off a loose branch to probe ahead of him for any dangerous creatures that might be coiled there. From the branches in the grove, he stripped as many dried pods as he could, stuffing them into a vest pocket. Not far away he recognized some screwbeans, their pods tightly coiled like springs, and there he found a cat's claw mimosa; he dropped the pods from the screwbeans into his right pocket, and the mimosa into the left pocket of his coat. He returned to Shoshone Joe. Together the two crushed the pods of the mesquite and the screwbeans, removing the hard seeds. Despite the absence of water, they ate gingerly, conservatively. Lastly they ate all of the mimosa pods, which were sweeter and the seeds digestible. The meager meal helped, but it did not fill them or even begin to satisfy.

As the moon dropped toward the horizon and the first glow of dawn appeared, the two took refuge on a rocky bench overlooking where the hills and cliffs came together at right angles. "Down there, Pah-hah." Shoshone Joe pointed into the faint recess of a blunt wall. They waited impatiently until the violet of dawn creased the sky, before they dared move down; but first they surveyed their surroundings for any sign of Morton. Then they noticed a hump of crumbled earth at the base of the cliff below. Shoshone Joe's stoic face tensed. His eyes clouded with worried dismay. Landry felt heartsick as they climbed down. A sheet of rock had peeled away from above, a dry avalanche that blanketed the desert floor, strewing rocks and broken boulder, but piling largely in a six-foot heap at the cliff base. The half-breed looked disbelieving, as if in a daze, his hands clumsy and outreaching. Shaking his head, he dropped to his knees and pawed aimlessly at an outflow of rock and dirt.

"If it's a seep like you claim, maybe it's comin' out someplace else," Landry remarked without enthusiasm.

But the half-breed wagged his head hopelessly and continued digging.

As the sun's rays tipped the higher peaks to the west, the two men searched without success. The bone-dry stems of once thriving mesquite, a small forest of bushes, revealed that indeed some time back there had been water of sorts. But the source had long disappeared. "Nothin'. Nothin' nowhere," Shoshone rasped. Landry looked for animal sign, for anything indicating visitors, even the smallest of creatures. But to no avail.

Hollow-eyed, the two looked at one another. Without food they could survive for days, if they rested enough and did not burn too much energy. But without water they were doomed to an excruciating death.

With the heat of the day coming on, they had no choice but to wait it out. "We got to hole up, get out of sight, and out of the sun." Landry looked around and pointed to a knob of rock on one of the high mounds. "Up there," he said. "We can keep moving around it, keep opposite the sun there, and at the same time keep watch." Despondently they climbed the route they had come, rounded a narrow shelf and took refuge under the knob. A few parapetlike lava outcrops afforded further protection. Glumly, they sat in the long shade of the early sun, their coats off already. The halfbreed turned his puffy face aside and stared afar. With swollen eyes Landry looked at the white sky, and then at the measureless leagues of desert mountains. The shafts of slanting light lit the arid land in vivid hues—mauve, rose, dark brown, soft green, bright yellow, deep red—all blending in patches and streaks until the sun rose higher, leaving the land black and gray with the alkali, leper-white once again. Beautiful, Landry thought fuzzily—and all dead. Would they too die out there someplace, brutally at the hands of Morton if he found them, or slowly, torturously in the desert?

On the east side, in preparation of afternoon, Landry hollowed oblong trenches for them, some six inches deep, and laid out the softest of creosote bushes he could find, an old Indian method to allow air circulation and to reduce body heat. They rested then as the orange orb of sun blazened the morning.

"Ain't no other water near," Shoshone uttered despairingly.

Landry squinted at the corrugated hills ahead, with the high White Mountains gleaming beyond to the northwest, the year-long snow streaking in the eastern clefts. Thoughtfully he twisted around to study the flat open playa to the southeast that they had been crossing. The mountain bulk, site of Desert Roost, slanted dramatically above the desert, rising from east to west where it peaked and dropped abruptly to the flats. There was life-saving water there, and Thomas, and Temple, and the youths—all his responsibility. And yet to try and reach them, a day's hard hike in the open, was inviting the worst, even at night with Morton on the search; even if they were moving west of where he probably expected them. Landry judged that the outlaw would let him and the half-breed wear themselves out, let them grow progressively exhausted and weak, drained and suffering without water, perhaps even disoriented. Like the savage that specialized in torture of his captive, Morton derived much pleasure in such little games. But he would not wait long before tracking them into the desert, to extract what he desired from Shoshone Joe, and to finish Landry once and for all.

To continue north now, toward Silverpoint, would take them through a high formidable desert without water, an uncharted way, foreign to Landry, unless the half-breed were to lead—but the man could not be relied upon in his state. On the other hand, they would be assured of a rugged country where they could hide like a fox when necessary. If they could make it through, there was water about a half day from Silverpoint. If they could make it that far, they could then go on to that town with the availability of horses, supplies, and a posse.

Shoshone Joe looked at the marshal like a harrowed animal, gaunt in the eyes. "One more day without water, we will die," he said gutturally.

Landry did not reply immediately. In the direct inferno of a desert day, a man probably could not last twenty-four hours. Traveling by night in September, with the heat still intolerable, but waning, he might, if lucky, hold out three days before succumbing to an anguished death. "I know," Landry said at last.

From out of the shadows below they saw a jackrabbit, rangy and lithe, bound through the sparse creosote; it darted first one way and then another. Behind came a coyote, its body bunching and stretching with effort, its red tongue lolling as it raced after the elusive creature, only to fall behind. Suddenly, to the right, appeared a second coyote, veering the rabbit to its left. Terrified, the big jack increased its effort. Landry grasped his rifle but hesitated. A shot could alert waiting ears; and a cooking fire would signal their whereabouts for untold miles. Besides, meat would make them only thirstier, and if they attempted it raw, the blood and the impurities in uncooked flesh could eventually poison them.

But they needed salt. Soon, cramps in the arms and legs, and in the abdominal muscles, would begin. Landry had once come upon a man out in the desert, curled in spasms. It had been too late to administer any salt or water. He had buried the body clenched in a fetal position.

The marshal pointed the rifle, trying to follow the dodging animal. Again he hesitated. With any salt as from blood, they needed water—water desperately. Too, he had seen coyotes daringly scoop up a shot rabbit and carry it into the brush disdainful of any bullets leveled at it. The two men observed as a third coyote appeared, forcing the long eared creature back farther. Using a clever stratagem, the coyotes were chasing the rabbit into a circle. As one pursued, two rested, taking up the hunt as the rabbit came by, until they would exhaust the frustrated creature and capture it easily. Quickly they cycled around a hillock and out of sight. Landry expelled his breath and leaned back to stare listlessly at the southern horizon. Shoshone Joe closed his eyes and turned his head aside. It was then the marshal saw them—five riders spread wide, leading packhorses and a saddled mount that was riderless, all advancing steadily. "Morton." His voice had a hollow ring. "What the hell is he doing in this part of the desert?"

Vallee bathed the face of the reclining deputy, as the yellow dog sat watching, his tail slapping the hardwood floor in a slow rhythm. She and Temple had dragged the man into the house, to an old cowhide couch where they had applied crude bandages to the wounds from a petticoat torn into strips. Thomas for a time had been delirious from shock and loss of blood. Fortunately, the lead bullet had passed through cleanly. But Temple had confided to the girl his doubts that the deputy would ever again handle a gun with the adeptness necessary for a peace officer. The old man had soaked the bandages in cold water to increase coagulation, and together, from a sheet, they had fashioned a sling. She had stayed by the young man's side most of the night as he dozed fitfully, waking at times to mutter appreciative thanks for her care and to express concern for the fate of the marshal. At Temple's suggestion, they had lit only one kerosene lantern, turned low, while the old man waited glumly beside a window, the shotgun across his lap. "You think whoever shot Thomas, and maybe the marshal, that—," Vallee choked on the words, swallowed, and said, "Maybe whoever it is, is going to come up here, after us?"

Temple shrugged, but could not hide his concern. "No worry of yours, girl. Just takin' precautions—that's all."

"Don't treat me like a child, Billy. I know what I feel. And I'm asking you."

His bushy head bobbed. He looked apologetically at Vallee, and then at Seth, who sat quietly and slightly cowered, watching. "Yeah, me and you, we're thinkin' alike." He picked up his battered hat off a chair and pretended to examine it.

The night crawled by. The fire crackled in the black woodstove. A pot of stew simmered on a back burner, a rich brew of flour, spices, wild onion, and thick hunks of two grouse, bagged that morning by Temple shortly after the marshal and the deputy had ridden out.

The moon lit the mountainside, making ghostly patterns through the trees and stark mine shafts. Twice Temple stepped outside and prowled around the building, the dozing hound rising to accompany him. Mono acted nonchalant. "Appears that so far, whoever shot Thomas ain't come our way, at least for the time being," he said to the animal.

When they returned, Vallee rebuked him. "I don't like it when you leave like that. When I can't see you, it frightens me." She was holding the deputy's gun at her side.

"I understand," said the old man. "Worries me about the marshal. But I don't feel right, leavin' you in the morning to look for him. And we can't move Thomas, not yet."

Vallee heated more water on the stove and bathed the deputy's arms and upper torso. Thomas watched appreciatively. "You should be a nurse. It's your calling," he said sluggishly.

She smiled. "Just doing what I have to." When finished,

she rearranged a pillow to prop him up slightly. "I really won't mind leaving," she confessed, "if only I knew Papa was all right. It's been eleven days now." Moisture filled her eyes. "I'm just so frightened."

"You and Seth, you haven't remembered anything else that your pop said as to why he was leaving?" Thomas asked, becoming more alert.

"Billy has asked me that question a dozen times. No." Vallee chewed her lip and continued, "Just what I told you—that he had some important business in Silverpoint in addition to getting supplies."

"He never even gave me the satisfaction of knowing that much, me his partner," Temple said with obvious bitterness. "He just said to take care of you, that he'd be back. And he should of been back days ago, unless that important business took an awful lot of time."

"All I know is that when he hugged us good-bye, he said that what he was doing would make a big difference."

"Damn strange," Thomas said, more to himself. Then he looked sternly at Vallee. "But whatever has happened, you and your brother would be smart to get out for a time, until we know who's out there and what they want."

"You still think you're going to take us out shortly. Well, I don't think you're going anywhere for a time," Temple interjected. "Not in your condition."

"I can make it," Thomas said defensively, looking pale.

"Billy's right," Vallee said. "But when you can travel, and if we hear from Papa, I wouldn't mind leaving for a time. I'd like to see what's happening in the towns, see some people and hear them laugh. I'd welcome the change for a time. Here, it's dust and dirt, and spiders and cobwebs, and packrats, and, of course, snakes. I hate snakes. I live in constant fear of them. They're all around, you know."

"I know."

Listening, Seth boasted, "I'm the snake chaser."

Vallee giggled. "Yes, whenever we go out, especially at night, Seth clears the path with a broom or a branch."

"He's a good man, brother like sister." A healthy sparkle lit Thomas's eyes.

"Best you children get some rest," Temple said, disinterested in the banter. "I'll watch over the deputy. I owe him. Them sage grouse cookin' there, they cost a lot."

"You can't guard all night," said Thomas, wincing in discomfort. "Prop me up higher and give me a Colt and I'll relieve you for a time."

"You got lots of guts, Deputy—maybe too much. But I ain't allowin' you to die on us, and I ain't done in yet. You got lots of restin' to do. So leave it up to me."

"You underestimate me, Billy, I ain't done in either."

"I seen young cubs like you before—they got to get cuffed some before they learn."

Vallee winked at Thomas, and he smiled at her like a little boy, thoroughly rebuked.

# (5)

Temple dozed occasionally while the wind pounded the building and sucked at the stove pipe, causing the fire to roar off and on. Mono pawed the door to be let out a few times, but never did he register alarm. Thomas groaned uncomfortably during what little sleep he managed. Once he asked Temple to steady him in a slow trip to the outhouse. Twice in the night Vallee rose to give him water, which he gulped greedily, for a fever had enflamed his body. Even Seth was compelled to rise, to peer sleepily from a doorway, his frail face pallid in the faint light.

Frequently, Temple turned the lantern nearly off to peer into the darkness at the lashing sage and trees. His weathered face registered deep concern for his longtime friend Dirk Landry. Something had gone wrong. Temple had always believed that every man had his allotted time, because fate or God sometimes changed the best laid plans. Man was fallible and mortal. But Landry? The prospector could not conceive of the marshal dead; maybe in trouble, maybe hurt some place, but not dead. He had seen the most experienced, the most capable outdoorsmen—hunters, mule skinners, mining men, ranchmen, lumbermen—individuals of strength and skill and courage, succumb suddenly, unexpectedly, tossed by a horse or a runaway team; crushed in a collapsed tunnel or a rolled wagon; struck suddenly by pneumonia or cholera. He had seen it all. But certain ones, certain kinds, seemed to transcend the chance and the unexpected. Landry was one of those. It haunted him, that his shooting the sage hens might have brought Thomas back prematurely. Again the old man had an itch to go searching with dawn, but with a wounded deputy, and Vallee and Seth subject to whoever was out there, he could not chance leaving, not just yet. Besides, Landry would want it that way. He had entrusted their well-being to others, and that's the way it would have to be.

Shortly before sunrise the temperature dropped to near freezing on the high desert mountain. Billy Temple stirred the embers into flames and added chunks of wood that he and Seth had split earlier in the year. He was aware of Thomas's eyes watching him. "How you feel?"

"Stiff and sore, and hot and cold all over—but I'll make it. Hell, in a day or so I've got to get all of you out of here."

"Like I told you, it don't seem to me that you'll be travelin' much, not for a time."

"We've got to. No tellin' what them men I seen—the ones that shot me—are up to. They must have gotten Landry, for God's sake, and I've failed him. I should have found out about him."

"You should know by now that Landry's no fool, he don't ride easily into no ambush."

"Then why hasn't he come back?"

"I don't know," Temple said solemnly. "But I shore as hell wish I did."

Vallee appeared silently, gracefully, from her room. She went immediately to Thomas and leaned down to check the arm. Blood had oozed through the bandage and the sling. The girl frowned sympathetically. "I'll change that, and bathe the wound, after I've heated some water." She walked to the stove and stretched out her hands to warm. She wore a long blue dress with white ruffles around the neck and the sleeves where they ended above her elbows, an outfit that Temple had never seen, that he surmised might have been her mother's. She must have risen early in the cold, he knew, for her hair glistened in long waves from a thorough brushing. As the fire warmed the spacious room, Seth stumbled out, yawning, his eyes riveted curiously on the deputy.

"How you doing, partner?" Thomas greeted.

"Me? How are *you* doing?" Seth spoke with moving concern.

The young deputy grinned stiffly as the lantern light played across his day-old stubble, making him look older. "I'll be up and around shortly, good as new."

"I hope so," said the boy innocently. He fed the dog some scraps left over from supper, which the animal bolted noisily.

Thomas reached across his lap, removed the Colt revolver with his left hand and held it uncomfortably, shifting it some for feel and for balance. "While I lay here, I'm going to get the hang of this here thing. Ain't ever been able to use my left much. But I guess now I'm going to have to." He looked at Temple, who met him square on, their eyes interlocking in a shared realization.

"I was thinkin' just that, last night, when I seen that arm of yours."

"Maybe my arm will heal good as new, but maybe not." Thomas flinched with acknowledgment. " 'Bout as bad a thing that can happen to a lawman, to lose his gun arm."

"No, bein' dead is worse."

The lawman laughed—the first expression of mirth that Vallee had seen in him since his ordeal, and she smiled joyously to see his face crinkle. "Well, for now, I better learn fast how to use this thing and with this hand." He looked at his left arm fretfully.

Temple rolled his lips and ran a vein-knotted hand across his beard. "I'll say this, son, I admire a man who sees himself for what he is. It ain't going to be no easy chore to handlin' that gun like you was professional. It'll take time and work to do it, if ever."

By mid-morning the sun warmed the old town, until shimmers of heat played across the ragged slopes, distorting the landforms. Billy Temple and Mono had walked above the superintendent building into the hoistings for a wider view. He peered about, his puffy eyes squinting in the glare. The dog nosed contentedly about and began digging out the nest of a packrat at the base of a wooden frame. Mingled with resinous sage and pinyon came the aroma of freshly baked bread. The old man looked with fondness at the structure that had been his shared home. A man of fierce independence, he had lived his life alone, prospecting a few times with a partner, but choosing to survive the rigors with a burro as his only companion. Now the Crawfords had introduced him to the pleasantries of family life, although he still preferred sleeping under stars. He had come to love Vallee and Seth like grandchildren.

A half mile down, below a block of the mountain, a movement of animals wound their way upward. Temple's aging eyes could not focus clearly. Concerned, but a little excited, he returned immediately to the superintendent's building. Seth, tending to the animals, saw Temple's haste and hobbled after him. Thomas, who was appreciating Vallee at work in the kitchen, looked at Temple curiously. "You got some field glasses?" the prospector asked.

Thomas motioned toward his saddlebags. "There's a pair in there. Why?"

"Someone's comin' up the mountain." His words had the impact of ominous thunder. Vallee paled, wiped her hands on her apron and joined the old man outside, Seth close behind her. Thomas struggled weakly to his feet and found his way to the door, the .45 in his left hand. Temple, with the two youths almost beside him, walked some two hundred feet to a promontory that opened upon the winding road far below. He adjusted the lens.

As his face cracked in smile, Vallee squealed joyously, "Papa. It's Papa!" She hugged her beaming brother. And then hugged Temple, who lost his sighting momentarily. He tried again, adjusting the glasses and bracing his elbows on his hips, his big stomach thrust forward in balance. For certain it was Noah Crawford, chunky and solid, riding on his bay, leading six mules, all packed with goods.

"What the hell's he got?" Temple growled.

By the time Crawford came into sight of the buildings, Vallee had reached him to be swung up behind. As he lined the braying mules before the superintendent's building, she was talking to him excitedly, while draping a full green dress down the length of her right side.

"Figured you'd like it," he said, glowing, "special design shipped from Frisco." His eyes settled on the deputy leaning against a doorjamb.

When Crawford drew rein, Seth went to him, clutching a boot with emotional abandon. He acknowledged the boy warmly and handed him a small package wrapped in butcher paper. Anxiously the boy ripped it open and held up a multiple-bladed jackknife for all to see.

"Vallee tells me there's been troubles," Crawford said to Temple, still looking at the deputy. Vallee looped her dress over a shoulder and embraced her father from behind with both arms, her eyes squeezed tightly.

"Hell yes, there's been trouble. And just where in the hell you been?"

Crawford did not attempt to dismount. "At least you can tell me what happened." He avoided the question and waited while the prospector glowered at him. The mules continued braying gustily and stomping in anticipation of a rest.

Spitting sharply near his feet, Temple, his eyes dark purple, did not look away from Crawford. "When you didn't return, I went looking for you a ways, 'bout as far as I dared go with them kids in my fold; and then when you didn't come back, and when they was about to go over the hill after you, I decided to get the marshal. I figured he'd know best."

"You left Vallee and Seth here alone?"

"Didn't feel I had a choice. But I see now, I shouldn't of left 'em. I should of stayed. 'Cause apparently you had no concern."

Crawford stretched haughtily. "Ain't no cause for you to get uppity, Billy. I did have cause. Good cause." He tilted his head toward the canvas-covered packs. " 'Cause all that on them mules will make me and you rich. Rich all the rest of our lives."

"What the hell did you do, Noah? You got more than staples there."

Crawford removed his hat and wiped his brow with a forearm. "It's our dreams come true, Billy. There's no stopping us from now on."

"Well, it better be God damned good, 'cause we got a few problems without you gettin' us more in debt." Temple's eyes strayed toward the deputy.

"Who's the lawman? And what the devil happened?"

"That's Dale Thomas." Behind the grizzled beard, Temple could not mask a satisfaction in relating all their problems, a satisfaction in seeing Crawford squirm slightly in the saddle. "He got shot going after the marshal, because we don't know where the marshal is. Like I told you, I went after Landry for help after you was so long overdue. In fact, while you and me was gone on our missions, there was some stranger prowlin' around up here. Scared Vallee and Seth half to death, and even Mono here." The old man looked affectionately at the dog. "Fortunately, they wasn't hurt none."

"The marshal ordered me to take your family out of here after we tracked what looked like a half-breed," Thomas said. "There's a gang out there somewhere that's dangerous. But before we do anything, we better find out what happened to Landry."

Crawford dismounted slowly. Grimly, he absorbed the fortresslike ramparts above the dead town. The sun highlighted his features. Vallee had inherited much of her good looks from the man. Although not big, he had broad shoulders and confident features, with a pronounced jaw. His bristly mustache and porkchop sideburns puffed in a dignified gray. Now, his piercing blue eyes crowded with defensive anger.

But Billy Temple was not intimidated. With a cool insolence he mouthed his words matter-of-factly. "I asked you, where in the hell you been? Your kids here have been worried almost sick. And I was about to give up on you. Figured you might of got done in somehow, somewhere. And what's all this? You ain't answered me that." He pointed a horny finger at the mule train. "Me and you, we shore as the devil can't afford this yet, not all them mules and whatever you got in them packs.''

Crawford looked at his partner with gentle understanding, as a father might view a child. "But I got 'em. I got a deal. Everything we've ever needed, we got now." He punctuated his words with a pointed finger. "Yours and mine. I not only got grub, but new tools, and hoppers to carry our ore to a mill. In fact, I bought a rocker table, and a small crusher we can use right here. Yes, right here. You understand that? Me and you can be independent. Don't have to rely on some big operation now." His eyes sparkled. "Under them canvases there's everything we'll ever need. Equipment for washing and sorting. Even got some dynamite in one of them boxes, and the newest chemicals and apparatus for assaying.''

"You got all that? How? With what?''

"Grubstaked it.''

"Grubstaked it? God damn. You gave somebody half the rights for everything?''

"Not half, one-quarter.''

"How did you do that? To grubstake, it's always one-half.''

Crawford looked somewhat smug and pleased with himself. "Silverpoint didn't have the goods or the deal I was lookin' for. So I went on to Virginia City. That's what took so long. Talked to plenty of people there. It was the proprietor at one of them equipment outlets there that gave us the break I was seekin'. When he saw a sample of our ore, the rest was history.''

Temple calmed some. "I agree this is what we need someday, but I don't favor bein' indebted to somebody, not till we get ahead a little. Don't like havin' another grubstake, not till we pay the first off. It ain't smart gettin' more in debt.''

"But don't you see, now we can pay them debts off. Real fast. That's why I figured it was an opportunity I couldn't turn down. We've puttered around long enough, partner.''

Temple ruffled some again. "That's right. I'm your partner. So if I'm your partner, why didn't you tell me what you was thinkin'—what you was schemin'?''

"Hadn't planned it when I left. Things just kind of happened. Besides, Billy, we are partners, sure, but I am the one in charge of finances, remember?''

"Still ain't right what you done."

"Didn't think this would rankle you so much; thought it would please you.''

Temple thrust his jaw out. "Don't matter so much now. We'll hassle this out later. Guess you didn't hear the deputy clear; we got trouble with the marshal missing and a shot-up deputy and people dangerous out there. Don't make sense why somebody would be prowlin' about up here, unless they want our stake.''

Crawford grew concerned. "We got too much to lose, Billy—you and me; we've worked too hard to lose out now.'' The man's eyes skirted the rimrock again.

Thomas, who had been listening, walked out on shaky legs, his eyes like embers. Vallee moved to him, supporting him physically. Crawford regarded the action with conflicting emotions. "First we're going to find Landry,'' the deputy announced, "and I'll need your help. Then, depending upon what we learn or find, I'll have to follow his orders and take everybody out.'' Thomas's face was taut and combative. "You can rest your animals for now, but plan to move out of here soon.''

"You can't travel, not yet,'' Vallee said, alarmed.

"She's right, son,'' Temple added. "You ain't in no shape to travel, unless you want to bleed to death.''

Crawford looked incredulously at the lawman, his face hardening with resistance. "I don't intend leaving, Deputy. Not now. I'm sorry about Landry, sorry about whatever's happened. I care, but I ain't leaving now. You can't force me off my own place, son.''

"All this happened because of you,'' said the deputy, becoming professional. "And I can order you to do whatever I feel you best do.'' The two men measured one another. Vallee looked at her father with disbelief. Seth stood loose-mouthed, not understanding, but glancing back and forth between his sister and his father.

"I brought the marshal and this deputy back because of

you," said Temple, taking a step forward with gusto. "You owe them something. If you ain't goin' to help look for Landry, then I'll go alone." The old man started toward the shed that housed his mule.

"No offense, Billy," Crawford called. "Didn't mean no offense. First help me unload these animals. We'll set 'em to pasture, and then I'll go with you. There's time. Still plenty of time."

Vallee smiled in relief and assisted Thomas back inside.

"Get down and keep down," Landry ordered. He watched the riders coming slowly.

"They've found us," said Shoshone Joe. "They picked up our tracks." He commenced breathing heavily. "They trap us up here—with no water." He sat up some, but with difficulty. "Better give me a gun," he rasped.

"Not yet, my friend. We don't know they've found our tracks. And if they're on to us, they don't know where we are exactly, and I'm sure Morton remembers I can still shoot." Landry sizzled the words through his teeth. The thought of sailing Morton and his gang off their horses one by one was most pleasurable. Then he noticed the big man, called Wasatch, standing in the stirrups. He had both hands behind him on the cantle as if to steady himself. The marshal chuckled. He had heard the man cry out as he had crawled away. Wasatch had been hit and doubtless found it excruciating to ride.

Morton raised a hand and halted his men. He was looking around at the low, bare range where Landry and the half-breed hid. From his saddlebag he produced a pair of field glasses and surveyed the area. Reacting, Landry pressed himself as low as the slanted rise would permit. "Don't move, whatever you do."

"I tell you, they surround us, pin us down. Without water, we can't hold out long." The half-breed's eyes, heavy-lidded in the past hours, rounded darkly, hollow with fright.

"Shut up," Landry snapped. His eyes narrowed in scrutiny. Just audibly he said, "Voices carry in this godforsaken country. You know that.'' They watched the riders disappear below the rim of the hill directly under them.

''What they doin'? What the hell they doin'? They comin' up here?'' Shoshone Joe's voice was wavery.

''I said, shut up.'' Landry's words were harsh and grating.

For nearly an hour they waited, hearing the shivering neigh of a horse or two, but seeing nothing. The sun's rays grew brighter, more oppressive with heat, forcing the two to circle the rocky knob as the shade shrunk and rotated northward. ''They see us soon for sure,'' the half-breed wailed, moving with difficulty. He looked faint, shriveled suddenly, his neck more swollen and reddened, the streaks more inflamed. The neckerchief still covered the wound, but it had stained and dried a dark crimson. The wound was no longer bleeding, Landry realized. He could see a vein pulsing down the full neck.

They could not move, at least until the cool of night. While Morton remained, they had to remain. Landry knew now that the outlaw was holing up in some rocky cavern below them to wait out the heat. But why he and his gang deviated so far off course? Certainly the outlaw would have expected the two of them to steal away into the night, heading always in as direct a route as possible toward Silverpoint, but not to angle off for Pah-hah. Did Morton know of the spring? Could Shoshone Joe have shared the secret while riding with him? If so, that would end it here and now for them both. But he doubted it. Shoshone Joe was desperate and frightened for his life. He would not have guided Landry off-course to the promised spring, knowing that Morton might be waiting or would assuredly follow in time. From their high position he could see a partial tumble of earth that had covered the spring. So far he had seen no movement of men to reach the site. Then another, more disturbing thought stung him, one that nagged him. Could Morton have come across their tracks? A few impressions, one or two here or there, with the indentation of pointed boots or the distinctive wide soles of the half-breed, could have given away their direction. That, Landry decided, was what had happened.

And now it was to be a trying cat-and-mouse game, with Morton suspecting, waiting, and always watching. The warming air blew gusts of wind. Landry noticed little whirlwinds beginning, smoky streamers of dirt and sand out on the desert flats. Dust devils! As the barren flats warmed, a bubble of heat formed, a vacuum that would ultimately whirl into a fantastic twisting spiral. By late afternoon or evening, with the dramatic shift of temperatures, there could be a destructive windstorm, he surmised. It would endanger them in another way. But it would also halt a prowling Morton, forcing him to take refuge. Landry, seeing the half-breed sprawled, almost sunken in some loose shale, settled in for a siege.

From their water packs the gang members refreshed their animals, refilled their canteens and gulped the tepid water. "Be alert. Look around you," Morton warned. "We don't want to walk into no Landry ambush. He don't miss." They then settled the horses deep in a rocky enclosure for shade and set them to munching noisily on grain out of nosebags. Wasatch crawled with cumbersome deliberation from the saddle to waddle stiffly to a water pack. He filled his canteen, dropped his pants, opened the flap of his longjohns, and poured the contents across the welts that grazed the moon of his right buttocks and his upper thigh. He closed his eyes during the burning sting, and gulped in great swells of air. His heavy gut swaying, he shifted around to examine the seared wound. When he looked up, he saw the others staring. He barked, "Tunin, you son of a bitch, I hope you get yours someday." The men laughed, all but Morton. Tunin smirked at the blustery words and turned away. Wasatch glanced about and glared at them all, even at Morton, who watched glumly.

"Funny, but it ain't funny," Morton said firmly. His eyes roved over the others. "Any one of us hurt, could slow us all down, blow away good plans, make us sitting ducks to any posse that might be out there. If there is a posse." Those amused lost their mirth and looked away or at their feet. "Now we best get rested. It'll be damn hot for a time. Landry, wherever he is, ain't goin' no place.'' Morton looked out at the little swirls of dust and alkali, beginning here and there. "Might be a dust storm before the day is over."

"That won't help none to track Landry down," Liddicoat said, fondling his rifle. "Wish I could get that bastard in my sights just once."

"What slows us up, slows Landry up," Morton said simply.

"Landry and that worthless half-breed. You really figure they're around here somewhere?" Jenson asked skeptically.

"They'll hole up someplace; they got no choice," said Morton. "But yeah, we found them boot prints, a hundred yards apart, and both pointing this way. Seems to me this might be where they're headed. Bein' we ain't seen no other sign, we gotta follow what we got—'specially that rounded one, kinda like them farm boots that Shoshone Joe wears. See what I mean?'' Morton gazed around him and up at the stone walls. "It's just like Landry to pull me off course while he sneaks back up the mountain there.'' The outlaw's black eyes sparkled with enjoyment as they settled on the rise of Desert Roost. "Landry's been breathin' down my neck a good many years. But this time, I'm goin' to get him—and end it for good."

Unconvinced, Jenson challenged his leader. "But why out here? They ain't no water out here. Why didn't Landry head direct toward Silverpoint? Try and get through the desert quick as possible? Him and that half-breed could find good country to hide in between here and there. Seems to me we've been pulled off course, but not by Landry; maybe we just guessed wrong. We could be losing lots of time."

Morton considered this. He liked Jenson, who spoke his mind always, no matter what. Jenson warranted an explanation. "At first I didn't know. I just couldn't figure it. It didn't make no sense, except maybe he wants to circle back toward Desert Roost, like I said. And that makes sense. That's where he must of come from. There's plenty of water, and food, and guns up there with them prospectors. As I see it, he thinks that we expect him to cut straight toward Silverpoint. But you see, he don't expect us to figure him headin' back to Desert Roost. He's playin' the fox.'' Morton smiled knowingly. ''Yes, I think now that might be what he's going to do, try to make it back up there—back up that mountain.'' Morton stared confidently at the distant upthrust. ''So we're goin' to wait it out here until dark. Him and that half-breed will come out and try for it. They're going to hike through the flatland at night toward that big mountain.'' Morton punched a thick finger at the towering rise, gold-rimmed in sunlight. ''Landry thinks he's outsmarted me.'' Morton laughed with excitement. ''He doesn't know I come across his tracks, that I'm on to his little trick. So I plan to be waitin' when they try to make it. And Landry will be like a sittin' duck out there in that open country with nothin' but sage.''

''He's still got his guns. We try to shoot it out, some of us are gonna get hurt,'' said Jenson.

Morton squinted cunningly. ''They can't outrun our horses. All we got to do is cut them off and pin them down, then sit it out. They can't crawl their way out, and without water, it'll be only a matter of time.''

''Maybe they've seen us, maybe Landry knows we're on to him and won't try crossin' them flats out there,'' said Liddicoat, gnawing some jerky.

''Maybe. But it don't matter—whatever Landry decides, whatever he does, it's only a matter of time till we spot him and trap him. We got water, and grub, and time—lots of time.'' Morton chuckled, the baritone sound rumbling in his chest; a slight tremor flicked his droopy mustache. ''Then I'm going to see him squirm before I kill him.'' The outlaw worked his mouth furiously.

''Landry won't go down easy,'' Jenson remarked, spitting into the sand.

Morton grinned. ''But I lay any odds Landry's goin' for the mountain at night. With a moon and all that open stuff, we'll spot them in no time.''

''What if we don't?''

''Then he'll be hiding, not moving. Come daylight the sun out there will be like a furnace. They'll beg us to do them in." Morton stretched back luxuriously. "This time I got all the aces. And he don't have no trumps. God, I love it. God damn I love it."

# (6)

Cautiously, Temple and Crawford wound their way down the ancient Indian trail, the mule in a slow, choppy rhythm, Thomas's black, which Crawford had borrowed because of its fresh condition, sliding and stumbling often on rotting granite, the particles crumbling free. "Anybody out here will hear us coming a mile away," Temple grumbled. He pulled his mule up, and Crawford drew up behind. The vast desert stretched endlessly brown, pulsing and radiating as the noon heat intensified. Clouds billowed in dull yellow mounds across the far mountains, hazy and indistinct. Dark veils of movement wavered across the hot flats. "Windstorm beginin'," the old man commented.

The prospector's sunken eyes, mere slits in the glare, noted wheeling specks, perhaps a dozen, banking, rising, slanting, dropping, to sideflow and rise again, riding the updrafts. "Buzzards," he spat with distaste. "Come on." He nudged the mule ahead, clicking his tongue softly, conversing privately with the animal; and she seemed to understand, for her ears bent down and rotated and came up to cup backward, acknowledging his secret message. She picked up pace. Crawford slapped the black anxiously, as fast as he dared. The vultures continued in a slow, gyrating wheel. "Don't seem like nobody's around," said Crawford, not at all convincingly.

"Hard telling, but it don't seem like it. Come on, let's see what them buzzards want." Temple led the way and Crawford fell in line. Wisely, Crawford knew that he might be the brains and the decision maker in the partnership, but when it came to desert survival and the way of the land, Temple would have to take charge—complete charge.

As the two approached the area of the shootout, both men looked knowingly at each other and dismounted. Their eyes scoured humps of mesa, sunken crannies, and shadowed nooks, especially the points of upflung rocks. Where the earth softened in washes between the fluted walls, they could make out scuffed earth, punctured and thrashed by the hooves of tossing animals.

"Looks like some broncs," said Billy, examining the patterned ground. "Appears them horses was runnin' wild, like they was spooked and without riders." Overhead, the brown-black vultures pivoted, rising gradually higher, disturbed by the men's intrusion, although two flapped by in apparent protest, close enough that their heads, naked and knobby, blazed scarlet in the sun.

Then the two men saw first the dirty white shirt and black vest of the man named Evans, striking against the dun-gray rocks, his body bloating, pitched over, the wizened skin darkening like leather, a dried pool of blood beneath him. For forty minutes Temple and Crawford skirted the corpse, exploring the area, finding some spent shells and imprints of boots and horseshoes, but nothing more. "Sure don't see no sign of Landry," said the prospector, a lilt of hope in his voice.

"Don't seem like it. If him or somebody else was dead around here, them buzzards would let us know. But where could Landry be?"

"God only knows." The old man removed a small shovel. "Least we can cover the body so the buzzards and coyotes don't get it. We can do that much."

"Seems to be some buzzards swoopin' around over there a ways," Crawford remarked suddenly, gesturing toward a basin below.

"My God," Temple wailed, grasping his rifle. Expecting the worst, the two dropped into the opening. They saw Jenson's dead horse to the side of the chopped earth, its legs stiff. Side to side, rifles angled across their chests, the two approached the animal with careful steps. "Check it out," said Temple as they reached the carcass. He kept fretful eyes on the rimrock about them.

Crawford squatted down. "Shot through the lungs. Somebody removed everything but the saddle."

"I'll wager this animal don't belong to the deadman up there. From where the horse is here, and the man is up there—this belonged to somebody else."

"I'm sure you're right." Crawford rose. "Let's look around before we plant the guy."

Following a fruitless investigation of the area, they returned to the body and resumed the burial. Afterward they piled rocks over the shallow mound, and formed a small pyramid above the head. "Don't know his name," said Crawford, sweating. "But with his likes, I guess it don't matter."

Temple sucked in his cheeks, then said, "Landry must of put up a fight here."

"This man, he had this .45 out," Crawford said, examining Evans's revolver. "And one shot spent. He was firing at somebody. There's no doubt to me—he was no cowpoke, and certainly no miner, a drifter likely. One of them desert kind that prey on the lone out here. You think then it was Landry who plugged him and the horse?" He tucked the weapon in his belt.

"I'd lay odds it was. And it shore looks like there was a number of 'em. The mystery is, where they went. And where's Landry? Not a sign now of a living soul that I can see." Temple looked about and shivered some, despite a warm breeze that sifted sand and rustled the sparse creosote.

"Think they took Landry captive?"

Without hesitation Temple replied, "It would be a first. Besides, no drifter like them kind you mention is going to take a lawman alive. If they got a drop on him, they'd have killed him, shot him on the spot."

"Maybe Landry tried to circle back to Desert Roost; and maybe he's got whoever it was out here on his tail." Crawford considered his words with alarm. "But if they did manage to gun down Landry, maybe they're headin' up there on their own.'' He pointed high, toward the ghost town. ''Maybe they're after our claim.'' His eyes rounded. ''Maybe they want all that we got—all that's ours. You said somebody was spookin' the place.''

''I did, but if they wanted our gold, why wait until now? Why didn't they take it when the kids was alone?''

''You can't second-guess an outlaw.'' He motioned in dismissal toward the piled rocks. ''We got no time to waste,'' Crawford said fervently. ''We got to get back and damn fast, with the gold for the taking and the kids alone.''

''You go back, then,'' said Temple. ''I understand your worry. But I'm goin' to look further. See if I can find any sign of what really happened.''

''You're a fool to go it alone.'' Crawford began backing his horse away. ''Look what happened to the deputy.''

''I can't leave Landry that easy.''

The heat intensified, and the hours dragged interminably. Shoshone Joe moaned often, drifting off, his eyes closed, the monotone rising such that Landry thought he might have to muffle the half-breed. But he saw no sign of Morton and his crew. They had holed up in a draw or under an overhang on the southwest side somewhere. There they had an unlimited view of the flat wasteland that stretched back toward Desert Roost.

Shortly, the sun became a disk of molten brass swimming in the burned white of sky. With the direct rays overhead, Landry shook Shoshone Joe to his senses, but the man mumbled something incoherently, and blinked at the marshal with vacant, unfocused eyes. The half-breed's lips were puffed and split, as were Landry's. ''Got to move down into some shadows, down in those breaks there,'' Landry announced softly. He helped the sick man rise weakly, unsteadily, assisting him with great effort, a step at a time over the curved edge, down a ways, where a recess of cleft rocks formed cooling darkness. Twice the half-breed slipped, but was kept from tumbling by the strong but tiring lawman, whose leg now gave him more pain. Loose rocks clattered down a wash-board of stone siding, making a whooshing sound until they piled, an echo diminishing gradually. Responding, Landry lifted the man, looked to see what was ahead, and swung him into a shallow cave. The half-breed dropped to his back, hard, with a cry. Landry pulled his .45 and waited, expecting to hear Morton's men. But nothing followed.

A slow, rising wind blew up, stirring dirt into a stinging dust that pummeled the southeastern side of the low hills, shifting, roiling ever so slowly, beginning a peculiar hum that both Shoshone Joe and Landry had experienced before. Landry stiffened, listened, and waited; the half-breed awakened, suddenly aware.

"Got to get down farther, behind this hill here," Landry urged. He lifted the raglike half-breed to his feet and began dragging him over the checkered rockside which was dangerously split and broken by untold seasons of heat and freeze. Carefully he assisted Shoshone Joe, bracing him with his good thigh and hip as the wounded man swayed and commenced to topple. Sweating hard, Landry worked them both down gradually, half expecting the stone plates to crash away, to thunder and crumble in a momentous give that would drop them both. Morton would hear and would find them, and at last would be the victor. Painstakingly they made their way the last forty feet to crawl inside a low indentation, then sprawled in exhaustion. For half an hour they lay unmoving, the half-breed as if in a coma. Landry, watching, saw the man open his eyes at last. "Ain't no use, Marshal. It ain't no use." His voice seemed afar.

"As long as we can breathe and walk, we got a chance."

The half-breed's dry voice cracked as he struggled with words: "Morton—he track us down."

Landry answered solemnly, "While I can still shoot, some of them will end up buzzard bait. And I'll try my damnedest to sink the first bullet into Morton. Now, we rest a spell, and then we're going to slip along the hill here, we'll keep on the opposite side of where Morton is—go west for a time."

"In daylight?"

"In broad daylight."

"Why?"

"I want to work our way a little more west until we're at a point that if we break for it, we can reach the road to Desert Roost. If we can just get across those open flats out there. We'll try at dark. I don't know if Morton suspects us here, but I kind of doubt it now; otherwise, he would have come after us. A lot depends on that sandstorm building out there. If we could somehow get through that, we'd avoid Morton and he wouldn't find our tracks." Landry reached out and touched his prisoner gently. "Now don't waste your energy talkin'. Sleep if you can."

With ample food and water, the Morton gang relaxed while the sun climbed and the horses again munched oats in their feedbags. Tunin, the young blond, dozed, his hat shielding his face. Wasatch leaned on his side against a slanted rock to relieve his right backside. His square, bullish face was pallid. Liddicoat sat looking out on the flats toward the mountain rise of Desert Roost, while listening to Morton and Jenson talk.

"Just hope we ain't outsmarted ourselves," said Jenson, his narrow, twisted face contorting even more. "I'd of figured Landry to head north toward Silverpoint where he could get help." The outlaw looked questioningly at Morton. "Maybe them two boot prints pointed this way was somebody else's."

Morton shook his head slowly. "Only a fool would be out here without a horse. No, it was Landry or Shoshone Joe who left them tracks. That one looked wide, like the kind of boots that half-breed wears. And, like I said, it makes sense for Landry to head back toward Desert Roost. We been over all that. The way to Silverpoint is hell. In Desert Roost he's got grub and water, and maybe even some deputies."

"If they are, they could be on our tail shortly. Then what? Don't hanker to tangle with no posse."

"Maybe. If there was more than that one we shot, seems to me they'd been after us already, that is if they knew where to look. No, tonight Landry will try to make it across them flats out there. We'll close 'em off and pin them down. And like I said, we'll let the sun burn 'em out.''

''What if Shoshone Joe kicks in? What if we don't get the whereabouts of the money out of him? Or what if Landry holds us off or does make it?'' Jenson studied his leader for any emotion.

Morton's dish face widened with a curling smile. ''Then we go back to Desert Roost, like I said we might have to all along. Them prospectors may just know something about that money. And besides, they apparently found themselves a little stake that may be worth looking into. Come on.'' Morton rose and gestured to both Jenson and Liddicoat. ''Bring your rifle,'' he told the latter. ''We'll go up on the ridge before it gets too hot and see what's out there.'' He removed field glasses from his saddlebag.

Building a sweat, the three climbed the south side of the low range that stretched roughly east and west like a giant, elongated mole hill, denuded of all life. From the summit, roughly a hundred feet high, they peered toward the next ranges, a series tumbled in blocks and faults to the north, with the White Mountains tipping above in the northwest. Morton assessed the distance. ''Long, hard ways to go, if Landry decides that way.'' Unaware that Landry and Shoshone Joe were struggling west under the northern escarpment, he turned around with his field glasses and sat down to study the stretch between him and the imposing rise of the mountain called Desert Roost. The lenses magnified the wavery heat but penetrated the yellow haze. ''Before dark, with the coming of the moon, we'll come back up here. We just might see them out there. See them hightailin' toward that town up there.''

''But it don't look good,'' said Jenson, pointing. Morton swung the field glasses in the general direction. A little yellow-gray spiral of hot air hurtled across a playa, twisting swiftly for half a mile before dissipating. Then in his view he picked up a second, and then a third farther out, thrashing the sparse brush and lifting debris. Behind, south toward the

mountain, where updrafts shifted erratically, a sandstorm—
one to reckon with—was building, already pushing a form-
less cloud that would be on them with time.

Morton looked stoically at the upcoming menace. "Best
we stake down the horses and take cover. That could be mean
when it reaches us."

In the superintendent's cabin, Vallee secreted herself behind closed doors, posing in the green dress before her mirror. She adjusted a snug jacket over it, the latest style, a
complementary addition that her father had hinted was tucked
in a saddlebag—another exciting surprise. Living so far from
civilization, she had lost touch with feminine amenities, although sometimes on his trips for supplies, her father had
brought a catalogue with the latest fashions, pictures that she
had pored over, lived with, and dreamed about.

He had promised her and Seth a world of wonders from
the pocket of gold they had unearthed. He had assured them
they would all go first to Virginia City and to the International Hotel and ride the celebrated elevator. She had heard
about the spacious lobby finished in solid mahogany and
arrayed with overstuffed black leather chairs and tropical
plants. She had heard about the Babylonish luxuries, the flo-
riated chandeliers, the crimson curtains looped and fringed,
the parqueted floors with Persian rugs; the French clocks,
the Flemish paintings, the wall solid with plate-glass mir-
rors; the marble statuary everywhere, especially on the posts
of the white curving staircases; and all the plumbing, cus-
pidors, and doorknobs made of silver; throughout, a French
taste prevailed.

They would dine at tables made of mahogany and ebony,
inlaid with brass and ivory, set with crystal goblets and chal-
ices from Vienna. They would eat on handpainted dishes
from Flanders, the plates flanked with embossed silverware,
the napkins woven in China. And as a table center there
would be a candelabra, its multiple flames casting writhing
webs of golden light. When ready for dinner, they would
summon waiters with richly brocaded bellpulls.

They would dine on roast pheasant basted with white wine, or baked salmon shipped in ice from the Pacific. There would be lobster, quail, and squid with imported Roquefort: certainly there would be sautéed oysters on the half shell, and green vegetables railed from California, and maybe a dessert of ruby-plump strawberries with whipped cream.

Amidst the popping of champagne bottles, an orchestra would entertain dancers far into the night. Afterward, they would retire to one of the 150 rooms with their plush carpets, brass beds, and private baths.

She ran her slender hands down, over the swells and swales of her body, across the folds, and back toward the bustle—a bulkier contraption than she had experienced, one that forced the jacket to flare, giving her a high, pinched waistline. Underneath she wore a shirt, bloomers, and two petticoats to give the long skirt fullness. She loved the white lace ruffles on the sleeves and around the hem. The dress fastened in front with delicate white buttons, and there was a hanging pocket that matched, which substituted for a purse. Inside, following another hint from her father, Vallee found a little lace cap and gloves to complete the ensemble. Her father must have sought the best millinery and dress shops in Virginia City before purchase, she thought. And she was thrilled. Yet she felt a vague emptiness, a gnawing anxiety that left her unfulfilled and with a sense of shame.

The deputy, Dale Thomas, lay suffering with fever because of her father's exploits. And Marshal Landry, a man she respected and quietly loved, could be dead, or in desperate need of help—a fearful possibility that pained her such that she wished she could push them far from her mind. But she couldn't.

Her father had returned shortly with the news about the deadman and the horse, that it appeared there had been more riders. A few hours later Billy Temple had ridden in. Dejected and troubled, he had found evidence of at least a half-dozen horses or more, heading north into the desert; but they had long disappeared. Once more he had searched around the site of the shootout for any clue, even for the grisly find of a grave. But there was nothing attesting to the whereabouts or to the fate of the lawman. He doubted that the riders were after Landry, he had assured them. Why would the marshal flee straight into the hellish desert—unless he were somehow forced to? Temple lamented that the marshal was probably still hiding out in the area of the shootout. But there was no way the prospector could know for certain, although he had fired three shots—the traditional method of communicating in the wilderness. The shots had echoed over the chaotic land. No one had responded. After an extended effort of futile searching, the old man had reluctantly returned, defeated for the time.

With these thoughts bombarding her, Vallee swayed first one way, then the other, to observe her full figure in the mirror. She sighed, her chest concaving. She resisted taking the dress off, wanting to show the outfit to Dale Thomas, to her father, to Billy, even to Seth. Impetuously she pulled on white gloves and pinned the flat little hat above a puffed curl of hair, and pranced out in her high-buttoned shoes, all so new, so now in style.

A dozing Thomas, startled by her appearance, looked up, his eyes widening. He stared appreciatively, then smiled slowly, broadly. "You are beautiful," he said, pronouncing the words carefully.

"Thank you." She curtsied. "Can I get you anything? Some coffee?"

"You being here, that's enough," he replied, pleased with himself.

She giggled and adjusted a pillow behind him. Despite his momentary jauntiness, he looked weary, dissipated, his eyes and face gaunt and pasty.

Self-consciously he ran a hand over a blond stubble that was forming. "I would like some hot water and soap and one of your pop's razors, if I could. Yes, I'd like that."

"I can shave you," she said.

"You?"

"I've watched Papa plenty of times."

He chuckled, and it was refreshing, for she too smiled. "No thank you. I can manage," he informed her.

"I'll get you water," she told him, pumping some into a kettle and setting it on the stove. "While it's heating, I'll take some cold water to Papa and Billy. They been up at the mine hours already."

"To show off your new outfit?" He smiled weakly.

She looked at him coyly. "Maybe," and began filling a bucket. When finished, she moved swiftly, daintily, outside, where Seth was pitching dried grass to the mules. Taken back by a sister he did not know, the boy sidestepped off balance and nearly fell. He looked at the girl through new eyes, his mouth open and hanging slightly. Aware of his reaction, but ignoring him, she sashayed to the nearby well, removed a ladle hanging from a nail and proceeded to the pocket mine.

Billy saw her first. "My God," he boomed, his face split with a broad grin.

Noah Crawford, picking at a slab of hardened earth, looked up, disturbed. His pressured features melted into a boyish pleasure at sight of his daughter. "Was worth the money," he said to her, "now that I see you in it. Guess my little girl is growing up."

Happily, Vallee ladled some water and handed it to her father, who drank in swift pleasure, sighing loudly afterward; then another to Temple, who gulped it mightily and said: "You are no longer a child, Vallee."

"Well, you've seen it for now, so I'm going right back and hang this gorgeous outfit up," she announced primly. "I don't want to dirty it, not ever." She ran loving fingers over the garment. "It's so beautiful." She hesitated then and looked soulfully at the two men. "Mainly, I just don't feel right, you know, being happy with the marshal missing?"

Billy bowed his head. "Me neither. I just don't feel right workin' here. I just ain't up to it. I know I should be out lookin' somewhere."

"But where? We've done all we can," Crawford challenged. "Hopefully he'll wander in. You know Landry, he's always been on top of things. I feel it here in my guts." The man pounded his belly. "He's out there well and fine and he'll come back. I just know it."

Rejecting his partner's assurance, Temple waited, his face dour and sunken. "You finished now?"

"What do you mean?"

"I mean, somehow we're going to have to get that deputy, Thomas, back to town or go in his place. They need to form a search party, get some deputized men that know this country. You, me, all of us, we got to find the marshal."

"Well, that deputy, Thomas, ain't going to be going far very soon. He's mighty sick," said Crawford as he studied the diagrams to assemble a dry rocker.

"Well, I just may be the one that goes," said Temple. "We gotta get help. We gotta find out what's happened to Landry. And we ain't goin' to do it hangin' around here."

"Give Thomas another day or so to recover."

"Hell, man," Temple said heatedly, punching his shovel into the turf. "You yourself just said he wasn't going very far soon. And if he can manage it, he wants to take all of us out of here with him."

"I do think that Dale—I mean, the deputy—is much better," Vallee announced with youthful optimism.

"Give the young man a chance," Crawford persisted. "Landry is his responsibility."

Temple stood up straight, his coat seeming to expand. "Hell, just so you and me can work the claim a few more days? You forget, whatever problems the marshal's into is because of you. He come back with me because of you. And you alone." The old man pointed a finger like a saber. "And what of Landry? If he is alive, every hour that passes could be putting him closer to cashin' in. And you know that, partner. You know that."

His face flushing, Crawford turned his attention to his daughter. "You, girl, what you listening to? Damn it, you go down and see how the deputy's doin'. You hear me?"

She clutched the ladle in one hand, the bucket in the other, and stood firm, her eyes darting from one man to the other.

"You heard me, child. No disobedience." Crawford's words boomed.

Vallee's face puckered, her lips pouting in defiance. Swinging the ladle like a bat, she whirled around, her skirt billowing, and stomped dramatically away.

"What the hell was all that about?" Temple reacted.

"What's between you and me ain't her concern."

"You wasn't too concerned about them kids alone when you left them here."

Crawford bristled. "From the moment I rode in, I sensed you boilin' inside."

"You damned right. And I still am."

Crawford's face constricted with a livid red. "I left you in charge of them, Billy. You know that, damn it."

Temple confronted his partner squarely, "But you never explained why you was leavin'. Me, your partner. And then you don't come back. You don't come back, Noah. You hear me? We waited and waited, till the kids got sick at heart, and I was givin' up on you—thought maybe you was dead." Temple stepped forward, almost threateningly. "And then you do come back, all fancied up with presents and grub and equipment that we can't afford, that you've grubstaked on our mine. You forget it's my mine, too. I got a say in what you do. All the months of sweat and worry and backache, for what? Now you got us in debt up to our butts." Temple began pacing away.

"I know what I'm doing, God damn it." Crawford pointed at the newly purchased equipment and at the boxes of dynamite. "See that? See that? With all that we'll take out a fortune in no time." He shouted at his partner, both forefingers pointing. "Listen to me, Billy. Listen to me."

Temple clenched his fists and stopped. "At the cost of how many lives?"

"We don't know Landry's dead." Crawford stretched his husky squatness as tall as he could.

"We don't know he's alive, either." Temple's eyes strayed over the mountainside. "There's something bad lurkin' out there. Somebody spyin' on us and prowlin' around our camp here; Landry disappearin'; the deputy shot; signs of a half-dozen strangers down there; the deadman. I feel it in my guts. We best get the hell out of here, even if we got to pack the deputy on a stretcher. You hearin' me, partner? It's the gold that's botherin' you—well, that bothers me, too. But with all them mules you brung back, we could pack our sacks out.''

Crawford snorted and wiped an arm across his mouth. Defiantly he turned his back to Billy, grasped his pick and took a resounding swing that sent rocks flying. ''I ain't budging—not one foot just yet,'' he growled. ''I ain't abandoning this mine now. I'm not leaving all this new equipment for the taking.''

''Then maybe I'll have to take things in my own hands,'' Temple roared.

Crawford twisted around, his face knotted, eyes smoldering. ''You ain't takin' my kids, Billy. Not till I'm ready.'' The man crouched slightly, his feet parted.

Temple slapped an upright shovel aside. ''Well, you just think about it, partner! Meanwhile, I'm going back down again. I'm going to look for my friend again—my friend and yours—Dirk Landry. Remember? And I just may follow them tracks for a spell right out into the desert.''

Crawford relaxed some. ''You're a fool, Billy. If them riders are up to no good, they'll kill you if you stumble on them.''

''We'll see.''

''Go on, Billy,'' Crawford taunted. ''Go on your mission. But if you don't come back, you stand to lose a hell of a lot that could set you up for life. Set you up real good.''

Temple looked contemptuously at his partner; he raised and punched a gnarled finger as if it were a pistol. ''If I come back and somethin's happened to them kids and you're still breathin'—''

''You threatening me, Billy?''

''You heard me.''

''Then go, you old goat,'' Crawford stormed. ''You're as

bullheaded as that mule you hang on to. You old bastard. Go.''

"I am.''

Crawford snorted half in amusement, half in derision. "Yeah, you go, Billy. You look for the marshal, and may luck and God be with you. I want him alive as much as you. I know you don't understand that. I just can't see what more we can do. I really don't.'' Realizing that he was losing the trust and respect of his partner, Crawford pulled back. "But you try. When you're through, I'll be right here. I'll be right here workin' our mine.''

"I expect you to be here. Nothin' short of God himself could budge you out of here, I think.'' Temple moved away and grunted toward the superintendent's building as fast as he could manage his aged body.

# (7)

By late afternoon a howling commenced, low and steady, increasing in intensity. A yellow-brown cloud of dust and sand pummeled the south side of the low hills, poured over the top and spewed over Landry and the half-breed. The windstorm carried uprooted weeds, tumbling and bouncing; it blasted and scoured the rocks with dirt and thrashed the creosote and the patches of mesquite. In late summer months, with the increasing temperature contrasts between the hot desert air and the cold air at higher elevations, updrafts of great intensity formed. Landry knew that the only sensible thing in a sandstorm was to sit it out and wait as continuous dust devils ripped about. And yet, the storm would obliterate their tracks, would force Morton and his gang into seclusion. If they could tolerate the elements, now would be the time to move, he decided. When things calmed, the outlaws would commence searching. Pulling his neckerchief up over his nose, Landry urged the lethargic half-breed to a sitting position. "Come on, we're going to travel a ways."

"You crazy? Go, and we die." Shoshone Joe's eyes held a remote look.

"Only chance we got is to go now. Come on."

Before dawn, in the faint light, Landry had stolen away with his knife and cut some wizened strawberry and beaver-tail cactus that he found in a volcanic field. From a mesquite bush he had gathered dew which only made him crave more. Moisture in the cactuses was minimal, but enough to relieve their split lips and swollen tongues for a few minutes. He had then looked for barrel cactus, a heftier shrub with a more

**90**

pulpy substance, but had found none. The barrel cactus was not a spiny water container, as many easterners supposed. If one managed to cut through the tough, thorny rind, and managed to chop that inner pulp into pieces, one could squeeze out a strong syrupy juice that would sustain life.

The long hours of suffering continued, their conditions worsening in the heat as they struggled west along the north side of the stretching hill. Supporting the tottering half-breed in one arm, and packing his rifle in the other, he leaned into the sweltering air. Wind swooped over the rise, pelting them—the sand stinging. But on the lee side of the low range, the impact was minimal, much less devastating than it would be on the windward side, where hopefully it would force Morton and his men to take refuge.

On they plodded, step after step, Landry's left leg knotting, causing him to drag it with a more pronounced limp. Clouds of white alkali clutched at them, choked them. Thick, constant, the fine particles penetrated their very pores. Dust filled the air—became the air. It covered their bodies. It worked under the lids of half-closed eyes, clogged the nostrils, gritted in the teeth, soured the mouth, and burned the throat: salty, stifling, bitter, acrid. On they struggled.

Shoshone Joe's dark skin had further reddened. His flesh was burning with temperature, and he shambled like some primitive creature; his mouth hung open with labored breathing. Landry could feel the man's arms and legs contract in quick spasms. Landry had found the remains of numerous men who had perished in the desert, and it was not an easy way to die. And Shoshone Joe was dying, he knew. It was only a matter of time, unless somehow they could make it back to Desert Roost. He now questioned whether they could even make it across the desert plateau to Silverpoint, a world he didn't know. And Shoshone Joe was becoming a greater liability with every passing minute.

A sucking spiral of wind howled around the east end of the elongated hills they were paralleling. The rotational disturbance raised a dense and angry funnel that swelled and gained in power as it shot north. Then it suddenly reversed, coming directly at them. Before they could find cover, the hot gust of wind engulfed them, whirling viciously—a dust devil. Half blinded, Landry threw the half-breed behind a low boulder and flopped over the man as a pall of dust enclosed them, so thick and white that they could not see. They held on, their heads down, their coats pulled up. The roaring vortex came over them, flapping their clothing violently. Shoshone Joe's hat whipped from his head, broke the strap and whirled away somewhere into the yellow dark. For what seemed like an eternity the devil thrashed them. Then, as quickly as it had struck, it was over, passing on, dissipating. They lay half buried in ash and alkali. Slowly Landry dug them free and slapped the debris from their clothes the best he could. Shoshone Joe babbled something incoherently. Then he vomited, retching dry heaves. Landry tried to steady him, holding him without hope, until the shriveled little man, more bones than flesh, collapsed in a faint, his cracked and bleeding lips turning blue.

Landry too, was feeling dizzy. His head ached; a tingling had commenced in his arms and legs. Their exhausting travail had brought them perhaps a mile or two west, hopefully far enough that Morton wouldn't chance upon them. And surely their tracks had been erased thoroughly if God was with them. But more dust devils wracked across the wastes to the southeast, building darkly, approaching menacingly. "It's no use, we gotta take shelter," Landry throated hoarsely. He noticed a concave niche ahead, some hundred feet distant. He pulled the limp half-breed upright, thrust a shoulder under him and hoisted him up. Under the dead weight, Landry sank to one knee, but with determined effort he struggled up. He staggered a few feet then lost his balance, dumping Shoshone Joe into the powdered earth. The half-breed agonized loudly. Landry managed to drag the man into the stone break. There, he arranged the quivering form as comfortably as possible, and turned his back to the next sandstorm and waited it out. In the distance, on Desert Roost, where the mountain hid its head in clouds, he could hear the crack of thunder. If the rain drifted over the desert edge, it could mean life-sustaining water, but also the chance of flash floods. Landry braced himself.

With evening, however, the storm ceased and an eerie quiet settled over the empty land. The half-breed fell into a low, uneven breathing. With the rise of a red moon that washed the land in a bloody glow, Landry emerged alone. With strained effort he climbed a flank of the low hill, scanning the countryside. For a time he rested, his swollen eyes soothed by the moonlight. A soft cooling breeze blew refreshingly.

Then he saw Morton and his men emerge from below, heading south; one led the packhorses, while the others began spreading out. They were riding slowly, searching the open deserts, the stark flatlands between the elongated hill chain and the rise of the mountain and Desert Roost. He saw the man called Jenson on the buckskin—*his* buckskin—pulling the extra horse which doubtless belonged to the man Landry had killed. The sheriff realized one indisputable, sobering fact: Morton was speculating that he and Shoshone Joe would try to make it back to the ghost town. With a sinking heart he knew he and the half-breed could not cross the stretch now. They would be seen, hunted down—converged on and surrounded like wolves on stray sheep.

Despairingly, he turned back toward his prisoner. Some fifty feet away he noticed the silhouette of a prickly pear cactus, a plant smaller than normal, but its flat, fruit-shaped pads looked fat and pulpy. Impulsively he lunged, then staggered toward the precious specimen. Frantically he cut at the plant in the faint light, ploughing, gouging through the barbed outer skin until he reached inner flesh, which he sliced into crude pieces. He stuffed several of them into his mouth and sank his teeth into the stringy succulence, rejoicing as the bitter juice soothed his swollen tongue and dry mouth. He closed his eyes and chewed steadily, at last spitting out the remains and quickly filling his mouth again and then again. He looked at the chewed pieces and rubbed them over his face and neck. The remaining moisture enlivened his dry skin, briefly soothing, like medicinal balm. The thick, slimy green liquid did not assuage his thirst, but it satisfied him momentarily and gave a lift to his spirits. He remembered the half-breed and set to cutting up what was left of the plant. He cupped the mushy pads in a flap of his coat and moved on. But when he reached Shoshone Joe, the man had ceased breathing.

Landry felt for a pulse, first at a wrist and then at the throat. Nothing. Stoically he laid the body out, covered the face with the man's coat, and asked simply that the soul be received by the Father. He chewed the moisture out of several cactus chunks prepared for the half-breed, wetted his face and lips with a few, and tucked the remainder in his pocket, hoping to use them farther on, should he not find another plant. Then wearily he looked north into the half light, praying that he had the endurance and the luck to make it to the springs a half day south of Silverpoint.

Determined, Landry plunged into the moonlight, moving steadily without the burden of his prisoner. Despite his dehydration, he set an even pace at first, knowing that when Morton could not find them, he would reconsider and come back to search, figuring that they had chosen to move north, after all. Late in the night a cooling wind rose to blow steadily, gradually obliterating his tracks with a fine dust. And for that Landry was grateful. He chose the hardpan wherever possible, avoiding sand traps or the encrusted beds of alkali where he could be slowed and tired and where he would leave obvious indentations. Of course, if Morton had any trackers amongst his men—apparently that had been the half-breed's job—they could pick up the simplest of evidence: a turned-over stone, a split twig, a crushed plant. But to achieve any reliable success they would have to track by daylight. Hopefully he would be far ahead of them.

If they came in the moonlight, on horseback, they would be visible and easy targets, while he, although on foot, could hide effectively in the maze of washes and draws, with their hillocks and twisted shrubs. If they managed to follow him— if they did find his tracks—he would draw them into an ambush, he decided. Even if they approached in a spread formation, he could down two, maybe three of them, before the survivors could find cover. Especially if he could drop Morton—like he should have when he had had the chance—the others would probably be disheartened enough to simply steal away. And he might gain one of the horses. Whatever happened, he would give them one hell of a fight, for he had no intention of dying like a whipped dog.

Once, he saw the erratic flit of a bat overhead and wondered where it had come from. Surprisingly, he had not thought much of food, although briefly he had tried to club a big lizard that had darted nearby. But the whole ordeal had weakened him and he had not been quick enough. He had lost weight, he knew, for his clothes hung looser than normal. He had not eaten since the meager meals of mesquite pods and buckwheat stems shared with Shoshone Joe. Those dry particles had further reduced the amount of body fluids. He thought of setting an animal trap of some sort when he holed up again. There were many little animals that thrived in the desert, kangaroo rats and such. But the time and effort was really not worth it. To digest meat, it required water. Water was the essence now. Water if he was to live.

The moon arched high, dimming the landscape. Shadows of the stately Joshua and of the formidable Spanish daggers shrank and eventually withdrew. The wind hummed and moaned through scallops and hollows, carving as it had for a million years. Ahead, on the distant mountains, heavy clouds draped the peaks. Rolling thunder sounded with time, and streaks of lightning laced the sky. Someplace there would be rain perhaps, cold, clear, sweet, quenching water. He tried not to think about it, tried instead to think of the sudden flash floods that could form, that could be deadly to the traveler caught in a ravine or in a narrow canyon.

On he trudged into the night, laboriously, his steps faltering sometimes, his boots growing heavier. With each step he winced under the ooze of grated blisters. His constricted throat clenched tighter; every breath, every gasp, ripped through him, torturing his throat and lungs; his legs and thighs ached, and a tingling in his arms commenced again. The muscles of his back and shoulders tightened, sending spasms up and down, sometimes across. At last he had to rest.

He dropped loosely beside a moldering mesquite trunk. He removed the stinking boots; where the soiled socks had worn across the wrinkled curve of heel, white blisters puffed thickly, reddening at the rims, some already broken. Even in the moonlight they were distinct. Landry took his knife and punctured those building, to watch them wither in a spurt of watery fluid. He lay back, closed his eyes and recalled drinking from icy, pure streams in the High Sierras. He remembered once, after crossing the dry Carson Sink, how he had luxuriated before the snow-touched flow of the Carson River; how he had dipped his canteen in to watch it fill, gurgling and wondrous: water so fresh, so sweet, so beautiful. He had lifted the container to his lips, slowly, pouring the contents into his being, his mouth working, sucking, absorbing with exquisite delight. Again and once again he had drunk, filling every cell of his body with delectable, surging rapture—until finally fulfilled, his thirst quenched, his body satiated.

Landry rose with difficulty, taking several tries until he stood up, swaying slightly, his shoulders bowed. No longer could he differentiate his old wound from all the hurt and heaviness that wracked his legs. Methodically he followed a fractured ridge, there circling a saucerlike depression. Twice he heard the shattering clatter of hunting rattlesnakes. And in a clump of moon-laced mesquite he heard some creature shrill in death. A swift movement followed. Something shook the branches, snapping the brittle stems—a bobcat or a coyote making a kill, he guessed.

As the temperature plummeted in the early morning, Landry began lurching. His head throbbed, making him dizzy. He fell once, barely making it up to struggle on. He crossed a high volcanic plain; worked through a sinuous pass between more low hills, keeping always to the most solid ground in a desperate attempt to conceal his path. He wormed purposely through a boulder-strewn plateau and rested for a time under a frowning cliff. What concerned Landry was the tendency for people in the wilderness to veer off and circle back, especially at night. But the pale moon cast enough light that he could see where the White Mountains rose misty with cloud. They remained his beacon always to the northwest.

Sometimes he thought he heard running water, but he knew it could not be. Sometimes he touched his salty face, felt the leathery skin, the mesh of whiskers, grimy and caked with sweat and dirt, and he knew that he had to reach water shortly. In the lowlands between the White Mountains and the desert plateau, the shifted earth had created rents where springs flowed and water gathered in volcanic cisterns to form shallows of clear, cool water. A number of them jeweled the region. One lay in his path a half day south of Silverpoint. There would be ranchers there, utilizing lush meadows fed by the pools.

Because of limited visibility he slipped once while climbing over a dome of rock, and slid bumping and bouncing to land luckily in a gray mat of soft earth. To break a bone or to dislocate something now, would mean an anguishing, unthinkable death. He lay for a time, watching dawn whiten the east. Then he saw a movement in the sky, forms dipping and darting from the northwest, to flash over him. He sat up mesmerized as a flock of mourning doves winged past, blending with the purple distance. Doves, he knew, left their roost near water in the morning and returned in the evening. And Landry realized joyfully that water could not be far.

But his exuberance was short-lived. By daylight a blustery wind had risen, pushing him here and there with faltering steps. For another mile he proceeded with growing doubt and precarious movements, his body teetering until the sun flashed golden-white on the snow patches of the highest mountains, looming closer always, heartening him for a time. He looked at them through eye slits that had partially congealed. He had come a surprisingly, yes, an amazingly long way—twenty, maybe thirty miles, he estimated. He angled determinedly toward a battlement of rocks, figuring it offered the best protection and shade to hole up for the day. But the rushing drone of wind drew his slow attention. Behind, approaching fast, came a low wall of yellow darkness—another sandstorm. And out of it twisted a high dust devil curling in his direction. Hurriedly, dragging his bad leg, Landry managed to cross a wash toward a small cave in a low ridge shaped like a half-moon. The cavity was shallower than he had hoped, but he had no choice. He tossed in a handful of rocks, should some critter—animal or reptile—be there first. There was no response, so he moved in.

He crouched down, drew his neckerchief over his nose and mouth, pulled his sweat-stained Stetson low, crossed his arms and turned his back to the onslaught. The devil hit with a vengeance, grinding up sand, moving small boulders and hurling rocks, lifting the earth, churning it and reshaping the landscape. For nearly an hour the storm battered the desert. Landry endured. And when it waned, and calm came, the land lay pristine and clear in a silence that was almost palpable. The empty sky shed its dry light on the solitary expanse. Through the swollen cracks of his eyes Landry looked out and saw the area before him strangely denuded, stripped of topsoil, so that unrecognizable rocks and formations emerged. Exhausted, he lay back; everything seemed to whirl in his mind.

He rested, wondering if he should remain for the day, and after a time opened his eyes. Above him, where a part of the cavity curved over him, he saw a bright orange spider running across a marbling of mineralized strata. It struck him as miraculous that in the burning desolation there could be such fragile life prevailing. Then Landry's tormented eyes took notice, registering on an interesting formation. He studied a slab of quartz feldspar between what he judged as granodiorite and slate. The quartz was a lovely rose pink. Interlaced throughout, thickly, were dark metallic globules. Curiously, the marshal removed his knife and scratched at the metal. Where his knife probed, the globules gave like a hard malleable clay. And they glimmered a dull yellow. Landry dug with haste, chipping free some small nuggets. When he reached down to pick them up, he saw others that had fallen long ago into several little piles. All were the same rich pink; all were weighted with hunks of pure gold! A few were nearly solid nuggets. Had he not been so wasted, so fearful for his life, he might have whooped with rapture, for quite by chance he had stumbled upon a mine of fabulous worth. Having lived a lifetime in and around mining country, he had seen some prize silver and gold samples, but nothing like this; none, he knew, had been so valuable or so promising as what lay before him. He wondered if he were dreaming. With the strain of it all—was he hallucinating? Maybe when he saw the gold pieces in a different light, the discovery would diminish, would not prove so fabulous as he now judged. He fondled a nugget, examining it carefully then.

Hurriedly he stuffed nearly a dozen pieces into his coat pockets. He rose more jauntily than he had in days and looked around, trying to obtain a perspective, to instill in him any distinctive landmarks. But the serrated land, pocked, shredded, and brutalized by time, offered nothing memorable except the battlement of rocks that stretched to his left, north and south above a chain of steep bluffs. Already the heat was hazing the mountains. If he survived, he could find the place again, he assured himself: the wash, the ridge, the shallow cave below the bluffs under the battlement. But survive he must.

Landry assessed the situation. To attempt traveling by daylight could invite an agonizing death; but to remain another twelve or fifteen hours without water was also tempting fate. Enmeshed in a tangle of fuzzy thoughts, he tried to decide. The sun was just now casting long shadows, and the intolerable heat was only hours away. He could travel a bit more, he decided. He would avoid the open where the sun struck with blistering intensity, and where he could be seen by Morton. Ahead, past the cliffs and the battlement, there seemed to be a natural rift, a draw that wound through. It appeared to be a gradual rise that led to another low mountain. But if he judged wrong, if it proved to be a dead end, or if there were ravines winding about and splitting into a labyrinth of coulees, he would surely perish. He had neither the strength to climb out nor the will to return and try another route. But if it were a pass, he would doubtless reach the valley of life-giving water. He felt the pink nuggets jiggle in his pockets; he reached for one and pulled it out. But with the brightness, and his eyes heavy and puffed, leaving mere slits, he could not see them clearly. Willfully he set out.

Just when and where he lost control of his sensibilities he would never recall. There had been more dizziness, the head-aches again, difficulty in walking. His bloated tongue seemed to fill his mouth and throat, so that swallowing became pain-fully impossible. Then came the tingling, and the spasms again; then finally a numbness throughout his shriveled skin. His breathing became more labored. Slowly he realized he could not hear or see clearly. Everything ahead was dim and wavery. But some deep-seated instinct for survival drove him on.

Then he saw, in his mind's eye, a brute of a man, with heavy square face and swarthy body, his hair black and mat-ted, his clothes tattered. He was heavy-boned, with stumpy bowed legs on enormous bare feet. And he was beckoning, waving one massive arm in a slow gesture to hurry, to join him. Landry wiped his face and eyes with both arms and tried to clear his senses. But as he approached, the man drifted off, floated, hovered somehow, keeping the same distance between them. He was beckoning still, while steadily laugh-ing through pointed teeth, his eyes glowing white in a cadav-erous face parched and seared as if by the fires of hell. Landry tried to raise his rifle, but somewhere along the way he had lost it. He reached for his sidearm. And then suddenly the man was no more. Vanished.

Confused, Landry stumbled onward. Then he heard the noise of tumbling water. Soon he commenced seeing water: vast lakes, shimmering, lapping, waiting. Crystal blue mir-ages just ahead tortured his afflicted mind, made him rage in anguish as they receded always out of reach, so that when he saw the green of marsh and meadow with the sheets of shal-low blue ponds, he didn't understand. He did not see the barn and the cabin amongst the cottonwoods, nor the cedar fence with the cattle lolling, nor did he hear the dog barking. But some part of him sensed the presence of water, for he hurried, deliriously, falling, to crawl on hands and knees and finally reaching out to clutch the earth, grimacing to pull himself inch by inch.

Two days later, in Desert Roost, Noah Crawford busied himself selecting high-grade gold and sorting out the blasted rock from a dry shaker which he had constructed. The contraption was relatively simple but effective: a hopper, a wire mesh, a slanted box with riffles on a four-post stand, all geared to separate the smaller gold from dirt and rock particles. The freed gold was stored in sacks, small enough that he could drag one about and lift it into a wheelbarrow for transportation to a back wing of the superintendent's building for storage. Ultimately, when they had enough to form a mule train, they would load the bullion, head for Carson City, and sell to the mint there.

The evening before, the old town had shook and shuddered from several dynamite blasts, the first since the failing mines had given out. Although a businessman by nature, Crawford had learned much about mining—an industry that had always fascinated him, more with the passing years, until he had become addicted to the dream of developing his own fortune. He had watched and had consulted professionals, until he had become an expert in the use of detonators. With an auger and a sledgehammer, he had drilled several holes in the solid area of the pocket mine, a section not penetrated by pick and shovel. He had attached the fuse and cap, and had placed them carefully in a cartridge. With the crimper, he had punched a hole in the dynamite stick. Then with a tamping rod he had pushed the fuse and the explosives firmly to the bottom of the hole. Before each explosion, he had covered the hole with logs to prevent rocks and ore from flying. It took roughly one minute to burn two feet of fuse, time for him to take cover behind some old corrugated roofs that had given away.

Seth had come up to watch. Crawford had embraced his

boy before each lighting of the fuse, but had walked him a safe distance. After each blast, Mono went yelping into seclusion, emerging only long after the sounds of soughing winds and singing birds had returned to the mountain. Crawford went downslope after each blast, to be certain the concealed youth was all right. "Beautiful, ain't it?" he would tell his son. Or, "Hear all that gold come loose," or "The good life's almost here," and he would slap the boy on the shoulder good-naturedly.

Crawford had purchased a small rock stamp called a jawcrusher, which would eventually be placed on a platform below a bin into which they could shovel the shattered rocks. He and Billy would need to channel water from one of the springs for power. That was *if* Billy returned. But whatever the problems or the challenges, mining was an exciting undertaking. And as long as the gold pocket lasted, their wealth would increasingly multiply. Life, at last, was showing great promise for Crawford, his dream come true.

When breakfast time came, Crawford refused to take off the precious half hour, choosing to have Vallee or Seth bring him something so that he could continue working. He stopped sometimes to drink water and to glance around the mountaintop for signs of an intruder. His Winchester never lay far from his reach. But the confusion of battered hoistings and shafts and slag piles; the confusion of rocky outcrops and wooded benches, and stony promontories separated by fingery rock slides; the brushy slopes and shear cliffs, dotted and streaked by moving cloud shadows: all of it made quick or certain detection of anyone almost impossible. If someone were watching, the stranger would have the advantage. That fact bothered Crawford. He wished his fool partner, Billy Temple, had not rushed off like the Good Samaritan, but had stayed and worked like any sensible man would have seen fit to do. Crawford felt no guilt. Landry had come to help in good faith, it was true. But a lawman had to fend for himself. After all, that's what he was paid for.

In the superintendent's building Seth finished a bowl of wheat porridge and molasses. With a hot pad Vallee removed some golden biscuits and scraped them into a basket. Immediately, Seth grabbed one, whistled and tossed it into the air, caught it then dropped it on the table, to shake his hand in pain. "Serves you right, with table manners like that," Vallee scolded mildly as she wiped her hands on her apron. "Didn't you think they were going to be hot?"

Seth shrugged and, undeterred, reached again, this time managing to split the steaming biscuit. He layered it into a tin plate and poured from a pitcher of dark molasses, his brown eyes watching with anticipation.

Vallee observed him without really seeing. "I wish Papa would take time to come down and at least rest; and I wish Billy would return; and I pray that Mr. Landry is alive and all right," she said, distress in her voice.

"Well, Pop is sure in a good mood," Seth blurted, feeding his face. "Ain't seen him so happy in a long time."

Vallee grew serious. "I don't understand. He borrowed against our mine for all that equipment. What if it doesn't pay like he hopes?"

"It will," Seth said nonchalantly with a full mouth.

"Billy certainly wasn't happy about it when he left. He and Pop had a row, and it was over that."

"I wouldn't worry, Pop's doin' good. He's all right."

"What do you mean by that?" Vallee was quick to respond, her eyes narrowing in curious scrutiny.

"Nothin', just I think he's doin' good." Seth pushed the plate away and licked his lips like a big cat upon finishing its meal.

Dale Thomas, weak and unsteady, had slept fitfully, moaning and crying out through most of the night. He had refused to eat breakfast, despite a reprimand from Vallee. To avoid her admonishing eyes, he had walked out for air and for cold water from the spring. He had been drinking one dipperful after another, as if extinguishing some inner fire. He returned now, his eyes faded and feverish.

"Are you all right?" Vallee asked with concern.

"I don't know," he said with alarming directness. His left hand was caressing the bandaged wound. He winced.

"Sit down," Vallee ordered. He found his way to the old couch and sat heavily. She pumped water into a washbasin, took a rag, wetted it and pressed it across his perspiring forehead. "Let's see the wound. We must wash it again."

Thomas removed his jacket, fumbling the buttons with one hand. His broad, naked chest glistened. He could no longer wear a shirt, for the swelling and distress had intensified. "I've got to get you and the boy out," he lamented, a catch in his throat. "And Landry. God, what's happened to Landry?"

"You must think of yourself now."

"There's danger out there. No telling where those men are that gunned me."

Vallee gnawed her lips. A dark blood had oozed through the back side of the bandage where the deputy could not see. It would need changing, and she had only limited cloth. Carefully she cut the folds of the old petticoat and peeled it away. Again the deputy winced. Thomas could not see the girl close her eyes and look away. His arm rested easily in the sling, but where the bullet had entered, sliced its way up the arm and out the back shoulder, was all creased red. Gently she touched the swelling. Thomas cried out. "I'm sorry," she apologized. The flesh was hot. "I've got to boil some water, you're festering." Her heart was pounding. "You've got to have a doctor, Mr. Thomas. There's only so much we can do for you here."

"It's Dale, please," he corrected. "And a doctor's three days away. We'll wash it for now, then take water with us. If your father is fool enough to stay, then I'm taking you and your brother out of here without him."

"You're too weak, and I know you're in great pain," she protested. "What if you can't make it? I don't know if Seth and I could get us and you to Silverpoint."

"Don't worry, I can make it. At least I can save your necks. Then I'll find a doctor."

Vallee rose. "I'm going to boil the water."

"Maybe I can talk some sense into that bullheaded old man of yours." Thomas struggled up, swayed, reached and suddenly toppled backward, hitting the couch and sliding flat on his left side to the floor, his eyelids fluttering.

"My God," Vallee screamed. She rushed to him, dropped down to cradle his head in her lap. She could feel his breathing, but it was noticeably labored. "My God," she uttered, "he's going to die on us." Gently she lowered his head to the floor and hurried to the door, a shaken brother behind her. "Papa," she called, her voice high and urgent. "Papa, come, hurry. The deputy. It's the deputy."

# (8)

Landry had awakened to a man's voice saying, "He's lucky to be alive, and he may not make it yet." Then he heard another man's voice, and then a woman's. He opened his eyes to a blur of swimming forms that came into focus gradually. A large man with a pointed beard was leaning over him; a younger man was peering down, his hands on his knees. Landry became vaguely aware that he was lying on a slant of hay in a small log barn.

"Where am I?" he asked, his voice weak.

"On the Withers' place," the big man replied. "Don't know where or how you come out of that desert, Marshal, but I couldn't believe it when I seen you staggerin' this way. Then you fell and started crawlin'."

"Don't talk," the woman said. Through fuzzy vision Landry saw her on her knees, a black dog with loppy ears at her side. She wiped a wet cloth across his lips, then lifted his head and held a bowl to his mouth. Landry drank and choked. Then he gulped the water, feeling the cool, refreshing liquid revitalize his mouth and tongue, his throat, his body, his being. "Easy. Not too much," she warned.

"More," he begged. "Please, more." Again she tilted his head, and he drank most of the bowl until she removed it. Then he became aware that he was wet, that his coat and boots had been removed, that his shirt was open. With alkali-stained hands he felt himself and looked down with surprise.

The big man held up a bucket. "Been keeping your body cooled down best we can. You was dried out like you'd been roasted when you come in."

"More water, please." With harrowed eyes, Landry watched the woman pour pure, clear water from a pitcher into the bowl. This time he took it in both hands. He gulped it again, desperately, tipping the container too fast, so that it sloshed around his face and down over his whiskers. When finished he lay back.

"You rest, and then we'll get some food into you," said the woman. The big man added something, but their voices seemed distant again; a drowsy heaviness settled over Landry. Never had he felt so tired. He slept as in death.

When again he awakened, he saw early afternoon shadows outside the barn. "His eyes are open, Melba," the young man called from the barn door. He had been sitting on a box a few feet away. "You sure did sleep, Marshal." He grinned. In his twenties, the man had broad shoulders and strong arms, the sleeves of his shirt rolled up above his elbows. He looked squat in the bibbed overalls. He had a thatch of blond hair and dimpled cleavages in his cheeks. "There's more water beside you." On a box next to Landry lay the bowl and the pitcher. Landry sat up and helped himself.

The woman entered the barn carrying a second bowl that steamed. She handed it to Landry, who smiled appreciatively. The delectable aroma of beef broth reached him. He took the bowl and savored the wispy steam, then tasted the richness, his eyes closed. The woman watched him. She was tall and straight, with raven-black hair parted in the center and pulled around in a bun. She had a pronounced forehead and wide brown eyes. Pleasantly attractive, she had once been quite comely, Landry judged, but the desert and the frontier life had robbed her early, as it did many women.

"I thank you," he said hoarsely. "Didn't think I was going to make it." He closed his eyes again and sipped the hot soup.

"We wasn't sure you would, either," she said, her hands folded in front of her across a yellowed apron. "Next meal will be more substantial. I'm heating some water for a bath, thought you'd want to soak out the desert, and I'm going to wash them clothes of yours. I'll have Ted bring you some of my husband's duds, he's big like you. There's a tub back of the barn. My brother-in-law, Ted here, will help you. I'm Melba Withers, and you talked with my husband, Jake. And who are you, Marshal?''

"Dirk Landry, U.S. government, out of Limbo City. And I'm much obliged. You people saved my life.''

" 'Course we're ponderin' how you come to get in such a predicament. Ain't often we see a half-dead marshal stagger in out of the wilderness—not out of that part of the desert.''

"It's a long story. But first I need to talk with your husband.''

"He's been waiting to talk to you, too. I'll fetch him. He's out in the lower pasture forkin' hay to our heifers.'' She turned to the young man. "Get the clothes I laid out and help the marshal. Bring him that water boiling on the stove, and when he's in the tub, bring me his duds.'' She took the empty bowl. "I'll take this back to the house, then fetch Jake.''

"Show you the tub out back,'' said Ted Withers as he helped the unsteady lawman to his feet and picked up his boots. The boy saw Landry's limp and looked away self-consciously.

"You know where my coat is?''

The young man suddenly regarded Landry intently, his expression strange. "We hung it yonder in the stable there.'' He pointed. "You come on foot, how far?''

"Familiar with the old town of Desert Roost?''

"Yep. Heard about it but never been there.''

"All the way from the base of that mountain on foot.''

Withers looked at him incredulously and shook his head. "Jacob Breyfogle country,'' he said. "Nobody but a fool lookin' for it goes in there.''

Landry luxuriated in the big tub that Ted Withers had filled with buckets of scalding water heated on Melba's stove and tempered with a bucket from the well. Afterward the young man had brought a straight razor and mirror. Landry kept rubbing the lye soap over his body and pouring panfuls of

bubbly water over his head. He lathered his hair in a shampoo
made from the wild soapwort that the family had collected,
crushing it and blending it with water; it was good too for
boils and blisters, he knew. Afterward he would massage it
into his battered flesh and aching muscles. Landry soaked
and took pleasure in his smarting skin. Frequently he interrupted his bath to guzzle the cold water in a pitcher on a stool
next to him that Ted had conveniently placed there. A few
times he gargled the water to let it tingle his throat, and then
spat it out through his teeth, to watch it sink in the soft, fertile
earth.

The setting was idyllic, with the small log house, tidy
barn, sheds and cedar fences shaded by hefty cottonwoods.
To the south, this side of the desert mesa, sheets of spring
water with green meadow surrounding them caught the blue-
white of cloud and sky. To the northwest rose the wooded
skirt, the base of the White Mountains in shadow, the peaks
still glimmering in sunlight.

Landry finished his bath, toweled himself dry, and tried
on the clothes. Jake Withers was bigger in the gut but not as
tall, so the trousers hiked high and loosely. With the last of
the warm water, the marshal lathered his face and began
shaving his whiskers. What he saw in a mirror on the barn
wall shocked him so much that he lowered the razor in fear
of cutting himself. Never had he seen such a haggard, tired
face, the gray eyes, blotted with blood specks, the puffs underneath, sagging and dark. He appeared a wild man, a madman. Landry was appalled, but pleased that the family had
been so receptive and so accommodating, despite his appearance. As he finished shaving and began dumping the
bathwater, he saw Jake Withers approaching.

The big man walked with a slow, swaying gait, his stomach projecting over a broad rawhide belt, the brim of his
floppy hat rippling in the wind. "Feelin' a mite better,
huh?" he opened.

"A mite better, thanks to you all."

"The missus tells me you want to see me." Despite his

swaggering assurance, he had anxious, unsettled eyes. Landry sensed a hidden side to him.

Landry ran slow fingers across his sore mouth. "After all you've done for me, I hate to ask you favors, but I have to, because it's official business. Do you understand?"

Jake Withers removed his hat and swept his arm across a sweaty brow. "Been expectin' it, Marshal. Don't every day have a near-dead lawman come staggerin' out of the desert. The missus tells me you're Dirk Landry. Heard lots about you. Honor to meet you." Withers extended a thick, pawlike hand.

Landry smiled and accepted a firm grip. "How far from here is Silverpoint?"

"Less than half a day's ride."

"I figured about that. You see, I need your help. I'm asking to borrow one of your horses and ride there now. It's damn important, since time's short. I'll return the animal, and your clothes here. In fact, you tell me how much, and I'll rent the horse. But I must get to Silverpoint."

"Happy to oblige, Marshal. But I don't think you can make it, not in your condition. With all due respects, a mile from here, you'll fall on your face."

"Well, Mr. Withers, I have to do what I have to."

"Then follow me, Marshal, and pick your flesh. I'd suggest that big roan yonder in the corral. That gelding can carry the biggest of men easy."

"It'll do."

Ted Withers, who had commenced slopping hogs, looked up curiously. Jake took a bridle from a post, crawled through the fence and whistled to the bulky animal. "Fifteen hands high," Jake boasted. When the animal reached him, he fit the bit between its teeth, steadied the tossing head, worked on the straps and buckled them. A powerful man, he held the horse well, his large paunch swaying. Then he turned the roan around and sidled it up to the fence. "Get the blanket and saddle on," he told Landry, who took the blanket from a rail and placed it across the broad back. The magnificent animal stomped impatiently. Next Landry lifted the saddle down, gave it an aiming sweep and tossed it. But to his embarrassment, instead of landing it, he went off balance and fell flat, to send the heavy leather contraption bouncing in the milled dirt. The roan pulled away, wild-eyed, to swing its rear from side to side. "Just as I figured, Marshal. You ain't ready for much of anything for a spell."

Landry shook his head, sat up and dusted himself off, removed his Stetson and stared at the saddle. He raised an eyebrow in humorous surrender. "I guess you're right." Jake Withers offered a hand and pulled the lawman to his feet. They walked a few yards, Landry's leg bothering him noticeably, as both found rest under a cottonwood. The rancher tried not to stare, but his eyes kept coming back to the lawman's bad leg.

"Looks like it's going to be me that runs your errand," Jake said, clearing his throat.

"Guess it is, if you're willing. I'm sorry, but it's damn important."

"You can trust us all, Marshal. Me and my brother and the missus, we work close. And we keep quiet."

"Do you have a pencil and paper around?"

"The missus does in the house."

"I've got to write a constable, a Bull Dunlap in Silverpoint. Do you know him? That's who I was going after. Got to reach him."

"Yeah, I know of him." Withers was not impressed.

"I'm going to ask you to ride to the town today; give him my message. If it's possible, have him bring as many deputies as he can spare plus the supplies and stuff I need. If he can't make it, or can't afford to release a deputy, then bring the supplies. I'll need a good horse, saddle, and bridle; a rifle, ammunition, canteen, blankets, several changes of clothes, and a new hat. I'll give you my sizes and list it all. And enough grub for at least two days' ride. He'll know what I need. And the U.S. government will reimburse him, but he knows that." The two stood up, Landry still a little wobbly.

"You don't need no constable to protect you. Me and my

brother can shoot. When you're able to go back in the desert, we'll go with you.'' Jake swung the loose saddle onto the roan and began cinching it.

Landry stopped. "I don't think you understand. I had a bad run-in with Leander Morton—Rattlesnake Morton and his men, a few days ago.''

"That son of a bitch is in the area?''

"He is. There's an outside chance that he might have tracked me this far. We must keep our eyes peeled, in any case. But I don't think so. I'm certain I fooled him, that I shook him off my trail. He won't dream I got through. My concern is for a prospector named Billy Temple, his partner, Noah Crawford—Dunlap knows both of them—and Crawford's two kids. All are mining in the old town of Desert Roost. A deputy of mine is with them, and I have good reason to believe they're in danger. With Dunlap's help we might just surprise Morton and his men and finish them once and for all. That's what I'll be writing him.''

With a calloused hand Jake Withers stroked his pointed beard. "You are sure as hell dedicated, Marshal." His eyes strayed to his brother Ted, who was approaching timidly. "Don't know if I'd want to go back into that hell." He looked out at the edge of the shimmering desert. "There'd have to be something awful important out there." He looked back to Landry questioningly.

"I see you found the contents of my coat." Landry's words came like the clap of thunder.

Ted, who overheard the statement, looked both foolish and guilty. But Jake coolly acknowledged the fact. "Pretty hard not to. When we took your coat off, it damn near weighted the both of us down.''

"I was half out of my mind when I found them. I'd like to look at them again myself. You see, I don't remember much about them, except at the time I felt I'd stumbled on to some real rich ore.''

"Rich!" Jake expelled a deep breath explosively. "I've lived all my life in this country. I seen prospectors and mines and speculators come and go. And I seen more ore than you could shake a stick at. But I seen only one other sample as rich as you was carryin'. That was a nugget in Austin, behind glass with special-built bars. It set on some black cloth. And Marshal, yours and it look just alike. Both near solid gold, both set in pink rock. And that piece in Austin was brung in by Jacob Breyfogle in 1867. You've found the Lost Breyfogle Mine, Marshal. I know you have. Ain't no doubt in my mind.''

"Well, I ain't ever seen nothin' like it either, Marshal,'' Ted blurted.

"You're supposed to be sloppin' them hogs over yonder,'' Jake said harshly.

"There's time, big brother. Hell, one don't ever see the likes of what he brung in, not in a lifetime. I want to know how he found 'em.''

"That ain't none of your business. Now go on back.'' Jake pivoted a hand to shoo the young man away. Ted backed up a little and stood his ground. "Go on. Get your chores done. You'll have time to jaw with the marshal tonight over supper.'' Ted hesitated for a time, glared at his brother, then looked down angrily before returning heavy-footed to his work.

"I can't thank you and your family enough, Mr. Withers, for saving my life,'' Landry said, twisting into an awkward position to ease his leg. "But I have to ask you not to say anything to anyone about my find. Understand?'' Landry spoke firmly. He recalled the haunting vision—the beckoning creature in the desert—but did not say anything.

Jake shook an assuring finger at Landry. "The less who knows, the better for those of us who do. I ain't as dumb as I look, Marshal.''

"One whisper, one glimpse, and there will be a stampede into this desert that won't stop for years to come.'' The marshal assessed Jake. "Tell you what, you can take one of those nuggets. But it must be kept undercover, at all costs. Except you can show it to Dunlap in private if you see him. What I know of Dunlap, it might be a nice little encouragement to join us. Let him know I brought it and more in.''

Jake Withers grinned broadly. "It's a nice little encouragement for anybody. Sure would like to know its assay value. Sure would."

"Well, if you agree to run my errand—get what I need and contact Dunlap, you can keep that nugget, but don't get itchy about assaying it just yet. Got me?"

"Got you. And you got yourself a partner, Marshal. Damn right I'll help. When you plan to go back after it? God, what I'd give to see the likes of that mine."

"When my job's done. When I know my people are safe, and Morton is dead or headed for hanging."

Jake grinned and shook his head in disbelief. "As I said, Marshal, I sure admire you for your dedication to that badge. But when you do go searchin', I know this country mighty good. You wouldn't come to near perishin' again with me."

Landry smiled inwardly. "Remains to be seen. All depends how well you do for me. If you can get Dunlap and my supplies back here—maybe afterward."

"They're yours. And if you need an extra gun hand, you got me, too."

Jake led the roan toward the house, a low sprawling building made of pine logs and mud, the roof nearly flat with a mud-hardened mesh of brush and crude boards. A number of washtubs hung from the siding, as well as knobs and hooks for axes and shovels; a multitude of deer antlers adorned the eaves. Behind a cedar hitching rail lay a cavernous porch that harbored a cord of stovewood, sawhorses, and an emery wheel. But Landry noted that along the front of the home, someone had lovingly made a narrow rock garden, blending the colorful stones found throughout the Basin country. White curtains in each window enlivened an otherwise bleak abode.

Melba was beating Landry's boiled clothes piece by piece on a stump. Behind her stretched a clothesline between two sheds. Waving there in the dry wind, the hung clothes would be ready in a few hours, he knew. Jake hitched the roan to the railing, walked over to the nearest shed and said something to Melba, because she looked at Landry. Jake then emerged with saddlebags, rolled blankets, a canteen, and a yellow tarpaulin. "Need some grub and a change of shirt, and I'll be ready," he said more to himself. "Ain't gonna spend no money for food or lodgin'."

Landry followed the big man inside the house. The main room was simple; shelves with dishes and spices lined one corner, with most of the pots and pans hanging from nails. Melba had the convenience of a drainboard with a sink and a pump. The table and round-backed chairs rested in front of a cooking stove, and on the opposite side of the room was a rough-hewn couch and lounge chair, upholstered in cowhide, the brown and white faded from use and time. A rug, the skin of a mountain lion, lay in the center. Three pictures, reprints of idyllic settings: the Rockies, the Shenandoah Valley, the Hudson, and a twisted piece of bone-white juniper, gave life to the walls. A large kerosene lantern hung from the ceiling. A rock fireplace filled the south wall. Landry could see two adjoining bedrooms.

Jake Withers wandered into a pantry and came out with food wrapped in cloth sacks. He stuffed a plate, cup, silverware, and a coffeepot into the saddlebags and disappeared into the first bedroom. Melba entered, her face perplexed, and behind her a dozen paces came Ted, obviously curious. When the woman saw Landry, her expression changed to a pleased surprise. Before she could speak, he explained, "Your husband has graciously volunteered to ride to Silverpoint for me. It's urgent, but for him there will be no danger. I assure you. Now I will need some paper and a pencil."

Melba went to a drawer, removed the requested materials and handed them to the marshal, who immediately arranged himself at the table. The woman watched him favor the left leg. "I must say, you look mighty different than that near-dead man who crawled in here." Her eyes danced.

"Thanks to you."

Jake emerged with some clothes as Ted stepped in the door. "You forgot to wipe your boots, as always," Melba said to the younger brother.

Embarrassed, he looked at the marshal, backed out and scraped his feet on a soiled rug.

"You and the missus got to hold down the place," Jake said to his brother. "I'm runnin' an errand for the marshal here. Plan to be back by mid-morning, tomorrow."

Melba looked searchingly at her husband. "What's happening?"

"Don't have time to talk, the marshal will fill you in. Quick as he finishes his message, I'm leavin'. And you, Ted, you mind my woman."

"When haven't I?" Hurt, the young man scowled defensively.

"He minds me, always," Melba protested. Landry saw her smile at the young man with a motherly devotion.

Landry returned then to the note, writing in large print and simple sentences. All lawmen were required to read and write, but he wasn't certain how capable Bull Dunlap was of deciphering complex sentences or of understanding professional terms. When finished, he folded the note and handed it to Jake, who pushed it into a vest pocket.

"I'll be back with everything, and, hopefully, Dunlap." Jake gave him a smart salute.

"I appreciate it."

"You just may be able to do me a favor someday," said Jake, stepping out and swinging aboard the roan to rein it away north. Landry watched from the door until the rider had disappeared over a low rise; then he returned to the table and drank the hot cup of coffee that Melba had placed down.

She happily set utensils and a white napkin before Landry. With ease, she then sliced sandwiches of thick day-old bread and hunks of cold beef. "You must be famished. But it's best not to eat too much too fast. Suppertime, I'll fix you something hot."

Landry smiled appreciatively and watched her every move. When the food arrived, he munched it slowly, taking exquisite pleasure. The first solid food in days tasted better than anything he had ever experienced, he decided.

Melba sat down in front of him with her own mug of coffee

and watched him eat, as Ted poured himself a cup and joined them, straddling a chair backward. "My husband was his usual informative self," the woman opened, "so naturally I have a female's curiosity. You was near death when you come in. What happened? And what is Jake up to? I realize you're in no condition to travel yet, but what exactly are you asking of him?"

Landry filled her in briefly with the details of the vanished Crawford, of his children, of Temple and Shoshone Joe, of the harrowing escape from Morton and his men. He purposely avoided mention of the gold.

"Those people on the mountain must mean a lot to you," Melba said, studying him, "that you would risk crossing any godforsaken desert again so soon."

"It's important, ma'am, or I wouldn't entertain the prospect."

Seeing his reluctance to talk about it, Melba let it go.

Landry ate slowly, finally pushing the plate away with only one sandwich eaten. "Guess my stomach's shrunk. I'll have the rest later."

Melba rose and poured him another cup of coffee. "I shouldn't wonder that it's shrunk. Anyway, the dog loves leftovers. I told you, you're gonna have a hot supper. You want some whiskey? Jake has a bottle or two in the cupboard. It might relax you."

"Not right now. Later I'd like some." Landry's mouth curled teasingly. "I can tell it's on the tip of your tongue. You're curious about the nuggets in my coat. In fact, you're dying to ask about them, aren't you? Well, I'm curious, too."

Melba blushed and looked down, but Ted beamed and grinned wide, so that the clefts in his face deepened. "Golly, yes." His eyes sparkled and rounded. "My brother says them nuggets are the richest he's ever seen. He thinks they're the Breyfogle gold. You think they are?" He leaned over the chair back like an excited kid.

Landry shrugged.

"You remember where you found them?"

"Ted, that's none of your business," Melba cautioned.

"It's okay, because no, I'm not exactly sure. I was pretty dazed when I came across them," Landry said with a shiver. "It was a nightmare by then, although it got worse. But to retrace those steps—I don't know, it remains to be seen."

The woman said gently, "Yes, you was a dying man when we found you crawling in—dying and a little out of your head. If you empty those pockets, I'll wash your coat." Landry looked at Ted. "Why don't you fetch the garment for us."

"We can look at them again?"

"Certainly, I'd like to see what I found."

Ted rose, almost knocking his chair aside, and thundered out.

Alone for the time, the man and woman felt an awkwardness. Landry broke the silence. "I don't know how I can thank you people."

"We may all be asking something of you, Marshal, before we're through."

"Meaning?"

"It doesn't matter right now."

"I'm tired," said Landry. "After your brother-in-law brings my coat and we look, I'm going back to the barn and lie down."

"You can lay on my bed or my husband's."

Landry looked at her strangely, but did not pursue it. "No. No, I don't want to impose."

Melba glanced toward the barn as if to watch for Ted. "I feel uncomfortable—we so seldom have visitors." She turned back, looking directly into Landry's gray eyes. He noticed then how liquid-brown hers were. "I hope we can talk some. Tonight maybe. I need your help." Then she stiffened and leaned back as Ted entered and handed the coat over.

Landry hung the battered garment from a chair. "Got something to lay them on? Nuggets can carve up tables," he asked.

Melba moved to a cupboard and pulled out an empty flour sack. "Here, you can keep this to carry them in."

One by one Landry removed the nuggets. One by one he

examined them, placing each in his right hand, where each nearly filled the palm. Ted stared, captivated. Melba sat entranced. Landry marveled at the rich pink of the rock, nearly solid with pure gold. He had not been hallucinating; they were the finest specimens that he had ever seen, let alone held.

"God. But my God, you're rich." Ted emphasized the last word and looked hard at Landry. "You got to go back. Right away, as soon as you recover. You got to stake it. My God. Look at them."

"With all that waiting for you, you'll never have to risk your life again as a lawman," Melba reminded him.

"Yeah," said Landry, "if it was just that simple."

# (9)

Morton had led his men in a desperate thrust west, following his intuition that Landry would try and swing back to Desert Roost rather than attempt crossing a forbidden desert to reach the distant springs. The blanketing dust storms, however, had forced them to take refuge, while the brutal winds had shifted over the earth and erased Landry's movements. In a whim of desperation, they even traveled several miles west of where Landry would have logically cut for Desert Roost, chancing that he had attempted to fake them by circling wide.

Finally, baffled and commencing to bicker amongst themselves, they had backtracked and then shifted north, deeper into the high desert, in hopes of uncovering or chancing upon a clue as to how Landry had evaded them. Morton, frustrated and morose, grew progressively irritated, then angry, and finally enraged, threatening his own men if they did not find the marshal. Morton kept looking for buzzards or ravens; he doubted if Landry had succumbed. The man was too wilderness wise, but the half-breed might have. He admitted they could lose the chance to wrench more information from Shoshone Joe. Earlier they had seen a dozen wheeling vultures, gradually circling then dropping into a hollow. The spot drew them miles out of their way into stifling heat as the day lengthened. Exhausted, their horses wet with lather, they had at last come upon the attraction—the remains of a small antelope, apparently killed by coyotes. "Can't afford to follow out these things too often," Jenson commented with practical cynicism.

Morton glowered at the little man but knew he was right and therefore didn't say anything. With the glaring heat, and the beginnings of another dust storm, they found haven in a walled gully. Impatiently they waited for the cool of evening. Morton wandered off by himself to sit on a rise above the ravine. Disdainfully he watched the thick engulfing approach of the dust devil, heard its ominous hum. He could not shake his obsession with Landry. Where was the man hiding? Had he miraculously evaded them, he on foot with a hurting half-breed? They with food, water, and on mounts. It was unthinkable.

Sullenly he watched Jenson climb out of the gully, apparently to join him. He resented the intrusion, but Jenson had been one of his most loyal men, practical, capable, one that could always be relied upon. "Looks like a mean one coming in," Jenson said, looking at the thickness whirling toward them, but it was obvious that was not his main concern.

"What's on your mind?"

"I been thinking. We know Shoshone Joe didn't have the loot on him. But when Wasatch hurt him, he yelled—that it wasn't there. Do you think maybe he was tellin' the truth? Maybe when he went back to steal that money, it really wasn't there. Or maybe he moved it to another place, and when he went back it was gone. Somebody else found it. Did you think of that?"

"I've tossed the idea about, yes. At first I thought if Landry hadn't butted in, we would have got the truth out of the Indian. But maybe not. He was hurt and scared. He knew we meant business. Maybe what he told us is all he knew. That's why I want another couple of days trying for him and Landry, just to clear things up. Then if we don't find nothing, we'll visit that old town up there. If Landry had a posse with him, they'd of come lookin' by now. That deputy we shot, I lay odds that was all Landry had with him. He was hurt, so he won't be no problem."

"Yeah, I think you're right." The two huddled down and adjusted their neckerchiefs in preparation of the devil bearing down. "You going to look in on them prospectors?"

"They're as likely suspects as we've got. If they know anything about our money, we'll soon find out."

When Noah Crawford reached his daughter, a bleary-eyed and woozy Dale Thomas was partially sitting up. "What the devil happened?" Crawford demanded as he entered the door.

"The deputy, he passed out—dead away."

"Never had that happen before," Thomas said, a weak, embarrassed smile forming. His ashen face looked much older than on the day he had ridden in.

Behind Thomas, Vallee motioned in silence to her father, who sidled next to her as she pointed to the enflamed arm. He grimaced, bit his lip, and moved around in front of the deputy to seat himself. He looked directly into the young man's eyes. "I ain't gonna lie to you, son, but you got the beginnings of a bad infection."

"I know. I've felt it coming on."

"We're going to have to poultice that, suck out the poison somehow." Crawford gestured to Vallee. "Get some of that powdered rose stem. And you, Seth, get us an axe and a hatchet." Vallee went into a cabinet in her father's room, where a number of medicine bottles filled the compartments. Some were professional concoctions such as tinctures and oils, and there was also a number of home creations, all carefully labeled. Vallee returned with a bottle. "Stir up the fire," Crawford ordered. Obliging, Vallee dumped wood sticks into the stove burner and vigorously prodded it to a roar. In a kettle, Crawford stirred a spoonful of the powder with melted lard from the back of the stove, then set it aside to cool. "When that salve is to the point of not burning him, rub it on the infection. And cut up one of them old flour sacks for a poultice. Seth and me are going to get some alder bark."

"Alder bark?" Thomas questioned.

"Yeah, alder bark. Learned that from a cook in a mining camp I once worked."

The boy came shuffling in with an axe and a hatchet.

Crawford strapped on a large knife and took his rifle and a cooking pan. "We'll go down into the ravine below here, where all that water runs through," he said, taking the axe from the boy as the two left.

Vallee checked the salve and withdrew her finger to wave it. "Ouch, still hot."

"Never swooned like that before," Thomas repeated, obviously self-conscious still. "Don't know what's come over me; no little infection should do that."

Vallee looked at the deputy with sympathy. "That's no little infection. You're not all that well. Besides, you've had a shock to your system and you've lost a lot of blood. What did you expect?"

"To be riding out of here, your family with me. And I intend to do just that."

"Well, we won't be leavin' just yet." Her voice caught. Thomas looked at her and saw deep concern, and a great fear that she could not conceal.

Northeast and a hundred yards below the superintendent's building, some of the springs converged in a watery little run that splashed and gurgled pleasantly down the mountainside. The continuous water made the rocks and banks mossy and produced a rich canopy of white alder, the wide leaves bright green, the bark smooth and silvery. Crawford set to chopping out some limbs. With his knife he sliced strips of bark. He showed Seth how to smash the strips on a flat rock, mushing them into a pulp which they washed in the cold water and scooped into the flat pan. "What we do with this, Pop?" The boy looked perplexed.

"When we get home, we'll mix a spoonful of this with flour and hot water. Then we pour it into a flour sack, fold it over and place it over the swelling on the deputy. It will suck out the poison."

"How did you learn all this?" The boy looked impressed.

"I studied it; learned about it, just like I learned about mining. If you're goin' to survive in this world, you better be prepared. Remember that, son.'' He placed a hand around the nape of the youth's neck.

"You think we can save Mr. Thomas, Pop?''

"I don't know yet, but he's a pretty tough young fellow.''

"I think him and Vallee kind of like each other.''

Crawford looked curiously at his son but did not reply. So engrossed were they that they did not hear the rider approaching slowly through the trees. Crawford sensed the intrusion more than saw it, and grasped his rifle, which leaned against an alder. Billy Temple called out, "It's me, Noah.''

"You sure startled me, Billy. Could of shot you.''

"No, much more likely I would have shot you if I'd been up to no good.'' He heeled the mule from cover and rode up. "Heard some pounding and wondered what the hell was happening.''

"The deputy Thomas, his wound is festering bad. We're getting some bark here for a poultice.'' Crawford paused. "You apparently seen nothin' of Landry.''

Temple bowed his head despondently. "No sign of him. But there was no sign of anything dead out there, and I traveled a good ways into the desert. However, I have a good gut feeling about something.''

"What's that?''

"I followed tracks of at least five riders and what looked like two or three packhorses to where they camped.''

"Five of 'em?''

"There was no remains of a campfire or a cooking fire anywhere.''

"Meaning?''

"Meaning, if they was just travlin' casual like, they would have heated something—coffee, at least. But they must have eaten or guzzled everything cold.''

"Maybe it was too hot. You know the desert, it can burn your socks off.''

"Not in the evening or early morning.''

"I don't follow.''

"To me it appears they didn't want to give away their whereabouts with smoke or fire. I think Landry is out there, and they're tracking him—or trying to. He may not be too good off, but I think he's alive and holding his own.''

''How come you didn't follow 'em further?''

''Hard to track at night, and in the day I was a sitting duck with five against one and me on a mule. And I got to worrying about you people.''

''Why would Landry be fool enough to head into the desert?''

''Maybe he had no choice.''

''Well, Billy, I'm glad you're back. I need your strong shoulders for the gold. And we may have a deputy on our hands that won't make it.''

Landry stretched languidly in the hay, feeling relatively good, despite the aches and the pains of the ordeal. A kerosene lantern from a barn wall cast cheerful light over the place. A few horses munched contentedly in their stalls. Melba had fixed a fine meal: fresh biscuits with chokecherry jam, chunks of hot beef and beans with wild onions, a side dish of canned tomatoes, a raisin and rice pudding, and cups of scalding black coffee. Ravenous, this time, Landry had eaten as if to restore his loss with one meal. Ted had been with them, not speaking much, but eating seriously. Landry smiled, thinking pleasantly about it.

Melba was as starved for talk as Landry was for food. She asked about the latest gossip and styles and happenings in Virginia and Limbo cities. She had probed about the reason for Landry's predicament in the desert. He freely admitted that he had misjudged Leander Morton, which had nearly cost him his life. At her insistence he elaborated on the mysterious disappearance of Crawford, about Temple and Thomas, and about Vallee and Seth in the old town. She listened with great interest. None of them mentioned the gold, until Landry repeated the desperate need to get back to Desert Roost. Melba was clearing the table, then stopped and placed one hand on a hip. ''I know you're a lawman, that you have duties and responsibilities, but most men I have ever known would abandon everything to find that gold.''

"Your husband said something to that effect."

"The desert is fickle. You should not waste too much time. If what you come across is the Breyfogle, men have given their lives looking for it. You are very fortunate; you must find it again, soon."

Landry shrugged. "Like I said before, I don't know if I can, but I know I gotta try. I'd be a fool if I didn't. God has given me a chance to be comfortable for the rest of my life. I know that. A lawman doesn't get much of a retirement, you know." Landry's eyes wandered afar. He came back to himself suddenly. "But first I gotta help those who are relying on me—those on that mountain. I have to."

"You're the only man I ever met so loyal to his duty."

"Not really. There are plenty of others who would do the same. Besides, those people are more than duty to me."

When Ted left to do the evening chores, Melba became noticeably relaxed. She talked then, about the isolation, about the loneliness, about the hard work, about how the farm had hardly paid for itself after nine years of struggle. Landry did not question, but she seemed to want to tell him that her father had been a failing Pennsylvania farmer who had pursued a dream by moving the family—her mother, two older brothers, and a younger sister—west to California in the latter days of the Gold Rush. But the dream had become a nightmare—with the sister dying suddenly from cholera before they had reached Fort Kearney, a tragedy that neither she nor her mother ever really recovered from. And then near South Pass the younger brother, one she was especially close to, had been thrown from a spooked pony. For two days they had carried him unconscious in the wagon, until he too had succumbed. She would never forget the windy openness of that high plain with the small pile of rocks for a headstone and the Wind River Mountains towering behind.

California mining had been no better for her father than had Pennsylvania farming. Ultimately he had managed to open a small merchandise store, barely making enough to keep the family from starving, as the mother, sick physically and emotionally, withdrew further into herself. Melba had helped by taking in washing, until she could move out to support herself by working in a boardinghouse. She had met Jake through her surviving brother. Both were teamsters. At age fifteen she had married him, living almost alone the first years, as he was gone much. But when the silver strike turned the eyes of the world on Nevada Territory, Jake had realized his dream, to have land, to be independent, and with their meager savings they had homesteaded and started the ranch here near the White Mountains, a site Jake had often passed and coveted in his hauling days. And that was Melba's life ever since. Landry felt somewhat sorry for her; but she, like so many others in the vast land, had been fated to a bleak and drab existence. There was nothing he could do except listen.

In the barn, thinking about the pleasant evening, Landry sat up. His smile faded as his concerns turned to serious business ahead. Mechanically he began cleaning and oiling his revolver. The wait for Jake to return would seem interminable, he knew. He wondered how successful the man would be with the assignments.

He removed one of the gold nuggets from the flour sack and watched it shine dully in the yellow light. He thought of the rich mine, of the fickle desert, as Melba had phrased it. What was visible one day would be buried the next. The landscape changed constantly with the shifting sands. Even landmarks took on changed proportion with the distortion of light and shadows.

He thought of Billy Temple, of Seth, and especially of Vallee—so blossoming and promising now—a fine gem for a worthy young man. What were they all doing now? Had they lost hope for his survival? Did they feel abandoned? And what of his deputy, Thomas? There had been that rifle shot while he and Shoshone Joe were together in the standoff. Why just one shot? Had the deputy come looking for him? It was certainly logical that he would. Had he walked into a trap? The sharpshooter, Lee Van Liddicoat, was adept at removing a rider with one shot. Could that have happened? How frustrating and useless to ponder.

Landry heard something outside. Quickly he punched some cartridges into the cylinder, rose, lowered the lantern and stole to the barn door. He waited to the side. Someone crossing the yard was carrying a light. The sound of swishing cloth reached him. Recognizing Melba, he stepped out, confronting her. ''What are you doing out here?''

She held out a roll of blankets. ''I thought you might need more.'' He smiled, bowed his head boyishly, thanked her and took them. Again there was an awkward pause, as he waited for her to leave, but he sensed she wanted more time. ''I appreciated your listening to me tonight. I must have bored you,'' she said timidly.

''Not at all. I like to know something about people I meet, especially people who have saved my life.''

She walked past him into the soft light of his lantern and set hers down. ''I just get so lonely out here, day after day, not seeing anybody. Just Jake and Ted. I miss people. Women especially. It's been so long since I've had a good woman's talk.'' She looked at him. Her voice was that of a sad little girl. ''Do you understand that?''

''I can appreciate it.''

She moved a step toward him. ''I don't want you to think of me as a brazen woman, Mr. Landry, but I want you to take me with you! Out of here.''

Dumbfounded, Landry swallowed and tried carefully to form his reply. Instead, he managed, ''Why?''

''I'm sick of my life here. I'm sick of this place.'' Her face held a chill of despair.

''But this is your life. This is your land. Yours and your husband's. You told me you've given nine years to this place.''

''But I don't want to die here. And I'm dying here.'' Her voice grew husky with conviction.

''But what of Jake? And what of Ted? The young man leans on you. He needs you.''

She looked at him with penetrating eyes. ''Jake can do just as much for him as I can.'' She stood vigorously erect. ''Ted won't stay much longer.''

''And what of Jake?''

"There's nothing there. We have nothing in common."

"You took vows, didn't you? And you've lived with him all these years."

"It was a marriage of convenience. Nothing more."

"You must have known what you were getting into."

Her eyes softened, dismissing him and his comment as naive. But she answered. "I wanted to get away from the drudgery of the boardinghouse, and what I knew was a hopeless future. But I didn't know we would end up in this godforsaken country." She glanced around at the stalls and at the rafters.

"You made a commitment, Mrs. Withers. Just as I made a commitment to some people out there on a desert mountain." Landry knew he was sounding condescending.

"I'm not asking to be a burden. I could help you. I could help the girl you spoke of. She must long for a woman's understanding." Her appeal had an edge of fright.

"It's too dangerous out there. The desert and Rattlesnake Morton. I'm trying to raise a posse. That's what your husband's doing for me."

She sighed. "Then when you come back." Her eyes mingled with his. "You will pass this way again, because of the water, and because my husband will not let you out of his clutch. Not now. Not with that gold out there. You see, Jake hankers for bigger things, just as I do, but we don't exactly hanker for the same things. But for certain he plans to be your partner, because you owe him something now for your life."

"Yes, I owe him, and I owe you and Ted. We'll see."

"When you come back, take me with you to Virginia City or to Limbo."

"Just pick you up, right in front of your husband?" Landry looked at her in disbelief. He tried to dismiss her as gently yet as firmly as possible. "Sorry, Mrs. Withers, that's not part of my job."

"I've threatened to leave him and this hellhole a thousand times. When I was working in that boardinghouse, when I met him, I thought he was my only chance." She laughed bitterly. "What a fool I was."

"You have a home now; where would you live? What would you do?"

"A home?" she scoffed. "It's a roof over our heads. You can't convince me otherwise. I've thought it all out carefully, for a long time. And I've saved a little money that Jake doesn't know about."

"You really sure you know what you're doing? Do you actually believe it would be easy going back to washing and scrubbing, if that's what you figure? It's not easy in those towns—a woman alone."

"I've been there before. It wouldn't be half as hard as what I do here. And there would be people to see and to talk to."

"Running away doesn't seem the answer. There must be something you and your husband share besides this place."

"If anything, we've grown apart. You don't understand, Marshal. I'm a barren woman. I can't have children. Maybe it's because I don't want to give Jake a child or be next to him. Or maybe it's because I don't feel like a woman. Anyway, for nearly twelve years we've lived like brother and sister, because there was nothing there to begin with." Her anguish and despair had turned to desolation.

"You're very much a woman, Mrs. Withers." Landry could feel her feminine presence strongly. "I'm surprised at your husband, unless you have pushed him away."

She accepted his insinuation without a blink. "He's never wanted or needed more than a cook and laborer. But I guess I asked for it. Marrying him, I got what I deserved." She was looking at him, and he detected a glint of moisture in an eye. "I could be a good woman for the right man."

"You're healthy, you're strong, you're your own person, as far as I can see. Why don't you just hitch up a wagon and leave? You'd survive." His tone invited confidence. "You don't need me or anyone else to escort you."

There was a sad insistence in her voice. "I'm an old woman at twenty-seven, Old and frightened." Her words had a forlorn tone heavy with dread. "I need somebody strong like you to help me with that first step. Can you possibly understand that?''

His face burdened but tender, Landry reached out and touched her hand. "It's getting late. You must go back. And you must think seriously about what you've said. To leave a husband of twelve years is a mighty big decision, it seems to me.''

"Maybe to you, it does.'' Then she nodded in mild consent and lifted his big hand and pressed it briefly against her cheek. "I will be waiting for your return.'' Then she was gone with her lantern. Bombarded by confusing emotions, Landry stepped to the door and watched her cross the yard. From a window, Ted was watching too, unaware that an indoor light silhouetted him darkly.

# (10)

Landry had been anxiously pacing when the Withers' dog began barking. Over the sloping rise came Jake on the roan, leading a sorrel strapped with goods. Two riders paralleled him. Melba stepped out of the cabin. Wiping her flour-dusted hands on an apron, she stood waiting, glancing frequently at Landry, who stood tall, his feet spread firmly, both hands on his hips. He had noticed earlier that she looked less haggard, and also happier, a rosy flush in her cheeks. The dog quit barking as the threesome reined up, but emitted sporadic growls at the strangers.

"Morning, Titus, most appreciative you could find time to make it," Landry greeted the constable.

Dunlap nodded, crossed his hands on his pommel and leaned forward. "Hear you had a rough time, that Rattlesnake Morton nearly done you in."

"Hasn't been easy."

"Hell, I'd like a crack at him." Contemptuously, Dunlap spat a wad of tobacco.

"Figured you would."

"Be a feather in both our caps if we done him in." Titus "Bull" Dunlap was a husky, barrel-chested man with a jowly, square face. His beetling brows, long bushy mustache, and wide mouth gave him a no-nonsense appearance. He had enormous hands and forearms. "Of course, it couldn't been all that bad, seein' what you found out there. My God, Landry, you must have fallen onto the Breyfogle."

"Remains to be seen."

"Sure would like to see you find it again. Think you can?"

Dunlap crouched in the saddle some, like an animal about to pounce, his eyes intensely interested.

"Hope you didn't tell nobody other than your man here. We got enough problems out here without ten thousand prospectors stumbling over us."

Dunlap guffawed deeply. "I ain't no fool, Landry. I like keepin' things amongst just a few of us. Oh, this is Joe Lasko. He's the only one I could afford to bring, and the only one I can trust in such serious matters."

The deputy tapped the rim of his hat. A gangly chap, he sat sullenly, his face sour, his narrow eyes assessing. A half-burned cigarette hung loosely from the corner of his tight lips.

Landry began checking the gear on the sorrel and removed a new Stetson tied on top. "With the likes of Morton, we could have used more men, but I know you did the best you could. I assume everything I asked for is here."

"Everything. And enough grub for a good five days or more, longer if we pick up anything off the land."

"I'm going to get out of my host's clothes." Landry removed new garments from one bag. "The woman here is the wife of Jake Withers." The constable and his deputy acknowledged her.

"Oh, yeah," announced Jake Withers. "I plan to go with you, Marshal. I know you need more gun hands."

"Could be dangerous and nasty," Landry said. "But I figured you would want to." He started heading toward the barn to change. "Best add what staples or clothes you may need, because we're heading out soon as I change."

When Landry emerged, Melba was waiting to take Jake's clothes. Landry thanked her graciously for her kindness and for her hospitality. "I could use Jake's help. But I'll try not to get him killed."

Her brown eyes caressed his face. "We both knew he would go. You have a partner whether you want one or not. And Marshal, I hope you find your friends safe, and that you find whatever else you want."

"Thank you."

"I'll be here, Marshal, when you return." Their eyes connected.

Although he knew she had made up her mind, he said, "Don't wait for me or anyone else. Do what you think you have to do."

Uncomfortable with the situation, Landry made long strides away. He adjusted the stirrups and swung onto the sorrel, a small compact animal that left the marshal's long legs close to the ground. Jake came out of the house with a sack—probably additional clothes or food—and said something to his wife, but he expressed no affection or concern that he was leaving her.

As they turned to head out, Ted Withers appeared on horseback from around the barn, the animal laden with gear enough for an extended trip. "What the hell?" Jake spouted.

"I'm going too, big brother."

"The hell you are."

"The marshal needs all the hands he can muster." Ted sat his horse firmly.

"We need you here to tend the place and help Melba."

"Then you stay, and I'll go."

Jake's face grew truculent. "You impudent pup, I should have whupped you more than I did. You listen to me and take orders." He stabbed a fat, hard finger at his brother.

Ted clutched the reins in his gloved hands. "No, big brother, you listen to me. I ain't going to die here sloppin' hogs and rootin' ground for you all my life." He twisted his horse from side to side, its tail swishing and flowing. "I know what you're after, and I got a right, too."

"God damn it, you stay put if you know what's good for you. I ain't arguin' with you no more." Jake yanked his horse away and shouted to the others, "Come on, let's ride." He pushed the roan into a gallop.

"You can't stop me," Ted called after them. "You can't stop me."

In Desert Roost, Vallee washed Thomas's wound and applied a hot poultice to the upper shoulder. The deputy sat on a chair, leaning forward. Color had come back to his face, and the swelling in the arm had decreased some, while the redness had lessened, but it was too early to predict. Seth and Billy Temple had made another trip to the canyon for more alder, and the day before they had ventured down farther for bark of the wild rose. Temple had brought the thorny stems back to pound into a powder, but he also brought back a number of stems with bright red leaves for Vallee, which she immediately arranged in several of her mother's prize vases, amenities she had insisted on bringing to the wilderness. The bouquets added a liveliness to the room, but not enough to raise Dale Thomas's spirit.

"Landry gave me orders to get you and Seth out, and I've failed that," he said, troubled.

"You couldn't help it; why, you could have died on the way. You know that, and we haven't licked this infection yet. And besides," she added mischieviously, "I think you like me waiting on you."

Her remark lifted the gloom from his face. "Of course I like you taking care of me. But that's beside the point. I'm getting you people out as soon I can."

"But there's been no problem, no threat of any sort. Nobody's been prowling around again." Vallee's comment revealed a sensible, practical side.

"It don't matter, orders are orders. And I've got to organize a posse and find Landry." He looked frustratingly at the slinged arm. "Except no sensible man would ride with me."

Vallee felt his despair. "With time, you'll use the arm. I know you will." She placed a hand on his forearm.

"No I won't, Vallee. Maybe I'll get some use out of it, but for speed and straight shootin'—a lawman has to have that. Otherwise he's useless; he's worthless." Thomas spoke with bitterness.

"What about Marshal Landry? What about that leg of his? And that doesn't stop him." Vallee felt feisty, unwilling to tolerate any of the deputy's self-pity.

"Landry is a remarkable man; that's why I believe he's

holding his own somewhere. Landry is the best lawman alive, now that my old man is dead.''

''Have you ever thought of using your left hand?''

He looked at her with shocked disbelief and immediately dismissed the idea. ''I was never good with my left, let alone with a gun in it.''

''Have you ever really tried?''

He slowly reconsidered the question. ''No.''

''That's something that could keep you occupied while you heal.'' She laughed with a girlish lilt and moved the poultice down to his elbow.

''You know, I always wanted to be like my old man, to follow in his footsteps. He was a fine sheriff.'' Thomas wanted to talk, to confide.

''Billy told me a little about him.''

''Then he told you that he was—'' Thomas hesitated. The words came hard. ''—was murdered?''

She looked down. ''Yes, I'm sorry.''

''Ambushed outside of our town. He was riding home in the evening, had been out to one of the ranches. There had been a ruckus about some water rights. He'd stayed for supper and was alone. And somebody was waiting.''

''There were no suspects?'' Vallee asked with dismay.

''Every lawman makes enemies. Sure there was suspects, but no one we could prove. I've always had my suspicions. He had chased Leander Morton and his gang out of the county shortly before. Morton had threatened to kill my old man. But that again is a guess.''

''How old were you?''

''Seventeen.''

A soft moistness formed in Vallee's eyes. ''Just my age. It must be terrible not knowing.''

''It eats at your guts every day of your life. Every gunman, every criminal I've ever run across, I can't help but wonder, is this the one?''

''But you shouldn't take it personally.''

''I can't help it. And now here I am, half a man trying to be a lawman.''

\* \* \*

Early that evening Landry and his men reached Baxter Springs, a soggy green meadow where a half-dozen or more tricklets, sweet and steady, made the area lush. There was a quiet pool of placid water where cattails and rushes grew tall and thick at the lower end. Blackbirds flitted and clicked about the stems, and coots and gallinules pumped across the surface. A flock of widgeon settled warily out of gun range. The men built a smoky fire of dead sage branches, hoping to ward off the myriad mosquitoes. They hobbled the horses to feed on the rich browse, and then set to cooking flapjacks and bacon in silence. The sun set in a pink flush. A sudden rush of wind brought the pungent scent of sage and rabbit bush, riotous now with yellow flowers. After they had eaten and sat drinking coffee, Bull Dunlap broke the silence. "How do you figure to take Morton?"

"Damn carefully," said Landry. "He's looking for currency from a recent bank robbery. He hid it in a mine somewhere above the old camp of Desert Roost. He'll go back looking for that if he hasn't done so already. That's why I'm worried about my friends and my deputy there."

"Lookin'? Don't he know where it is?"

"That's his problem. Apparently someone found it or a member of his gang double-crossed him."

"How'd you learn that? The note you writ me wasn't all that clear."

"I rescued a half-breed from them, a former gang member, who they suspected of going back and taking it. They were torturing him for information when I came upon them. That's when I got into problems; a man hiding in the rocks nearly done me in. They got my horse, and if it hadn't been for some bad dust storms, they would have got us. But with luck, we managed to escape them."

"Where's the half-breed?"

"Dead out there. As I said, they carved him up some before I got him away."

"And did he take the loot?"

"Yeah, he did. I got it out of him. He hid it in another

spot, and if you can believe it, when he went back for it, it was gone again. He had no reason to lie to me.''

''Who could have taken it?''

''Anybody's guess at this point.''

The darkness began to close in. A pair of coyotes took up chorus, and a third answered them from across the valley. His eyes riveted on the fire, Dunlap said, ''This could be a wild-goose chase. Morton could be long gone.''

''He could, but he won't leave before he gets what he figures is his; he's going to look for that loot, for a spell at least; that's why my people are in danger. He may think they found it. But if he gets occupied, we could take him and his gang. No way in the world will he suspect us, so we have the element of surprise if it's not too late.'' Landry looked around at the men. ''But we can't be too careful when we go up that mountain. Morton's no fool. That's why he's survived so long. For certain, he'll have a watch on guard up there.''

Jake tossed his grounds into the fire and made it steam. ''The gold—did you find it right away?''

''I'm not all that certain now how many days I was out there. But it wasn't long before I reached your place that I came upon it. It was after Shoshone Joe—that's the half-breed—died.''

''Not far from my place, huh?'' Jake sat higher.

''Hear you got more of them nuggets? Would you spare a look?'' Dunlap asked.

''Sure.'' Landry reached into a nearby saddlebag and removed the sack. They all sat silently in rapt concentration, their eyes shining. The deputy named Joe Lasko puffed deeply on his cigarette to make it glow. He let out smoke in a long, slow ring while running his fingers slowly over each nugget, as if imprinting their texture on his flesh.

''My God, Landry,'' Dunlap uttered. ''I never seen nothing like this before in all my life. Almost solid gold!'' He raised his dark eyes to Landry and they had a burning intensity, like glowing embers.

''Like I said before, Marshal, you got one hell of a strong call to duty,'' Jake Withers commented. He held out one specimen to let the mineral reflect the firelight. "If it was me, I'd be out lookin' right now."

"Well, you aren't me," Landry said quickly.

They bedded outside the light of a dying fire. The coyotes yapped to the fading moon for a time and quit. The wind increased and the night turned cold. Sometime after midnight, Landry awakened to the nicker of a horse and then another. He removed his nearby Colt from its holster and raised himself on one elbow. Again the horses protested. He saw Dunlap move. "Somebody or something's out there," Landry whispered. Withers and Lasko had awakened.

"Might be an Injun trying for our horses," Dunlap suggested, cocking his handgun.

Landry's sensitive ears caught the muffled but distinct rhythm of an approaching horse. "Somebody's riding in on us," he said. "Come on, scatter, and go quiet." The campfire, now red-glowing opals, cast little light, but the men understood the need to be separate. The four crawled from their blankets; all took their rifles, hunched over and slipped hurriedly into the surrounding sage. Landry lay forward, his rifle braced on a dead branch and pointing toward the sound of an oncoming animal. He could hear somebody breathing not far from him, probably Jake, he thought. Landry cocked his head and listened. The nearing horse had stopped. They waited. Nothing. Again their horses sounded. There came a snapping of twigs in the direction of the stranger. Then Landry made out an outline of a man leading a horse toward their camp, holding its nose for silence. "Halt," he bellowed. "There are four rifles pointed at your heart."

"I hear you. I hear you," came an alarmed voice.

"Throw up your hands. Identify yourself, and come up to the fire."

"Don't shoot, Marshal. Please, don't shoot. It's me, Ted Withers."

"Ted, you stupid ass, what the hell you doing here?" Jake yowled.

"I knew it was you four; just thought I'd sneak in and roll up in my blankets for the night. Didn't want to wake you."

All the men were on their feet. "Could of got your stupid head shot off, you God damned fool," Jake shouted.

"I guess I could of." Ted came into the faint light of the dying embers.

"You was to stay home, take care of the place. And what of Melba?"

"She understands—more than you do."

"Well, damn it, you're going to turn around tomorrow morning and go back."

"No I ain't," Ted announced resolutely. "I can be of service to the marshal just as much as any of you. Besides, I come to get my share."

In the early afternoon several days later, Vallee baked bread, packed food to go, and all the necessary clothes for herself and Seth. At dawn Deputy Dale Thomas would lead them, backed by Temple, down to Silverpoint and on to Limbo City, the lawman's home base.

Clean-shaven, bright-eyed, his hair freshly trimmed by Vallee, Thomas walked into the building and smiled at the girl. His right arm lay snug in a sling, and he was wearing a shirt, the swelling having gone down. Good food, time, medication—especially the poultices—had gradually sucked out an excess of infection. On his left hip rested a revolver, butt forward. For hours he had been practicing with his left hand, drawing, holding, manipulating, aiming, and dry firing, convincing himself that his left was all thumbs and that the positioning of the holster was impossible. Deliberately, he had refrained from shooting a bullet, for he did not wish to draw attention to their presence in the town. The deputy's overriding concern remained: how well could he handle the instrument under stress? The activity, however, had occupied his thoughts and had passed time as he had grown stronger. But not until the last day or so, had he been in any shape to travel.

"That bread sure smells good," Thomas greeted.

"Want some hot?" Vallee asked, pleased.

"No, save it for the trip."

She moved to him. "You know, I'm getting kind of excited, going back to the city for a time. It's been so long, I won't know how to act."

"Sure you will. You'll be at home in no time." Thomas sat heavily on a chair.

The girl studied him. "I just wish Papa wasn't so stubborn. I just wish he'd come with us at least for a few days. Getting away from here would do him good. He's so wrapped up in the gold." Her hands went to her throat in frustration.

"Well, I sure have tried with that old man of yours." Thomas looked at the girl for support. "I suggested he take what gold he's sacked with him on the mules. The mine ain't going to go nowhere. Besides, he's got a legal claim to it."

Although obviously agreeing with the deputy, she came to her father's defense. "Well, he always had something about claim jumpers; he's always feared that. He's told me that whoever was prowling here those nights was probably a claim jumper looking the place over."

"I know, but that's a guess."

"Besides, he says there's no danger anymore, not from those men who shot you. He thinks if they had meant us harm, they'd have followed you here. We've talked about that."

"Whether there's still danger or not, I've got to get back, organize a search party, and see if we can learn anything about Marshal Landry. Besides, how many times do I have to tell you people, his last command to me was to get you and Seth and Billy out of here, until things blow over." Thomas sounded peevish.

"I know the marshal placed you in charge, but this is our home and our lives, and we have rights," Vallee said huffily.

"Problem is, I have a gut feeling they ain't blown over. We're as much in the dark and as much in danger as ever."

"Well, you are a good lawman, you follow orders to the end, that I must say. And if your daddy was here, he'd be proud of you."

Thomas turned his head in troubled remembrance. "That's not fair."

Seeing his hurt, Vallee said hurriedly, "I'm sorry. Really, I'm sorry."

"No bother. I know you meant well. I always hoped to stand in my old man's shadow." Bitterly he added, "And now I never will."

She reached out, her slender fingers tenderly touching his good shoulder. "Please understand, I didn't mean it the way you think. I meant it from the heart—you will be—you are becoming what your father was. I just feel it." During his recovery he had talked again about his father, how he longed desperately to avenge the murder, if only he knew who the killer was. He had mentioned again how he wanted to follow in his father's footsteps, and how now, with his shattered arm, his future as a deputy—as a man—was questionable. But Vallee noticed that as he became stronger and the more he practiced with the revolver, the less he deplored his situation.

Abruptly Thomas rose and walked to the door, where he canvassed the mountain, from the steep drop below to the broken peaks above.

"What's the matter?" Vallee caught his edginess.

"I don't know. I just feel something's wrong. Wish we'd left yesterday, like I wanted."

"You was still too rocky. You couldn't of."

Billy Temple, who had been helping Seth tend the animals, came bustling toward the cabin, rifle in hand and at a pace surprisingly fast for a man of his weight and age. Seth gimped behind, keeping up. Thomas called, "What's wrong?"

Temple's droopy eyelids, an unconscious shield from decades in the glare of a desert sun, were abnormally lifted. "Me and Seth seen a horse and rider movin' through the trees about a mile down. I just glimpsed him and then I seen another. The two was spread out and they was avoiding that old trail up here. There may be more, couldn't tell, but they ain't up to any good. They was keepin' to cover. And they're coming in on us."

Vallee let out a little mew of fear.

"We'll set out the rifles, and I'll get the ammunition,"

Thomas said. "You can help me, Seth." He turned to Temple. "Can you manage to get up to Noah? Warn him we got visitors and to get back down here?"

"I'll get him." Temple shuffled out.

"Oh, God, what's going to happen?" Vallee said, her face pale.

"I just knew we should have gotten out yesterday. Felt it in my bones. I just hope to God that this ain't what Marshal Landry warned me about."

# (11)

Morton quietly signaled his men together near the end of the old Indian trail to Desert Roost. Jenson, ever suspicious, looked up at the jagged mountain that bulked hugely against the sky. Black thunderheads had billowed up in vast cloudy castles, possibly ominous and threatening by late afternoon. "Finding that loot Shoshone Joe took or maybe got taken from him is like looking for a needle in a haystack. It's a waste of time," the little man reminded. "It could be anywhere and we'll never find it in a hundred years."

"Don't intend to look just yet."

"Them prospectors, you mean?"

Morton climbed off his gray, picked up a twig and squatted in the shade. The rest followed suit, except for Wasatch, who sat sideways in his saddle, uncomfortable, his face glazed, the piglike eyes feverish. Morton began diagramming on the ground. "You, Liddicoat, you go to the right. I want you to climb up on that ridge under them peaks, near where we hid our take. There's a ledge up there with good cover if you leave your horse, and from there you can see their cabin and the pocket mine. You remember where?"

"Sure do."

"I'm going to climb to the left." He drew a pincerlike line in the dry earth. "Along that string of trees up there." He pointed to a dark spur of pinyon that crowned a small cirque, overlooking the old town and not far from where Crawford had picketed the mules. "Give me and Liddicoat a head start of near an hour, Jenson, before you, Tunin, and Wasatch move out." Morton's dark eyes engaged them as he spoke with quiet determination. "Spread out some, but keep in view of each other. I'd stay off the trail; no use givin' yourself away if you can help it. But if somebody does see you, it just might keep their attention enough that me and Liddicoat won't be noticed."

Morton spoke with exactness, working a design with his twig. "The cabin's here." He marked a spot. "You've seen it, it's the large one that was once used by the big shots. Tunin and Jensen, you'll take cover within rifle range. Wasatch, you handle the horses, keep 'em at least fifty yards down hill from Tunin and Jenson. We want them animals safe and ready. With your butt achin', that's about all you can handle."

"Yes, sir." Wasatch gave him a thankful look.

The men listened intently, excitement growing. "And don't worry none about me. But keep your eyes on the ridge where Liddicoat is." Morton turned his attention to his most trustworthy marksman, who was squatting too, bracing himself on his rifle. "Now you, Liddicoat, I want you to tie your neckerchief to a long stick. If you see them prospectors, they probably will be working their claim and be away from the cabin. Or there might be only one, like the last time we was up there after Shoshone Joe." Morton addressed his men seriously. "Now listen careful. If there's only one prospector, you wave that neckerchief once, stop, wave once again, stop, and wave a third time. Wait and do it again to be sure we understand. "You all got that?"

Jenson nodded slowly in acknowledgment.

"Now if there is two prospectors workin', you do the same, only wave twice. In otherwords: two, stop, two, stop, and two again. Wait and repeat yourself. If there's nobody up there, if it appears they're in the cabin, do the same thing only three times each. I'd like to take 'em alive, if we can— until we learn what we want. I don't worry about the young ones, it's them prospectors we need. You all understand?"

"Got it," said Liddicoat.

The others mumbled a yes.

"I just bet you do." The meticulous Morton asked Wasatch first, about the signal. He fumbled it. Then he asked Tunin, who did better. He turned to Jenson, who remembered exactly, and finally Liddicoat, who repeated the entire process twice for the sake of everyone.

"Stay back from the ridge," Morton suggested to Liddicoat. "Me and the boys will see you easy without much chance of one of them prospectors or their kids spottin' you."

"Just what are you going to do?" Jenson asked Morton, his eyes squinting with curiosity.

"I'm going to get into that main building behind them up there. Once I know where them prospectors are, I can take 'em. That's why you three down front will need to keep their attention. Maybe if I can locate them two kids, that would make things easier."

"There's that girl we seen," said Tunin, his mouth grinning wide with expectancy.

"Ain't your concern, till afterward. This is business now." Morton's voice crackled sharply.

"Where do I fit in next?" Liddicoat asked, always the perfectionist.

"You're gonna have to play it smart. I'll do what has to be done up there, but our success may well be in your hands. If it looks like I'm in trouble, and if you can set a bead on them prospectors, you may have to drop them. Whether you wing them or kill them, you got to decide. But if you kill both of them, we may never learn nothin'. Remember that."

"Just how you going to find your way inside them old buildings?" Jenson asked skeptically. "Abandoned mines ain't a place to crawl around."

Again Morton smiled, a side of his thick lips curling in superiority. "Once when the law shot up my first gang, I hung out up there for a few months. I got to know them buildings pretty good."

In the superintendent's building people hustled. Mono caught the tension and began barking, until Crawford swatted the dog. Then, with a rifle, the man took a stance next to a window, where he had rolled up the burlap covering.

"Don't make it too obvious that we suspect them, keep it normal," Thomas warned. He had found a burst of new life as he asked Billy Temple to check out the underground storage room for rattlers or any other unwanted creatures. With a kerosene lantern the old man worked down the ladder. "Vallee, you and Seth are going down where the gold is." The deputy pointed at the open hatch.

"I don't want to," she protested. "We want to be here with you. We can help somehow."

"I'll load guns," Seth piped.

"No. I want you safe and out of the way. Whatever happens to us, at least you two will have a chance."

"But I don't want to." Vallee crossed her arms.

Thomas looked at her firmly but with understanding. "I can't tell you how much I appreciate everything you've done for me, but now this is my job. So you must cooperate with me."

"I want to be with you."

"This is no time to argue," Crawford told his daughter. Vallee looked apprehensively at the hatchway.

"We don't know what's going to happen. Them men that Billy seen might be friendly hunters, but I doubt it." The deputy's demeanor became authorative. "Whatever happens, you two must remain quiet."

With a frail smile Vallee conceded. "I'll do what you wish, but I want a gun."

"Can you shoot?"

"They both can," said Crawford over his shoulder. "They can have that loaded revolver above the mantel."

Satisfied that Temple had cleared the premises, Thomas waited until Vallee and Seth were down until he handed the girl the .45. He was doing everything with his left, and it suddenly came to him that he was greatly limited. "Damn, damn." The words ripped through his throat. "If only I had my old gun arm."

An emerging Temple said, "Just be thankful you been practicin' with that left."

"Don't close the hatch until you have to," Vallee called.

Temple checked out his shotgun, took a rifle from over the mantel and cocked it to be certain it was loaded and ready. Industriously they all gathered ammunition, each piling cartridges near their positions.

"Best we use this cabin here as a fortress, if the need comes," said Thomas. "Splitting up would be foolish."

"Don't worry, son," said Crawford, "I ain't budgin' from this place with that gold down there."

Deputy Thomas stared at Crawford and added with barbed directness, "Or your children down there."

Crawford glanced back with quick hostility, his eyes raking up and down the length of the deputy. "Gold, children, I got a lot at stake here."

Temple took a north window overlooking the old town. Thomas opened the door slightly where he could point the revolver with his left. He cursed softly under his breath at the weighty awkwardness of the piece and at the fumbling uncooperativeness of his fingers.

"If trouble comes, you ain't going to be much use, except to growl along with the dog," Crawford said without looking at the deputy.

"I'll manage, don't worry about me," Thomas spat back.

A half hour crawled by, then forty-five minutes. Once, the dozing Mono lifted his bristly snout and rumbled low, alerting the defenders. But after he'd cocked his head, sniffed the air and rolled over into a sighing sleep, everyone relaxed.

"What's going on?" Vallee called.

"Nothing. Not a thing," Temple called back.

"Maybe you and Seth was seeing things," Crawford quipped.

"My eyes might be gettin' old, Noah, but not that old. I ain't survived over forty years in the desert, seein' what ain't there."

"Outside chance it could have been hunters comin' in to set up camp. I know there's some big mule deer on this mountain, a few panthers, and a herd of sheep up in the higher country." Crawford spoke hopefully.

"That's true," said Temple, "but what little I seen, they

looked businesslike, like they was comin' for a purpose. As I said, they was spread out, off the trail, like they didn't want to be noticed. No hunters would have done that.''

"Well, we just best sit tight for a time," Thomas advised.

In the spur of pinyon, Morton waited. The eastern pitch of the mountain left much of the old town in shadow now, but the sun's rays lit the higher peaks and the ridge where Liddicoat climbed. There would be ample light for several hours yet. Morton could see the pack mules and the horse that Crawford had brought in, plus Temple's mule and pack animal, and Thomas's black. Landry had started from here, he figured. The wounded man was probably inside the building, if he had survived. The mules had all arrived since Morton and his men's last visit to the dead mines. If his little ploy over the missing take from the heist didn't work, there was much high-grade ore stacked somewhere, he concluded, which the prospectors had taken from the pocket, and that could be an additional bonus.

Then from the ridge, back far enough that anyone in the superintendent's building could not see, Liddicoat stepped out onto a ledge, his slender frame clear in the golden rays. Morton could barely make out the movement. He could not see the red neckerchief. But he saw enough of the overhead swing to count three and pause and three again and then again. Wisely, Liddicoat repeated the performance. Satisfied, Morton moved from the shelter of trees, rifle in hand, his Colt loose in its holster. He worked quickly through high sage, then down a steep hollow of shale to a shaggy juniper, keeping it between him and the building, which he now assumed housed the prospectors.

He dropped next to a cluster of mahogany; there he waited. Confident he had not been seen, he slipped behind some decaying outbuildings until he reached the main drift. He climbed inside a loading door and moved cautiously along the tunnel-shaped building, the beams and siding angled and hanging in places. Abandoned ore cars stood rusting on old wooden rails. He found his way to an alcove where the doors had long disappeared. Stairs led down into the sunken dark. From a vest pocket Morton removed his matches. A quick blue flame lit the way. He stepped down, watching for reptiles, and proceeded along the familiar manway, until he suddenly saw the glimmer of light ahead. Waving out the match, he withdrew his Colt and advanced. In the light of a kerosene lantern sat a boy and a young lady. Like a stalking panther, Morton moved in on his prey.

High up on the ridge, Liddicoat found a perfect rock for a brace and settled down to hone his sights in on the building. He had a magnificent command of the whole setting and had watched Morton come down the mountain and enter the main drift. He had even picked out his three partners, two climbing on foot, the suffering Wasatch remaining below as a backup. Anxiously the sharpshooter prepared for action.

In the trees below the superintendent's building, Jenson and Tunin took positions within view of each other, but far enough down that they could still see Liddicoat wave his signals. Jenson, a veteran in such tactics, had feared that the impulsive Tunin and the hurting Wasatch had not taken enough caution in their approach. He recalled that Morton had not been that much worried about detection, and that gave him some solace. Jenson, who had taken great effort to find adequate concealment under an arch of sage, was appalled when he saw Tunin rise like an advancing infantryman and spring forward, his shoulders hunched, his rifle in front, as he attempted a closer, more strategic location. A gun barked from the building, the bullet lifting a plume of dirt in back of the racing feet. Another bullet serrated a rotting log, sending chips flying as the young outlaw plunged safely behind it. The bullet ricocheted and whined into the distance.

"God damn, I missed," Crawford wailed, and ducked as two of the outlaws returned his fire with shattering lead that splintered the sill. Blindly, Thomas punched two shots and slammed the door shut.

"Close the hatch," Temple hollered. Thomas went for it;

still weak, he lost his balance and fell on his good side, crying out. He managed to squirm forward to push the hatch door shut. Against the confusion and the racket, he heard Vallee and Seth voice brief sobs of fear. "No tellin' how many is out there," Temple shouted.

Crawford edged up along one side of his window. But as he positioned his rifle, a bullet smashed through the rolled burlap, breaking it loose to drop noisily, striking his shoulder and bouncing away. He lurched sideways, tumbled to his buttocks and rolled to his back. The bullet hit the kitchen siding and knocked a frying pan off the wall before sinking into the woodwork. Crawford blinked and tugged at his puffy white sideburns. "Son of a bitch," he howled and came to his hands and knees to upright himself before another shot whizzed through the same window, twanged off the stove and lodged in some shelving.

"We're in for it," Temple yelled. "They know where we are, but we don't know where they are."

"What the hell do we do?" Crawford shouted to Thomas.

The deputy was crouched on his feet, waving the revolver in his left hand. "Hold 'em off. They got to cross open ground to get closer to us. So we hold 'em off no matter what." Mono, who had crawled under a bed, came out to rumble a deep growl near the hatch. But another crashing bullet sent him scurrying back to cover.

As they ascended the base of the mountain, Landry and the men heard sporadic gunfire. "Trouble up ahead," Dunlap affirmed like a warrior readied for combat. "There's a sizable reward on Morton's head, damn sizable. Too bad us lawmen can't collect."

"Yeah, too bad," said Landry, cocking his head to listen.

"But the sooner we get Morton, the sooner we get on to other business. Right?" Dunlap nudged his horse and it pulled upward, whinnying. All the horses were wheeling and backing under their bridles and shaking their heads, to make their bits clink as their hooves thudded with uneasy anticipation.

"Whatever," Landry said vaguely.

"Hell," Jake whooped, "me and my brother, we ain't no lawmen. We could have it all. Every bit of the rewards." His last word rolled like disappearing thunder.

Landry had a distant, calculating look. He licked his dry lips slowly. "We're not rushing into this. We're going to come on to them slow and careful. There's five of them." Landry ran his hand thoughtfully over his face.

"Well, Dirk, you know this bastard better than any of us. You call it all the way," Dunlap said.

Landry looked at the high ramparts prickling over the rise ahead. He spoke with an air of confidence, like a field general. "I figure they've sneaked up an old Indian trail and Morton went in himself, first. Morton would figure only he's good enough to do that. He knows this old town. He hid out here once. So he's after that heist money and whatever else he can get his hands on. He knows Crawford and Temple have been mining." Landry tried to steady his horse, which kept nosing forward. "Wasatch, the wounded one, will stay back with the horses. Keep aware of that. The others will move on the town or the building, wherever my people are— all except Liddicoat." The marshal scrutinized what he could see of the high peaks. "Liddicoat and his rifle—that's our concern. He'll station himself someplace overlooking the whole thing."

"Where you think he might be?" Dunlap asked.

"He'll be somewhere to the right of us, somewhere up in that rough stuff where all the ridges and some of the old mines are. It's the only place he can go to see over everything. So we have to be sure we keep him from seeing us, that we keep cover between us and that high country."

"So now what?" Dunlap pursued.

"We'll leave the road here and cut around to the old trail— that way we can come in behind them. Sounds like they've got my friends pinned down, probably in the cabin up there." Again they heard an exchange of gunfire. "You take the brothers and your deputy in and be careful," the marshal told Dunlap.

"And you?"

"See that line of pinyon yonder?" Landry pointed to a steep hollow of shale with a finger of trees. "I'm going to lose myself in that; then I'll get back of the superintendent's building and try to come in behind. Give me time to get up there—shouldn't take long. And when you see me leave that grove and start down, move in. You got that?" Landry drummed the ribs of his sorrel.

"We're with you." Dunlap's barrel chest expanded with readiness. His squarish face and thick eyebrows made him look like a lion about to pounce.

In the storage basement Vallee sensed the shadowed movement and alerted Seth by her startled jerk. She thrust her hands to her mouth in a soundless scream, then reached for the .45 as Leander Rattlesnake Morton announced, "Don't, girlie, or you and the boy is dead."

# (12)

With care, Landry let the sorrel pick its way up the spur
of pinyon, as he kept the line of trees between him and
the old town. The gunfire continued off and on, in a casual
way that revealed a standoff. But for how long? Landry
knew that Liddicoat would be watching from somewhere
with that unerring rifle, and that Morton would be attempting access to buildings surrounding the holdout. At
the end of the spur Landry left his horse. He removed a
large nugget from the saddlebags and tucked it in a vest
pocket, took his rifle, checked his Colt and stepped out
into the high open sage, his heart pounding, a sweat building over his back and shoulders. If someone were hiding
anywhere in the chaos of ruins and saw him, he would be
an easy target. Moving quickly, directly, he reached a large
juniper, waited, looked, but saw nothing. He hoped that
Dunlap, Lasko, and the brothers had seen him leave the
spur of pinyon and would begin their advance. Several
smaller mahogany trees dotted the slope between him and
the decaying outer buildings. He decided to use them as
cover in a step-to-step dash to the main drift.

On the ridge high to the north, Lee Van Liddicoat rested
languidly against a slab of rock, watching. He sat alert, his
eyes narrowing. He had seen movement on the upper end of
a long row of trees. Or had he? He waited, rifle in hand. And
then he saw a man with a hitching stride come out of the
same trees that Morton had used—saw him drop rapidly down
slope and disappear behind a shaggy juniper. "God damn,"

he muttered. "Landry! Could it be Landry? Can't be." Immediately he sprawled down, rested the rifle on a low rock and tried to judge the distance and the trajectory. He raised the sights high in an attempt to lob a bullet when whoever it was came out.

Dunlap, his deputy, and the two Withers brothers watched anxiously until they saw Landry emerge from the dark trees. "That's it. Come on," said Dunlap. "We go in. Keep off the trail and keep something between you and that ridge up there where that sharpshooter might be," he warned. On foot, they separated some fifty feet apart, but in view of one another, and began closing in on the Morton gang.

Vallee reached for the revolver that lay before her on a sack, but Morton was there, wrenching it from her, his leering face close to hers. "No, no, little girl," he hissed. "You scream and I'll kill you and the boy." He plunged her gun into his belt and smiled triumphantly, showing his gappy teeth, his long, droopy mustache twitching. He grasped her by the wrist and jerked her to him. She cried out involuntarily as he dropped his own gun into his holster and, with the free hand, cupped her face, muffling the cry. Her eyes widened in fear. The heavy odor of sweat, dirt, and horseflesh engulfed her. Seth jumped up and lurched awkwardly at the man, pummeling him with both fists. Morton backhanded the boy, knocking him over some gold sacks, where he fell hard, to lie stunned and whimpering.

Fighting against a swoon of fright, Vallee sank teeth into the thick, callused hand. "Ow, damn you," Morton sputtered. "You little bitch." He threw a muscled arm around her waist and lifted her off her feet. She grunted under the crushing power. "You're gonna cooperate now," he said coldly.

Wasatch, more concerned about his painful wound than with the shootout, lay not far from the horses. He was quite content to let Tunin and Jenson fight the battle. He broke off a huge quid of tobacco and chewed mightily, his bovine features momentarily relieved. He sat munching, listening to a shot now and then, his ponderous jaw working up and down. Gradually he became aware that some of the horses were tugging at the tied reins; others were snorting, shying back and forth, their eyes bugging. He looked down the trail then and saw Deputy Joe Lasko crouched low, running from tree to tree. "Holy hell," he exploded, just as the deputy saw him. Wasatch levered a half-dozen wild shots, forcing Lasko, Dunlap, and the Withers brothers onto their bellies. Upslope, both Jenson and Tunin turned around from behind cover, confounded by the sudden, intense fire. "Behind us, God damn it. Behind us," Wasatch roared, as Dunlap and his charges punched shots in the general direction of the big man. Wasatch threw his arms over his head and ducked, burrowing into the brush. The horses screamed.

As Landry bolted from the juniper in his hitching stride, he heard the whistle of a bullet. He dove for cover behind the first outbuilding just as the lead splintered away a section of roof above him. Landry waited, then peered about. He concluded that it had come from a ridge on the shoulder of the mountain. He made it to the next building without response, but as he plunged for the main drift, three bullets almost found their mark, one over him, one behind, and one into the siding as he reached the oblong building through a loading door. Only Lee Van Liddicoat could be so accurate from that distance. Quickly, Landry walked with a swinging stride past abandoned ore cars, along some wooden rails and under precariously hanging beams. Through an alcove, he stepped down some wide stairs and proceeded along a man-way where light glowed ahead.

"Something's happened, someone else is down there," Crawford bawled. Aware that the attackers had turned their attention elsewhere, both Thomas and Billy Temple left their positions. Vigilantly they joined the man, to hear a lively exchange of shots. "What's happening?" Crawford looked at the two with perplexed eyes.

Temple's face registered hope. "You think Landry, maybe?"

Then they heard Vallee: "Please, we need help, please open up. Please let us out."

Surprised and confused, Thomas called, "What is it, Vallee? What's wrong?"

"Please. Open up. Please."

Befuddled, both Billy Temple and Deputy Thomas scrambled to the hatch and lifted it at the same time, to face a grinning Rattlesnake Morton standing on a rung, holding the girl in front of him, his gun to her throat. Temple and Thomas froze, their faces stricken.

"Greetings," said Morton. "Lots of nice bullion you got down here."

"Morton. Leander Rattlesnake Morton," Thomas erupted, as if he were spitting out spoiled meat.

A slow recognition came to Morton's eyes, "Well, young Thomas. Son of Jesse Thomas—the late sheriff. Well, well, a chip off the old block, I see. Looks like my boy, Liddicoat, messed your arm up a little bit."

Seeing Vallee clutched in Morton's burly hold, Thomas turned pale. "Take me, Morton. Let the girl go."

"Oh, no, she stays with me. So does the boy." Below, Seth was sitting up, blinking and shaking his head. "Now throw your guns down here. All of them down below me. And do it real careful like." Both Temple and Thomas obeyed, handling their weapons gingerly, each dropping a revolver and a rifle onto the sacks below. "Now whoever else is up there, step over here and drop your guns." Morton stepped up another rung so he could see, and pushed the girl up in front of him, but not so high that her head appeared.

"Ain't gonna do you no good," Crawford rumbled. "Hear that shooting out there? Your gang's under siege."

Morton listened to the gunfire exchange. Momentarily troubled, he caught hold of himself. "Long as I got this little girl and boy, I ain't worried about nothing. Now you there, you step over here and toss down your guns.''

"No."

"For Christ's sake, he's got Vallee," Temple said to Crawford, as Morton cocked his gun and pushed it deeper into the girl's throat.

Morton spoke precisely and with great confidence. "I talked to a half-breed just before he died. He said one of you found some money that belongs to me."

"I don't know what you're talking about," Crawford said, his mouth twitching.

"Oh, I think you do. Now if one of you tells me where it is, this little girl and boy ain't gonna get hurt." Morton freed the girl's arm and encircled her waist to lift her into view. She cried out pitifully in fear and discomfort.

"We don't know what you're talking about," Crawford insisted.

"Well, we'll start with the kids here. First the girl gets it, and then the boy, if you don't smarten up. Or maybe just the boy, and I'll take the girl back to my men. They need cheering up."

"Don't hurt them," Temple said beseechingly.

"You touch her and I'll kill you," Thomas warned with vitriolic hatred.

"You and who else, boy? Now, I asked a question."

"I told you, I don't know nothin'." Crawford's voice ripped gutturally through the room.

"If you know something we don't—then speak up," Temple said to his partner.

"Yes you do, Papa," Seth called from below, his voice shattered with fright and confusion. "Yes you do, Papa."

"Shut up, Seth."

Immediately Morton addressed Seth without looking at him. "Speak up, son."

"Papa . . . I saw Papa hide a big bag down here. I looked and it has money."

"Where?"

"Over there under some stuff."

"Get it for me," Morton snapped. Seth moved mechanically, as if in a dream. In a corner, under a slat of tin roofing, he retrieved a fat bag and brought it to the outlaw leader. "By God, that's it." Morton's eyes had a lustful light of joy. "Open it up, son." Quivering, Seth unlatched several clasps and timidly raised the flap. "Seems to me you been lyin'," he shouted to Crawford. Then to Seth he said firmly, "Hold it up higher, boy, and let's see what's there. It don't look as full as I remember. Take it out, boy. Lay it all on them sacks." Quickly Seth dug in and set out the currency. Morton made an assessing glance. "It ain't all here. You," he snarled at Crawford. "My money, it's not all here."

A flustered Crawford looked around as if for help or assurance. "What do you mean?"

"It ain't all here. And you better damn well know what happened. You hear what I'm sayin'? You bull me one more time and I hurt this girl. You hear me this time?"

"Yes."

"You're lyin'."

"I know," said Crawford meekly. "I bought a few things for my mine."

"Hell," said Temple disgusted, "so that's where you got the money. You lied to me, you lied about grubstaking our claim. You was going to cheat me by having us pay back a debt that don't exist."

"No. No way was I going to." A wrinkle of strain formed between Crawford's eyes. "I was going to tell you about it, eventually. You must believe me. All of you must." He suddenly looked shrunken and trapped. "Take it, Morton, and leave my children be." His voice broke with an emotional plea.

"Oh, no. Not yet. First throw down your gun."

Crawford obliged, tossing his revolver into the hole to land on a cushiony sack. Then he slid his rifle over the floor to where Temple kicked it down the hatch. "I'm coming up," Morton announced, "the girl with me, and you, son, you bring the money after you. Any of you try anything and the girl gets it, and then all of you get it.''

"Don't hurt them," Crawford pleaded. His eyes had settled on Billy Temple's shotgun leaning against a north windowsill.

Morton saw. "I wouldn't try it, mister."

"I wasn't goin' to try nothin'," Crawford said.

"That's better. Now you're going to call off whoever else is out there," Morton ordered.

Before Morton could continue, Landry stepped from the dark. He reached up deftly, caught the barrel away from Vallee's throat, and caved Morton's hat over his skull so hard that the outlaw screeched like a dying animal all the way to the ground. There, he collapsed in a twisted heap, pulling a screaming Vallee on top of him. Seth and the others gasped in shock. Landry swung the girl up into his arms as both youths hugged him and broke into tears.

"Landry, you son of a bitch, you're alive," Temple whooped, dropping to his knees to look down.

"Praise God," Thomas roared. "I feared you was dead." He too came to his knees, forgetful of his injury, to peer into the gloomy storage room.

Crawford, unmindful of possible bullets, bolted to his feet and rushed over.

"I damn near didn't make it," Landry said, "but that's a long story. Now help me get Morton out of here. You got some rope?"

"Should be a coil down there," Crawford said.

Landry found it and fashioned a loop under the outlaw's arms. Meanwhile Seth and Vallee scrambled up the ladder to be assisted clear by Temple and Thomas. "Keep low," the deputy warned. "They're still shooting out there."

In an enveloping bear hug, Temple embraced the brother and sister. Vallee and Dale Thomas squeezed hands in thankfulness, all holding low in fear of stray bullets. But when Crawford attempted to clutch his children, Vallee drew away.

"Why, Papa? Why did you lie? Why? You could have got me and Seth killed!"

"I didn't mean to," Crawford wailed, sounding indignant. "You have to believe me, I didn't think he was that serious. Please, you gotta believe me." Outside, the posse members and the beleaguered outlaws exchanged a sudden and intense fusillade. Everyone in the room hit the floor, although no bullets reached them. Landry retrieved their guns.

"Hurry, get this man up there," Landry commanded when the shooting eased.

Guiding the dead weight, the marshal eased the unconscious form up the ladder as the three men pulled the rope, lifting Morton into the room, where they sprawled him on the floor. Landry brought up the money and the lantern. Then he cut an eight-foot section of rope, bound Morton's hands behind his back and secured them to the man's belt. He wrapped the end around the booted ankles.

Landry gestured. "Come on, help me get him over to the door." Tossing the crushed hat aside so that the features could be seen clearly, Landry, assisted by the other men, hauled Morton toward the porch, held him upright and swung the door wide. As they pushed Morton in front of them for all outside to see, Landry bellowed, "You down there, Wasatch, Jenson, and whoever else. We got your man here. We got Leander Morton. It's all over. Come out slow with your hands up."

From cover, Jenson and Tunin looked at each other in stunned disbelief. "That you, Marshal Landry?" Jenson inquired.

"It's me. By God, it's me. And if you want your boss healthy, come out with your hands high."

"He don't mean nothin' to me," Tunin yelled, and started to crawfish away.

"You son of a bitch," Jenson hissed at Tunin. "Morton ever learns you said that, he'll gut you on the spot." The testy little outlaw turned back toward Landry. "Let us go,

Marshal. Just let us go and we'll clear out; that way no one will get hurt."

"No way," said Landry. Then he shouted, "Dunlap, Withers, Lasko, you all hear me?"

Dunlap shouted back from below the outlaws, "We hear you."

"Hear them, Jenson? You and your men are surrounded." Landry felt his voice flow and extend down over the mountain. "You have no chance. Give up now."

Liddicoat, on the ridge overlooking the action, could not hear any dialogue, but he could tell that the occupants of the superintendent's building had someone who looked disturbingly like Leander Morton in their clutch. The shooting had ceased. Then, for the first time, he saw the interlopers. Dunlap, Lasko, and the Withers brothers had crept from cover, all coming to their feet, hunched in preparation of arresting the remaining gang members, yet unwittingly exposed to Liddicoat the sharpshooter. The man's tongue darted wetly over his dried lips like that of a snake before the strike. He swung the braced gun toward the emerging posse members, took a trajectoral aim, and fired.

The first bullet sliced a limb from a pinyon above Jake Withers's head. The man flung back and fell over a tangle of roots to sprawl hard. The second bullet sent Ted diving into a bed of sage. Dunlap took refuge behind a gnarled mahogany and tried to see where the bullets were coming from as a third slug plumed dirt in front of Joe Lasko, forcing him to retreat. Ted poked his head up, but a fourth piece of lead whined closely, knocking slivers of rock away, making him howl as one splinter sunk into his right hand. Using his little finger and thumb like a tweezer, he plucked it out and crawled deeper into the bed for better protection. Dunlap came out of the mahogany to try and find the whereabouts of their tormentor, only to be stumbled backward as another bullet splintered the tree trunk. He rolled over and crawled quickly away. "God damn, that bastard can shoot," he cursed.

Meanwhile, Tunin and Jenson found their way down a brushy draw where Wasatch was attempting to lead the animals. They overtook him, mounted and headed out, low over the horses. Only Joe Lasko managed a shot at them, but he was quickly distracted as Liddicoat dropped a bullet less than two feet from the deputy's head. The marksman remained cool and indifferent to a barrage of lead that sang harmlessly over him. Several shooters from the cabin were attempting to reach him, snap-shooting from the windows and from a side shed. But he was safely out of their sight, for they were only guessing his whereabouts.

Liddicoat watched with deep satisfaction and chuckled to himself. "God, what fun." His pinched features melted in a sigh of repose. He lay back, threw his head up and laughed, laughed in a wild, raucous way. Those below lay at his mercy; with his unerring ability, with a commanding view, nobody, not one, could escape him. Satisfied that his partners had made it, he watched them disappear along the mountainside. Then, reluctantly, he took leave to join them.

Sometime after the shooting ceased, Dunlap, Lasko, and Withers lay hiding, certain that the sharpshooter was waiting for them to emerge. It was Landry's assuring voice that finally brought them out. With rifle in hand he had left the cabin, walked across the opening to the wooded edge where the mountainside dropped away. He and Temple had tried futilely to stay Liddicoat's deadly aim. Sensing that the sharpshooter had departed, Landry coaxed his men out, his voice edged with disappointment and disgust—disappointed that the gang had escaped, and disgusted that his men had not dropped or captured one of them. But he took solace in having taken the big one— Leander Rattlesnake Morton.

Upon rounding up his and Morton's horse, Landry showed Temple the precious nuggets. The old man stood in awe, speechless, rotating several specimens, admiring them, feeling them, scrutinizing them again. "It's the Breyfogle, Dirk," he responded as last. "I've been lookin' for this all my life. Told you, I seen a sample in Austin, those many years ago. And I'd never forget it. This is a spitting image."

"I took one in my pocket," said Landry, replacing the nugget with the others. "I thought I might use it to distract Morton." Temple remained silent as they joined the others in the cabin. Landry gave Vallee the fresh bandages he had brought. Thomas was bleeding again. Landry asked for someone to stand guard outside, and Joe Lasko volunteered. "We're leaving in the morning, all of us, you and Billy, too," the marshal announced, looking at Crawford. "We'll help you load up your gold."

"Don't see no danger, now that Morton's a prisoner," said Crawford, handing a bottle of his whiskey around.

"Don't underestimate Morton's men."

"There's no honor amongst thieves, you know that. Why would they risk their necks for him?" Crawford gestured toward the prostrate form of the outlaw leader.

"Maybe not with that young blond fellow or the guy they call Wasatch, but Liddicoat and Jenson are two men to be reckoned with. They've worked for Morton a long time; in many ways they and him are like brothers." Landry hitched his gun belt. "They'll be back. Besides, we have their haul, and all your gold here as well. And Morton has additional insurance—he's always had a habit of being the only one who knows where some of their biggest takes are stashed." As the men drank deeply, they all stood looking down at the bound figure, his squarish head puffing with purple bruises.

"Good sight to see," said Dunlap. "Eases some of the embarrassment of lettin' them gang members get through us. That rifleman up there on the ridge. Jesus Christ, I never seen such shootin'. He must have been as far as a half-mile, but he was dropping 'em in on us like we was a couple of hundred feet away."

"One of the best in the whole Basin country," Landry said. "Let's bring Morton around. Several of you help me." Landry reached for a bucket of water beside the sink, while

Temple and Dunlap lifted the outlaw by the arms and the feet. They walked out on the porch, where the marshal threw the water over Morton's head. The man groaned and shook himself.

Ted Withers moved over to Vallee, who was washing her hands in a basin. They both had eyed each other upon first meeting. She had noticed he was attractive, broad-shouldered and strong, with dimpled cheeks and curly blond hair. He and Marshal Landry had removed their hats immediately upon entering the room, and that had impressed her.

"Can I help you with the bandaging? I done some on my brother Jake, when he got bunged up on a plow once." Ted had never seen a girl so pretty. Granted, he didn't see many females, except for his sister-in-law. The women in Silverpoint or in the larger Limbo City were either wives of ranchers or farmers, all chunky and work-weary, with a passel of kids. Or they were clerks or owners of a shop, matronly and businesslike. Most of the girls in the saloons were used, haggard wretches to be pitied; all drank too much, and many eventually died from smoking opium. The few farm girls he had met at picnics and church socials had been plain, often dull, and all hungering for marriage. He couldn't take his eyes off Vallee. She was like a perfumed breeze off the sage after a spring rain. "Can I help you?"

"Certainly, if you wash your hands. The soap is there." She pointed to a washbasin. Dale Thomas watched them. Some fresh blood was oozing through the covering over his elbow. Ted pumped water into the pan and vigorously lathered his hands, arms, and face.

Crawford and Temple were helping an unsteady Morton back into the cabin. His dazed eyes had a fire of hatred, like a wild animal in a trap. "Here," said Landry, handing the bucket to Ted. "You can fill this again." Inside, they bound Morton to a chair. He remained quiet, his face defiant. Both Seth and Vallee kept staring at him as if he were some loathsome reptile that had just crawled out from under a rock.

Landry motioned to both Temple and Crawford to join

him outside, while Jake and Bull Dunlap kept a watchful eye on the prisoner. "It's none of my concern what has come between you two and your partnership," the marshal opined when on the porch and beyond hearing range of Joe Lasko. "But you realize, Noah, that I must take you in. You're going to have to face the consequences of knowingly using money that was stolen."

"I cain't ever forgive you for that," said Temple icily.

"I'm surprised and disappointed in you too, Noah. It's not like you to let greed get to you. That's not the Noah Crawford I remember, that I came here to find." Landry's eyes held steadily on the man, who looked away, obviously uncomfortable. "We're longtime friends, Noah. So why?"

Crawford's eyes looked back and forth between the two men. "I was up yonder in one of them old tunnels, looking for a cool but dry place to store our dynamite," he began. "You know what I mean—far enough away from the mine and our quarters for safety. Near the opening, I seen where somebody had been digging. It was fresh, maybe a day or so before. So I checked the spot, dug around, and that's when I found the bag."

"You knew it was stolen money."

"Hell, yes, I did. It was in a Wells Fargo bag with notes and cash inside from a bank in Dayton." Crawford's eyes were remote and strange. "I never in my life seen so much money. I knew it could buy all the equipment and mules that Billy and me had been hungerin' for. I knew I could cut years off our labor with it. But I knew Billy wouldn't go along with me. He's always fretting about how much we owe. So I did it on my own." Crawford looked at Landry and at Temple with chagrin, but not with apology or shame.

"You was going to take my share to pay a make-believe grubstaker." Temple bristled with hostility.

"I would have worked something out, Billy, I wouldn't have cheated you." Crawford acted hurt. "You know that. I just couldn't let you in on it yet, mostly for your own sake."

Billy muttered to himself.

Landry cautioned both men, "We don't have to make it obvious to Seth and Vallee. We'll take out what gold you have, and when we get to Limbo City you'll just come with me, Noah."

"What will a judge do to me?" Crawford's voice was calm, but his stance had become rigid.

"I don't know. Because you don't have a prior conviction, and because you've been a respected citizen, maybe you'll get off light."

Crawford looked earnestly at Landry. "What's the chance of prison?"

"As I said, it depends."

"My kids—what will become of them?"

"Should of thought of that before, Noah." Temple stalked off.

A roll of thunder split across the peaks so close it shook the buildings slightly. Landry strolled out to his horse and removed his gear and saddlebags as Temple entered the cabin, followed by Crawford. Joe Lasko, who had been smoking constantly, stamped out a cigarette stub and rolled another. "Bet we see a big downpour," he told the marshal. "Maybe a flood in them canyons down there."

"Sure as hell hope not. It will be miserable enough traveling out of here as it is."

Landry saw that Ted was bathing Morton's head, which had ballooned with swelling. Vallee was again dressing Thomas's wound; the young man sat sullenly, glaring at the prisoner.

Landry moved to his deputy. "You've been through a lot. How do you feel?"

"Better now that we got Morton. If I could prove he was the one that killed my old man, or that he had anything to do with it, you'd never get him off this mountain alive, Dirk." Thomas looked at his boss, his face livid with anger.

"He's not worth it, Dale," said Landry.

Vallee beckoned the marshal to her and whispered, "I'm grateful to your man, Ted Withers. I didn't want to tend to that Morton. I couldn't bear to touch him."

"I understand," Landry said softly.

"I don't see what's so great about nursing scum like Morton. The animal should be shot on the spot," Thomas said, loud enough for the outlaw to hear.

The marshal walked over to his prisoner. Sullenly Morton looked up, his black eyes mocking. "You'll never get me back to prison, Landry," he announced quietly. His words were not arrogant, not venomous, not taunting or threatening, just matter-of-fact.

"I got you there once," said Landry, smiling slightly, taking a surprising pleasure in his dominance and control. "And I'll get you there again. I've been to hell and back to get you this time. And I'm not losing you."

As Ted finished wrapping cloth around the other man's skull, the outlaw leaned over and spat at Landry's feet.

Unfazed, Landry said, "And Shoshone Joe. He never told you about any money. Because he died before my eyes."

Morton cocked his head back with a superior look. "Yeah, I know. The buzzards led us to him, all tucked in a little cave under his coat. I took a chance that somebody here had found the money, and it worked." He tossed a snear at Noah Crawford, who listened gloomily.

"Well, something worthwhile came out of the hell I just went through, besides getting you." Landry reached into a saddlebag and produced a handful of pink nuggets. "I stumbled across this out there." The marshal thrust them under Morton's nose.

Morton's haughtiness vanished. His face blanched. His eyes opened wide. "The Breyfogle," he said, barely audible.

Dale Thomas rose to his feet, his eyes squinting. "Lord alive," he gulped.

A lethargic Noah Crawford came to life and pressed forward, reaching for a sample. "Where the hell did you find that? My God. My God, that makes our stuff here look like fool's gold." Aghast, he looked at the marshal with bewildered eyes. Seth and Vallee pressed behind the men, to peer over their shoulders.

"He come upon it out there in the desert while trying to

escape Morton here. Fell across it by chance," Billy said from across the room. "Sure as God will strike me dead, it is the Lost Breyfogle that he's found. It's pink feldspar and pure gold. Nothing like that has ever been found again, until now."

"Did you map where it is? Can you find your way back? What the hell happened?" Crawford asked anxiously.

Landry told briefly of his ordeal: the shootout, Shoshone Joe, the nightmare in the desert, his discovery, and the wandering about out of his mind. Morton listened to every word.

"But can you find it again?" Crawford interrupted, licking his lips.

"I don't know," Landry said, his eyes expressionless.

The thunder continued, ominously, and a few jets of lightning lit the sky. Jake Withers and Bull Dunlap had asked Landry to meet them outside. While Joe Lasko, still on guard, watched curiously, Dunlap addressed the marshal with dead seriousness. "I don't have to remind you, Dirk, that you enticed me here with that little sample of gold you gave to Jake Withers to show me. You wouldn't have done that if you didn't have some plan for me and you—after we got Morton, of course."

"That's right," said Landry, knowing exactly what was to come.

"And me and my deputy did come to your rescue, and we got the man you wanted, and it looks like we scattered his gang for a time."

Jake took a step forward and reminded quickly, "And me and my brother we'll help you get Morton back."

"Yeah, we'll help you escort Morton back to Limbo City. Just in case his gang tries to wrestle him from you," Dunlap added, tugging at his bushy mustache. His square face formed into a hard, calculating look.

"Well, I appreciate that mightily," said Landry, smiling with humor, "because I believe Liddicoat and Jenson will talk the others into coming after us before we can get Morton to jail. But I think mostly what you're trying to say is that on the way back we could follow the route I took to where the gold might be. Right?''

"Exactly," Jake gloated. "If you think you found it a day away from my ranch, then it's a natural. From here we could cut straight across the desert to my place. We could take Morton with us. You could retrace your steps. Afterward, me and my brother will help you take Morton all the way to Limbo City. Together as partners, we'll get Morton behind bars and maybe find your gold along the way.''

"As partners, we could be richer than kings," Dunlap crowed. "Richer than that fellow, what was his name—King Solomon?''

"Yes, it might be practical," said Landry coolly. "Billy Temple claims that's why Breyfogle never refound the mine— he waited too long and lost his sense of direction. I'd sure hate to make that mistake.''

"No, you don't want to make that mistake," Dunlap agreed.

"Yeah, you can't waste too much time," Jake Withers added.

"I been expectin' this. But I don't like taking Morton along. Goes against my instinct, know what I mean? It's not smart putting all our energy into a search for gold while taking along a dangerous prisoner, and with his gang still on the loose.'' Landry shrugged. He didn't like the game they were suggesting; it went against a deep inner grain, going along with the two men, both smitten blindly with greed. And yet a part of him had gone soft, a little dizzy with the wonder, the headiness of it all. The Lost Breyfogle. He had found a legend, a fortune so great that he could be wealthy beyond his imagination. He felt torn by conflicting emotions. Sometimes a man had to be practical. The gold was there for the effort, and he had enticed Dunlap, and certainly he owed the Withers family. All of them could form a partnership, a company. And Morton— what the hell, together they could drag him along. His discomfort, his frustration, his witnessing the discovery, might be the ultimate coup after all the years it had taken to recapture him. "What the hell," he said, "we got much to lose, but more to gain."

# (13)

Although the thunder crackled and lightning lit the peaks, no rain came. Landry organized a guard system in which all the men, even Thomas, participated; two at a time, with one outside, overlooking the building, the second inside, beside a window. The kerosene lanterns were turned down to emit a yellow smear of light. Morton's hands were bound in front of him for a time to permit eating and drinking. Vallee, although repulsed by the outlaw, prepared his food and drink. Protective of her, Landry or Dunlap served him. Thomas sat rigidly, obviously suffering, never taking hateful eyes from Morton. Aware of Thomas's discomfort, Crawford offered the deputy a whiskey bottle, which he accepted. He twisted the cork free, tilted the bottle and took a hefty swig. He coughed and sputtered as his eyes moistened. He handed the bottle back. Crawford offered it to Jake, who thrust it to his mouth; he too absorbed a hefty gulp, which had no noticeable effect. The bottle went the rounds and back to Thomas.

After binding Morton to a chair, his arms behind, Landry called a meeting. Thomas sat guard at the window. He kept nipping at the bottle and staring into the dark. Ted leaned over to Seth and whispered. "Sure reckon the deputy likes your sister, but is she sweet on him?"

"I think so," said Seth.

"We're heading out early tomorrow," Landry announced. "With your gold on the mules, Crawford. You, Vallee, and Seth, will go with Dale on the route along the mountains to Silverpoint and on to Limbo City. As you well know, there's water here and there along the way, and a few isolated ranches if you need anything. Me, Billy, Dunlap, and the Withers brothers will take Morton across the desert to Silverpoint.''

"Going for the gold, right—only sensible reason that a man would go into that hell country," Crawford said shrewdly.

"Maybe I'm crazy taking Morton along," said Landry, "but he's my responsibility, and I'm not letting you folks try to take him in.''

"We can handle Morton," Dunlap boasted. "From here we can let you find the exact route you took to the mine.''

"What about me?" Lasko asked, a cigarette bobbing in a corner of his mouth.

"I want you to go with Crawford." Landry looked at Bull Dunlap, who was apparently agreeable. "They can always use a good gun hand.''

"I don't like it." Lasko removed the cigarette, his narrow eyes tightening. "I want to be in on the Breyfogle find, too.''

"It won't matter," Landry said in a lazy voice. "We're all going to draw up a contract tonight, a partnership. So it won't matter if you're with us or not.''

"It'll be all right," Dunlap said to his deputy.

"In that case, I'll volunteer to go with the Crawfords," Ted Withers piped up. All eyes centered on him. "I trust my brother. I'll just leave the decisions to him.''

"You ain't going after the Breyfogle?" Jake asked incredulously.

"I said I trust you.''

"Good." Landry smiled.

"In that case, I want to go with Dunlap into the desert," Lasko challenged, looking at his boss.

"No," said Landry, "the more armed men with Crawford, the better.''

"I ain't no old woman," said Thomas peevishly. "I ain't in a wheelchair yet. You implyin' I can't hold my weight?''

"You're a fine deputy and I'm proud of you," said Landry carefully. "But don't be a fool. Don't let pride cloud your thinking. You know better than anyone that right now you can't fulfill your duties—and won't be able to for some time.''

* * *

Throughout the night, thunder jarred the mountain. Vallee, Seth, and Crawford retired to their rooms. Ted rolled out in a corner of the main section, while Billy Temple sat guard over a dozing Morton. Thomas sat sullenly by the porch window, still guzzling the liquor off and on. Landry sat guard with his rifle above the building, while, at Landry's suggestion, Dunlap, Jake, and Lasko rolled in their blankets outside in a glade that fronted the building. Anyone attempting to sneak up on the place would surely rouse one of them.

The night wore on. In the big cabin, Thomas rose, approached Morton and looked down at him. Immediately the outlaw was startled awake, his dark eyes patient and unafraid. "I think you had something to do with the backshooting of my old man," the deputy snarled. "But I can't prove it."

"I don't know what you're talking about."

"The hell you don't. You was in the county at the time. And there was rumors and more rumors."

Morton's eyes took on a smoldering contempt, his thick lips twisted in a haughty smile. "Never heard of a judge hangin' a man on rumors."

"You cocky bastard! If you wasn't tied in that chair, I'd knock that smile off your face and your teeth with it," Thomas hissed.

"Why don't you take off these ropes and try, sonny." Morton's lips curled tauntingly.

Flushed with hatred, Thomas advanced closer.

"Don't do anything foolish," Temple warned. "Don't you see he wants you to hit him. So don't ruin your career and life for the likes of him."

"You stay out of this, Billy." Thomas shook his left fist in Morton's face. "Count your blessings that I ain't going with you and Landry, 'cause if I was, you wouldn't make it back."

The outlaw scoffed at the deputy. "Then they'd hang you, because I'm innocent."

"Innocent hell. You lying bastard," Thomas screamed.

"Back off," Landry growled, standing in the doorway. "You can be heard a mile away; heard you above the thunder."

Jolted by the order, Thomas stepped back. His face livid, he begged; "Give me five minutes alone with this scum here. I'll have the truth once and for all."

"That isn't your right, Dale. No one knows that more than you. The court must decide Morton's fate. Now you go outside and cool off." Landry took the whiskey bottle and set it on a high shelf.

Defiantly, Thomas stared at the marshal, then looked back at Morton, his face registering hurt, frustration, and outrage. "Nobody can prove he murdered my father. For that, my old man will never rest in his grave. But I think Morton had something to do with it. We should hang him to one of them headframes out there right now." Disdainfully, he turned about and marched into the night.

As a red sun painted the cloud-dappled peaks, the men finished readying for their journeys. The half-dozen mules stood patiently in line, blinking and waiting, the gold sacks, goods, and personal belongings packed on five of them, the sixth at the end linked to the others but draped with a blanket so that Vallee and Seth could ride. "Sure as hell don't like leaving the mine," Crawford grumbled.

"It'll be waiting for you to return," Landry assured him.

"I sure as hell hope so."

Ted and Landry helped Vallee and Seth onto their mule. Vallee wore trousers and a shirt under one of her father's old coats. With her hair pulled back and tucked under a Stetson, she looked cute and somewhat boyish. "It's light enough now, best you get going," Landry suggested.

Those heading down the old wagon road between the mountains and the central plateau toward Silverpoint, mounted. Lasko led, guiding the pack train, with Vallee and Seth on the last mule. Ted Withers and Dale Thomas followed directly behind, with Crawford bringing up the rear. They moved out, the horses stomping and snorting gustily. The others watched them wind down the mountain, northwest, down the same route Crawford had come, until they were out of sight. Satisfied that they were well on their way, Landry motioned the others to mount. Billy Temple was already aloft, leading the pack mule carrying their provisions and water packs. The men were in good spirits, excited and anxious to be moving, but Landry was worried. Somewhere out there were Morton's men.

"We just might never have to work again," Jake said happily.

"We just might end up dead, if we don't keep on our toes," Landry cautioned, his eyes roving over their surroundings. He leaned forward on his sorrel, readied, then waved them forward. Behind him, the reins lashed to his saddle, came the gray, carrying a dour-faced Morton, tied on securely. The first thunder of the day rattled the mountainside as dark clouds boiled about the peaks.

Above the old town, from the mouth of a mine shaft, the opening partially covered by brush, four outlaws watched the two units depart. "It don't make sense why they're takin' Morton down that old Indian trail—that just leads to where we come from out in the desert," Liddicoat pondered. "I can't figure it; why don't they all go out together with the mule packs?"

"Whatever their reason, I can see our Wells Fargo bag over Landry's saddle horn," said Tunin, his young eyes concentrating.

"Don't matter at this point," said Jenson, his mouth pinching as he studied the train below, some 150 yards away. "I've been thinkin', they got all that gold on them mules. If we keep to the high cover, we can shortcut over the mountain and drop down in front of them. If we take out that deputy in the lead, and maybe that young fellow that was with Landry, we can stop the others, or at least send them hightailing it. Them others are just some kids, a wounded lawman, and an old man. They wouldn't know what hit 'em. We'll store the gold back in the big cabin, right where it was. Then we'll go after Morton and our money." He laughed, pleased with himself.

"Me and you, Jenson, we been together too long. I was thinkin' exactly the same thing," Liddicoat added.

"Good idea, but me, I'll stay by the gold and guard it good," Wasatch offered. "Don't feel much like traveling."

"And the girl with 'em, leave her for me," Tunin said wolfishly, his eyes eager. "She's all mine."

"She'd probably scratch your eyes out." Wasatch guffawed.

The young blond glared at the big man. "There ain't no she-cat I can't handle."

"Well, we ain't takin' no female with us," Jenson warned.

"Who said I want to take her with me?"

"We're wasting time. Let's get them. I like the smell of gold." An expressionless Liddicoat moved out ahead of them all.

An hour and a half down the old road, the mule train progressed steadily, the drop gradual. Lasko held his eyes on the snaking route ahead; Ted and Dale watched the slopes above and below, with Noah Crawford overseeing them, often twisting around to make certain they were not being followed. Mono, the mongrel, trotted close beside him, its red tongue lolling. Ahead, from a clump of sage, the impact of a rifle shattered the silence. Lasko never knew what hit him. The bullet shuddered the point man, lifted him from his saddle to spin loosely. He landed hard in a mushroom of dust, rolling some twenty feet downhill. Vallee screamed. Mono yelped and ducked into a few scrubby trees to cower. The mules broke from the trail to tromp downslope as Noah Crawford's animal whirled sideways. Ted Withers's horse screamed and reared. Thomas's beast kicked its heels high and bucked away, throwing the deputy end over to the ground to writhe in anguish.

From rocks overlooking the chaos, Jenson stretched up and fired at Crawford but hit his horse instead. The bullets caught the animal's windpipe, cutting short a squeal of fear, dropping it in death; a bubbly spurt of red poured from its throat. Crawford lurched away and managed to crawl off the trail, where he lay stunned.

With a Bowie knife extended, Tunin stepped out of a tree clump to grasp the halter of the mule carrying a frightened Seth and Vallee. The animal balked, veering to the side. Braying in terror, it kicked its rear hooves high, dumping Seth. "I like you, little girl," Tunin shouted through gleaming teeth. He tugged the mule toward him, wrenching its neck back, and sliced it free of the others. Vallee caught up the tie rope and lashed him viciously; the young blond cried out in surprise, throwing his hands in front of his face. "You God damn little she-bitch," he shrilled.

The released mule began pivoting. Tunin rushed at the girl and reached for a leg, but she kicked him and lashed him again viciously. The spinning mule knocked him back. Once more he threw up protective arms. Seth came slowly to his knees, picked up a rock the size of his hand and hurled it at the young outlaw, missing him.

Ted Withers saw Vallee's danger, but dared not shoot. Impulsively he spurred his panicky animal ahead, off the trail and directly at Tunin, who had to dive away, somersaulting, to keep from being hit. As the outlaw came to his hands and knees, Ted wheeled his mount around, bolting it after the man, forcing him again to roll away as the hooves nearly trampled him with timed perfection. The rancher dropped from his horse then and struck the outlaw a resounding blow to the side of the head as Tunin struggled up. Down he went again, groaning. But as Ted reached to pull him to his feet for another blow, Tunin found a large granite rock which he swung at the rancher's head, missing, but ramming it into his left collarbone. Ted, ducking aside to avoid a lethal blow, wailed and fell. Vallee screamed for fear of his life as her mule seesawed away. The girl clung desperately to the animal's neck and somehow managed to remain aloft as her Stetson sailed away. Tunin dropped the rock and pulled his sidearm to kill Ted.

Dale Thomas sprawled, his back lodged against a rock to

avoid Jenson's gunfire. The deputy watched the struggle below. Desperately he raised his Colt with his left hand and
pulled the trigger. The bullet grazed Tunin, spun him so that
he went off balance and fell rolling, over and over down a
steep knoll until vanishing in brush. An exchange of gunfire
continued, mingling suddenly with the crackling of the building storm.

As the mule slowed, Vallee dropped free. Seth ran awkwardly down to her, ignoring any danger, falling twice.
Crouching, brother and sister clutched each other. Liddicoat
saw the pair, but was not interested in killing them. He headed
off the mule train and caught it some fifty yards downhill,
where the animals slowed. The gold was still aboard each
animal, there for the taking. As the animals calmed, he banked
them around a rocky outcrop and guided them back toward
Desert Roost, picking his way through the rocky rise of sage
and screening timber that paralleled the old road above. Jenson levered a half-dozen bullets at Crawford and Thomas,
who lay pinned and unable to respond. After delivering the
barrage, Jenson disappeared, keeping the landscape between
him and his adversaries. He crossed the road and cut south to
intercept Liddicoat. Thunder rumbled closely overhead.

A frightened Tunin first crawled then ran downhill, cupping his left arm, where a flesh wound oozed mushy red. He
too joined Liddicoat and the mule string.

With great effort Dale Thomas advanced on the rocks
where Jenson had hidden and found the little outlaw gone.
He came back to Crawford, who lay bewildered, his mind
still foggy. "You all right?" Dale asked, squatting.

Crawford blinked and shook his head. "My God—Vallee
and Seth and the gold."

"I think Vallee and Seth are safe, but the gold and mules
are gone."

"Gone. Gone? Goddamn." The older man came quickly
but shakily to his feet and stumbled to the trailside to peer
downslope. He could see the last of the mules curving around
an open bend. He fired a shot that went over them. From
somewhere near the animals Liddicoat returned his shot,

winging so close, Crawford had to duck. Still wobbly, he stumbled and fell face forward in the dirt.

A hundred yards south of the mule train, a mounted Wasatch, holding his partners' horses, awaited the approaching gold train.

Mono came out of the brush to lick Crawford's face. Angrily the man swatted at the dog, which bounced deftly away. Vallee climbed hurriedly up the steep hill to Ted Withers, who sat holding his painful collarbone. Seth limped after her. Crawford and Thomas slowly joined her.

"You kids hurt?" Crawford called, coming over to kneel next to Vallee.

"We're fine." She did not look at her father, but at Dale Thomas. "Thank you. You shot real good with that left of yours." Her words rang proudly. Thomas nodded acknowledgment. He looked pale and drained. She turned her attention to Ted. "I don't know how Seth and I can ever thank you, too. That horrible man just came out of nowhere, and you could have been killed." Her eyes encompassed him tenderly. "Did he hurt you bad?"

"Nawww." Ted attempted to dismiss the incident.

Crawford and Thomas helped open the man's shirt. The collarbone area had commenced swelling. Both realized the injury was more serious than Ted admitted. The younger Withers recoiled as Crawford touched the bone. "It's probably broke. What happened?"

Vallee explained with rushed words, "This crazy blond man—he was like a wild animal. He tried to attack me and Seth. But Ted here rushed in and fought him. Then Dale shot him, but he got away."

Crawford stood up and looked down at the Withers boy. "Much obliged to you, son. Both you and the deputy need a doctor. Best you two young men get moving. Get yourselves and my kids on to Silverpoint. You can find a doctor there, rest some before getting on to Limbo City."

"Our farm is a half day this side of Silverpoint," said Withers tautly. "My sister-in-law Melba is there. She's as good a nurse as anybody. We can get good food, and rest there for a spell.''

Dale Thomas was scrutinizing Crawford. ''Just a minute, what are you trying to say, Mr. Crawford?''

''I'm going after my gold.'' Crawford backed away. ''I'll put my things on Lasko's horse.''

''Don't be a fool. You wouldn't have a chance alone.''

''Please, Papa. Don't,'' Vallee begged, still kneeling beside Ted.

''Please, Papa,'' Seth echoed.

Crawford waved his head slowly in a decided no. ''I ain't givin' a lifetime of drumms and work up to a few worthless skunks.''

''I'm ordering you to stay,'' Deputy Thomas said with authority. ''You forget that you got a little explaining before a judge about some money.''

''When I take care of my gold, I'll come back on my own. That's my word.''

''No you won't, because you ain't coming back alive. You ain't trained to go up against the likes of Morton's gang; they're hardened outlaws,'' Thomas insisted. ''One shot could nail you dead before you get within a quarter-mile of them.''

''I'll take my chances.'' Crawford started toward the dead horse and his gear.

''No,'' Vallee cried, and started to run to him, but Thomas caught her arm. She brushed him off with a swing of her arm, pushing the weakened deputy off balance. He dropped to his knees. Ignoring him, Vallee rushed to her father and tugged at his coat. He shook her off and continued.

Thomas withdrew his revolver with his left hand and pointed. ''Halt, Crawford. I'm commanding you.'' He cocked the hammer.

Crawford did not look back, but at the sound of the cocking he called out, ''Shoot me in the back if you have the guts, boy.''

''No. no, no,'' Vallee cried. Tearfully she turned toward Thomas and spread her arms, trying to shield her father.

"You ain't gonna stop him unless you kill him," Ted Withers said dully, holding his collarbone. "Let him go." Mono whined and started after the man, but then reluctantly returned to Seth.

The three watched Crawford remove his gear, round up Lasko's horse and mount. "Papa," Vallee called desperately. But the man did not acknowledge her. A shatter of thunder again rocked the peaks. The dark, slow-moving clouds broke slightly with cool, refreshing rain.

Landry and company had moved too far off the mountain to hear any distinct gunshots; however, both Landry and Temple pulled rein several times to listen, their eyes seeking each other. From long years on the trail, they intuitively sensed something was wrong. A roll of thunder crackled the peaks with lightning. Gray slashes of rain clouded the stony knobs and pinnacles. Resolutely they continued, dropping quickly toward the base of the mountain where the lush gray sage gave way to creosote and shad scale spaced far apart. Nearby the clouds ruptured suddenly, spewing a needling downpour that soaked them within seconds as they struggled to cover themselves with ponchos. Landry draped Morton's slicker around his shoulder. The man did not seem to notice. The stinging rain filled the brims of their hats and flooded off.

They dropped lower through a wash toward the old shoot-out site. "Best we climb out of here, in case of flooding water," Landry warned, moving them up an embankment. The circling vultures had been pushed off temporarily by the driving rain, but the men could smell the stench of Jenson's dead horse, although the rain tempered it somewhat. For fifteen minutes they rode in discomfort, but there was no cover, no relief from the pounding rain that continued unabated, becoming a blinding deluge that made the horses neigh and slip on the newly slick rocks and slushy rivulets.

There came a muffled rumble from above them. "Move, get the hell out," Landry yelled. "Fast, get to higher ground." Wildly, the men spurred their frantic mounts. Billy

Temple's mule balked at the sudden confusion, kicked out
its hind hooves once, then set its legs, it ears laid back.
"Take Morton's horse," Landry shouted at Bull Dunlap,
handing him the reins. Then the marshal swung his sorrel
down into the draw to switch the animal's rump furiously;
the mule gave a squeal of furor and began moving. But as a
broken wall of tossing water poured around an upper bend,
the animal came alive. Both the mule and Landry's horse
climbed desperately up the crumbling sides of the wash, the
animals humping and digging, their eyes bulging. They
pulled free as the raging water-force swept by, carrying trees
and brush and boulders, the latter crashing and clattering
under four feet of tumbling death.

High on the mountainside, the outlaw, Wasatch, lay on his
big belly across the saddle, supporting his weight on his left
foot in a stirrup. His pale face grimaced with each rhythmic
stride of the horse. "Don't know how much farther I can go
on," he moaned.

"You and Tunin won't have to," Jenson consoled him.
"Me and Liddicoat, we talked it over. You and Tunin—in
your conditions—would be more trouble than help. We're
gonna leave the gold right back at the old building, like we
discussed. There's plenty of graze for the animals, good water, and we'll leave you enough grub. That'll give you two
time to heal and rest up. Most of all, you can guard the haul
just like you wanted. But you two got to keep watchful. Some
of them, like the old man, might be fool enough to come
back after it."

A grateful smile flooded Wasatch's face. Tunin looked at
Jenson with ready acceptance, for he too was eagerly willing
to call it quits. The neckerchief around his upper left arm
had not contained the oozing blood that colored his shirt-
sleeve. His face had grayed in torment. "What you and Liddicoat plan?" he managed to ask.

"We'll help you take the gold off, and set you up. Then
me and him are goin' after Morton." Jenson took a chaw of
tobacco. "If we don't, he'll skin us alive if and when he gets

away. Besides, me and Liddicoat, we been with him a long time. He's like a big brother.''

"You just might get killed tryin' to bail Morton out. What good is that goin' to do?''

Jenson picked at his teeth with a thorny nail. "You suggestin' we should just abandon him now that we got them prospectors' gold?''

"I'm sayin', why get yourself killed?''

"Morton's been pretty goddamned good to you, kid. He wouldn't take too kindly hearin' you just now. So don't get no personal ideas about this gold here.''

"You ain't all that loyal, Jenson,'' Tunin said, his face combative. "I've overheard you. You, Liddicoat, and Morton—you got hauls from way back socked away all over the territory. And in some cases only Morton knows where. Without him, you won't get them.''

A quiet Liddicoat in the lead looked back to exchange glances with Jenson, who said, "Well, let's just say he's our necessary insurance.''

"The thing that I don't understand, that I just can't shake off, is why they split up,'' Liddicoat called back. "Why did Landry and his men head out across the desert? It don't make sense, and I don't like it, I tell you.''

"Yeah, it's strange. It bothers me somethin' powerful, too. Guess we'll find out when we get Morton back,'' Jenson replied.

"Ain't gonna be easy gettin' him away from the likes of Landry and his crew,'' Tunin told them bluntly.

Jenson looked at the youth with patient tolerance, like one might a naive child. "Never said it would be, but with Liddicoat able to shoot a fly off a horse's rump at any distance, we can make it pretty hard on them. On the trail, around the campfire, they're sitting ducks. One by one, we can cut them down. Then too, Morton's like a wild stallion, always sniffin' and seein', and always waitin' for a break.'' Jenson spat tobacco. "Come on,'' he urged, "let's get this ore up to the old town; me and Liddicoat got lots of miles to cover.''

On foot, leading Lasko's horse, a soaked and grim Noah Crawford watched the mules and the outlaws wind slowly, making their way toward Desert Roost. Checking his rifle and his sidearm, he kept above them and carefully out of sight as he worked toward the main drift behind the superintendent's building.

# (14)

Ignoring the putrid horseflesh, they explored the area of the shootout for a time, moving around the rimrocks and the draws, where the boulders of peeling lava had concealed the dead gunman. Billy Temple took them to the mounded grave. "Who was he?" Landry asked Morton.

Morton stared at the site, his face impassive except for a twitching mustache. "Name was Hank Evans."

"Hank Evans." Landry rolled the name, sounding it out. "That's familiar. I think I have a poster on him."

A lazy, mocking smile curled the sides of the outlaw's mouth, "He damned near got you, Landry."

Landry did not dignify Morton with a look, but replied with steely reserve, "Damn near—but I've had closer, Morton, I've had closer."

Landry led them to the spot where he and Shoshone Joe had taken refuge under the boulder with the browlike overhang. "We waited for dark here," he explained, swinging around in the saddle and looking back at the familiar columns of fluted rock where Morton's gang had stretched out. "Considering all the hell that I went through, I might have been smarter trying to make it through you and your men, Morton." The outlaw looked smugly at his captor; his obsidian eyes narrowed icily. Landry met the other man's gaze. "Alone, I would have made it through—but I figured not with Shoshone Joe."

"But then you wouldn't have found the Breyfogle." Jake Withers guffawed jauntily, his black floppy hat curling in the wind. His large face went wide in a smile so broad that it cocked his pointed beard.

The rain ceased. They left the lower skirt of the mountain through draws of thick greasewood and headed into the desert, the playas sparsely dotted with shad scale and blackbrush. The speckled yellow of creosote enlivened the seemingly endless stretch of ash-white. The damp cooling had made the creosote pungent, almost intoxicating. "Toward them brown hills, the other side of all this alkali, that where you're headed?" Bull Dunlap asked. "This flat ahead, we can't go across it in the dead of heat."

"We don't cross it, we go by it and cut northwest."

"Northwest!" Temple exclaimed. "I can't believe my ears, Landry. Whatever got hold of you? You know there's nothing but miles of dry rock that way. No wonder you got into trouble."

For a moment Landry ignored him and simply set a steady pace in the announced direction. No one noticed, except for Landry, that Morton took a sudden interest. He sat his gray higher, straining against the bonds to see, obviously intrigued and perplexed, but realizing then why he had lost Landry's trail.

"We should have enough water to hold us several days," Dunlap told Landry, "unless you get us lost and babbling out of our minds. Hope you ain't got nothin' like that up your sleeve."

"You mean you don't trust me? Solid partnership we got." Amused, Landry tossed the words over his shoulder.

"He don't mean nothin' against you," Jake said, quick to soothe.

"Oh, then our little contract still holds?" Landry was smiling to himself, but the others could not see.

"We're with you, Landry," Dunlap drawled. "I was just sayin' it ain't smart to cross a desert in the heat, especially one that much ain't known about."

"They're right, it ain't nothing to joke about, Dirk," Temple reminded, almost as if he were a correcting father.

"Well, you're right to an extent," Landry said casually,

unruffled. "The country ahead is a wilderness that I never saw before, until we tried it. And I don't hanker to ever see it again. But if we want the gold, I'm going to have to find my route, exactly as I did it, my way. Problem is, I wasn't payin' that much attention to landmarks. I just wanted get across to water. The White Mountains there, they were my guide."

"Still, you must have been mighty bad off, if you don't think you can remember where you found gold," said Dunlap.

The marshal reined his horse and pivoted. The animal shifted and danced, its nostrils quivering. The men all pulled into an arc facing him, except for Morton's beast, which Landry drew up beside him. His face suddenly humorless, Landry looked at them through slitted eyes, his voice brittle. "Seems some of you never felt your skin blister until it splits your face, or your eyes go blind from glare, or your tongue swell until you can't breathe or swallow. That's only the beginning. You get to where you can't see, you can't hear, and you can't think. . . ."

"No questions, no doubts. We ain't judgin' you, Marshal," Jake assured him immediately.

Dunlap swung a hand in dismissal, his face receptive and totally approving. "Me too, I'm with you all the way, Marshal. No problems. You just keep calling the shots."

"I've promised you no guarantees, except to try." Landry looked from man to man. "And I'm going to do my damnedest to find it. But at this point, I can't promise you anything."

"Bad piece of desert out there, Dirk," said Temple. "Most desert rats avoid it like the plague. Only thing I can figure, you chanced a dangerous route 'cause Morton here wouldn't suspect it. Ain't that it?"

"You're partly right." Landry turned his horse toward the wastelands and continued, the others moving up close, all listening. "Shoshone Joe told me about a seep twenty miles northwest of here, an ancient Indian watering spot less than a day's travel. He called it Pah-hah."

"Pah-hah?" Dunlap repeated doubtfully. "I been in these

parts a good many years and I ain't ever heard of no Pah-hah.''

"Me neither, Marshal." Jake was quick to join in. "And where I live, a lot of prospectors and lost souls come tumbling out of that waste, just like you, dying for water. Nobody ever said nothin' about a spring out there."

"It wasn't supposed to be a spring, just a tiny flow in the rocks, enough to keep a man from dying—that was according to Shoshone Joe."

Temple was thinking seriously. "You know, I heard rumors years back, rumors about some water out there somewhere. An old friend of mine, long dead now, mentioned in passing that he'd heard something to that effect from some Injun guide. I didn't give it no account at the time."

"Did you find anything?" Jake asked Landry.

"At first, I was like all of you. I thought he was crazy, or trying to trick me, but the more I thought of it, I realized that I was his only hope. Morton and his men were looking to kill him, once they learned the whereabouts of the loot, so why would he lie to me? That's why I chanced it, figuring it just might be there and I could dodge Morton, plus be able to swing back to Desert Roost."

"And?" Temple leaned forward over his nodding mule to hear better.

"As you will see, we didn't find a seep. But there had been one there once." A murmur of surprise arose from the men. "It has been buried in a landslide. But there were signs. Yes, it had been there." Landry steadied the sorrel into a brisk walk. "I remember us moving to a higher ground, toward those low hills, those with uneven tops." Landry pointed. Jake and Dunlap both squirmed high to get a better view of the irregular landscape, the bluffs weathered and rounded in places. The marshal squared his shoulders with a swell of confidence.

"Good God, this is something," Jake whooped. "Good God, I can't believe it. All that gold out there just waiting for us."

They rode through the forest of high Joshuas, not so ghostly

as in the moonlight, but imposing and fearsome nonethe-
less, with their spear-point leaves leathery stiff and dagger
sharp. The wind grew warm. Slowly, along a gradual rise,
they approached the low hills, time-battered and scarred.
Landry wondered if it was in this area that they had heard
the rattlers. In the more protected breaks the bright green
mesquite grew in sheltering clumps. They passed on, through
a draw where a second range appeared with an obvious elbow
of elongated hills that veered at a right angle. "That's it,"
Landry cried out.

"That's what?" both Dunlap and Jake Withers asked at
the same instant. Everyone stretched higher in his saddle to
peer, including Rattlesnake Morton. "That's where we found
the remains of Pah-hah."

"God damn," Dunlap whooped, too.

Hurriedly they rode, forcing the animals, lathering them
into a greater pace. At the base of a stretching lift they reined
their animals to rest. "Come on," said Landry. Both Bull
Dunlap and Jake Withers were off their beasts before the
marshal had finished his command. He looked at Temple for
support.

"You go ahead," said the prospector, knowing what the
marshal wished. "I'll wait here, keep a gun on our guest."

"We stayed the first night up there." Landry pointed at
the hump of the hill. They took care not to stumble and fall,
for the low hill held sinks of stone and loose rocks that made
travel precarious. They climbed laboriously to the summit.
Landry marveled that he and Shoshone Joe had made it at
night, although he informed the two that the weary half-
breed had fallen heavily here. Landry studied the waves of
mountain ahead, especially where the two thrusts of hills met
in an elbow. He looked for a flat rock that he seemed to
remember Shoshone Joe sitting on, but he could see none,
although in a tight rift between two bulges of bare promontories he saw an ample grove of mesquite, with screwbeans,
and cat's claw mimosa. "By God, that's where I got Shoshone Joe and me our only real grub, that first morning we
rested here." Landry stumbled almost deliriously toward the

site, but pulled up, not wanting to exhaust himself foolishly. With exciting ease he was finding his way back, he realized. But the setting brought back fearful memories of the fright and the excruciating suffering that was to follow. Without words, he returned to where they had a commanding view.

"Where now?" Jake blurted.

"Just give me time. I've got to set my directions."

"You see anything familiar up there?" Billy Temple called. He sat some ten feet away from their mounted prisoner, the shotgun pointed at the outlaw's belly.

"Yeah, I'm seeing things pretty good now." Landry then recognized the rocky bench where he and Shoshone Joe had taken refuge at dawn, where they could overlook the section of hills and cliffs that came together at right angles. "Down there," Landry pointed, "see that pile of rocks down there, kind of flowing out from the cliff?"

"Yeah," said Dunlap, leaning out over a short but dangerous drop.

"Well, that's where the seep apparently was."

"I want to see it, to believe it," said Jake.

"For now, I want you to go back down with Billy Temple," Landry drawled, "and bring Morton around to the base down there. If you swing east, you can get around here in an hour. I want to move on as far as we can before camping tonight. And, of course, soon we'll have to get out of the sun for a time. Another couple of hours and it will be damn hot."

"Why me?" Jake protested. "I want to be right here with you."

Landry growled at the man. "I don't want Billy to be out of our sight with Morton, let alone bring him around by himself. You want the gold, then you go with Billy."

"Do it," Dunlap said simply.

Swaying his shoulders like a disciplined little boy, Jake Withers cursed under his breath and headed down toward Billy and the horses. Landry stared at the patterns of tangled hills and cliffs beyond, knowing that for all his memory, it would not be easy to pinpoint the exact area of location unless they were lucky. But he intended to give it one hell of a try. An excitement was building in him now, a growing confidence. He led Bull Dunlap to the peak of the mounded rise, to the rocky knob where he and the half-breed had waited out the day. Dust storms had almost completely filled the spots, but they could still make out the shallow depressions where a few cuts of creosote bushes lay in place, anchored by the dirt. Landry squatted and ran a hand over a stem, grateful that he had survived.

They looked about. Landry squinted at the corrugated hills to the northwest with the high White Mountains gleaming beyond, the year-long snow streaking the eastern clefts. Then he looked to the south, at the open playa with the green of sparse forest that encircled the towering mountain, site of Desert Roost. They watched Temple and Withers take Morton eastward around the flank of the hill. In anticipation of their eventual arrival, they climbed down to the supposed seep of Pah-hah, to where a sheet of collapsing rock had strewn shattered earth in a six-foot heap at the base. Here the rubble of jointed rock had spread loosely, sheeting and thinning. They examined remains of bone-dry mesquite, a small but once thriving forest. Where the winds had scoured and scraped the bedrock, the sand had sifted clear. Landry bent toward some caked earth. With his knife he probed the brick-hard ground, breaking it to reveal evidence of a once rich soil, rooted with hairlike clots.

"By God, Landry, you was right," Dunlap exclaimed. "There had to be water here at one time." Landry could not reach the hardpan, although he managed to dig some six or seven inches, which revealed that there had been a lengthy and steady supply of water, not an extensive quantity, but enough to give sustenance to nearby wildlife or a passerby, and to produce green life. A miniature oasis.

With the heat beginning to pulse and shimmer off the flats, Landry remembered Shoshone Joe moaning, drifting off, his voice rising, threatening to alarm Morton, who had taken refuge in a draw somewhere on the southwest side. He remembered the sun, a disk of molten brass swimming in the burned white of sky. He remembered shaking the half-breed to his senses, then nearly carrying the man, whose vacant eyes and puffed features had taken on the foreboding wan appearance of death.

Dunlap studied the marshal. "You're thinkin' of something mighty hard."

Landry snapped to. "Just thinking back."

"Damn glad you are. You're doin' good, Landry. I take my hat off to you. Sorry I had my doubts at first."

"It was hot as hell that day, hotter than it'll get today. We had to find more shade. Shoshone Joe was in bad shape. I almost had to pack him off this hill here. Couple of times he slipped. Damn near fell a few times. He kicked up enough rocks that I was sure Morton or one of his men would hear. But somehow, no one heard us."

"So where'd you go?"

Landry moved ahead along a stony rise and pointed upward. "I got us away as fast as we could manage, to that little cave up there." They both stared at a shallow indentation. "We waited there, me with a gun drawn, figurin' sure as hell Morton would come looking. When nothin' happened, I got Shoshone Joe down here to the flats."

Dunlap whistled, slowing. "You come down off the top up there with a half-dead man?"

"Yes."

"Just look at them loose plates of rock. You're sure as hell lucky you two didn't get buried alive."

Perspiration began beading the marshal's brow. He chewed his lips thoughtfully. "Yeah, just talking about it makes my skin crawl. But somehow we made it. We rested for a time, before I pushed him west, along this wall of hill here. That's when a dust devil hit us. It was a hell of a sandstorm, but it forced Morton to take cover too, and it buried our tracks." Landry remembered the intensity, the uprooted weeds, tumbling and bouncing, the abrasive wind shearing the rocks and trashing the brush.

"You traveled in broad daylight?"

"For one thing, I knew if we waited for nightfall, Morton and his cronies would be out like bats on the wing after us.

And I figured he wouldn't ever guess that we would travel in the heat of day. Then too, I wanted to get opposite Desert Roost and as close as possible for a run to it."

"You wouldn't have had a chance out there, you two against Morton and them, all on horses."

"You're right under ordinary situations, but I could see another big sandstorm brewing. There were dust devils lining up, all over those plains to the southeast out there. I figured we had to move, if we had a chance at all. And that desert storm comin' would cover us from Morton's view, as well as cover our tracks, if it didn't do us in first."

From around the curve of hill, they watched Temple approach steadily with their prisoner bound to his gray. Jake followed a few feet behind them, his rifle pointed at Morton's back. Both Temple and Jake Withers showed disbelief and then amazement when they were shown what had been a seep. "Not even you, the desert fox, ever knew about this, did you?" Landry taunted Morton.

The smoldering eyes looked straight into Landry's. "If I'd known about it, you'd be dead now. As it was, Landry, I realize now, I damned near got you, 'cause I figured right. I figured exactly what you was going to do, and I'd have gotten you if it hadn't been for them devil storms."

"Almost, Morton. You were on the other side of this hill, Shoshone Joe and I were on this side. Not a quarter of a mile apart. Difference was—I knew it and you didn't." Landry looked up at the bronze sky. "It's getting hot, but we're going to push on."

"We're with you, Marshal, all the way," said Jake, rubbing his big belly as if he were hungry. "Except don't you think it's getting too damn hot? Shouldn't we take cover soon?"

"Not yet," Landry said, mounting. "We're going to move as far as possible." He showed them where he and the half-breed had braved it west. "Along here, Shoshone Joe and I suffered something terrible." Landry's voice cracked with emotion. "Shoshone Joe was dying. I knew, but could do nothing for him. His skin was afire, and his body got the spasms," Landry related. "I was going under, too. That's when the next dust devil hit. Struck us so hard we couldn't see our hands in front of our faces. We hid someplace along here and waited it out; it damn near buried us alive. But we managed to survive. I carried him to that little cave up ahead." Landry pointed to a concave niche. "We spent the second night there. God," Landry reflected. "It took us two days of hell to make it just this far on foot, and we've done it today in just a little over half a day."

"You stayed here the second night?" Dunlap pursued.

"Ahead in that little cave. That's where the half-breed died. I climbed to the top there when the moon came out and I saw Morton and his gang searching the desert between here and Desert Roost. That's when I knew I had to forget my hope of getting back to the old town, that my only chance was to head north toward the springs and Silverpoint. Out on that flat to the north, I found us some cactus, which I cut up, but when I got back, Shoshone Joe was dead."

As Landry approached, he felt heavy and a little queasy, for the place held dark memories, and the remains of Shoshone Joe would not be pleasant. But he stopped and blinked his eyes. In the shallow niche where Landry expected to see the sunken and dried body, nothing remained. Two dozen feet from the niche, out in the soft of desert, lay a mound like a grave.

He looked back at a smiling, self-satisfied Morton. "So you did find his body?"

"The buzzards did. We just joined them."

"Well, at least, Morton, you had the decency to bury the half-breed."

"But I hand it to you Landry. You pulled one on me. Wasn't till we seen them buzzards and investigated, did I realize that I was closer to you than I ever suspected. But by then them damned storms had covered any sign of you. That's when I decided to hightail it to the old town up there."

They rested then in some shade, took water and food and cared for the animals. "From here you was headin' in the direction of my place," Jake remarked. "Out there." He waved his hand slowly, almost reverently, his palm down, across the vastness of desert. "You found the gold between here and my place."

Jake flushed with excitement and stroked his pointed beard. "But I gotta give you credit, Landry, you've remembered everything crystal clear—everything."

"So far."

Jake looked disturbed. "What do you mean?"

"So far it's been pretty easy, but from here on . . ." He swallowed hard. "I don't know. A lot of it's fuzzy."

"Don't like you talkin' that way again. It'll probably all come back to you, once you see landmarks," Dunlap assured Landry.

Landry studied the field of volcanic rubble where he had cut the cactus, sucked on it and washed his face with it. He was not as anxious as the others to head into the next link, for in his mind's eye he saw his bones white and scattered in the wasteland, bleak, dry, encrusted with hair and tattered clothing, and he did not want to tempt fate again.

With the cooling of late afternoon they readied to travel northwest, when Billy Temple called their attention to yellow, smokelike clouds forming across the plains behind them.

"Damn it," Landry said with bitter distaste.

"Dust devils. A big storm growing," Temple acknowledged. "Could be on us within an hour."

"Best we move out, make some distance before it reaches us," said Jake.

"Best we start lookin' for good cover up yonder," Temple warned.

"But before we do," said Landry, "you and me, Dunlap, we're going to crawl up on the top of this hill once more."

The men, including Billy, looked at Landry as if he'd lost his mind. "That's wasting time," Jake bawled. But Morton looked curiously at the marshal, his stony face registering surprise, then cunning.

"Won't take long. Come with me." Landry motioned to an uncertain Dunlap.

"What the hell is so important up there?" Disgruntled, Jake Withers spat at the ground and slowly dismounted.

Landry, with his rifle and a pair of field glasses, chose an easy access, up a troughlike fissure between two rounded humps. Picking their way cautiously, they reached a low cleavage in a few minutes.

"Like Withers down there, I want to know what the hell you're up to, Landry." Dunlap was puffing.

"Just a gut feeling." As they moved into the cleavage where the playa came into view, with the jut of Desert Roost in the distance, Landry hunkered down. Instinctively Dunlap did the same. Landry surveyed the setting through his field glasses.

"You think somebody's tailin' us?"

"For the last couple of hours Morton's been looking around or back as if expectin' somebody. He tries not to be obvious about it, but I've caught him." Landry canvassed the vastness slowly, carefully, moving from right to left. He could sense a fidgety Dunlap watching him. Keeping his breath even, so as to steady the glasses, he examined the eastern edge of the playa. Suddenly he jerked alert to adjust the glasses. "By God, there is somebody. Damn, I lost them." The marshal hurriedly focused the lens. "There he is, and by God, it appears there's two of 'em. One of them's leading a packhorse or a mule."

"Let's see." Dunlap reached for the glasses.

"Far out to the southeast, they're moving up a dry wash and trying to keep out of sight behind some high banks." Landry handed Dunlap his glasses. "They're following us, I'd lay odds. There's no other reason why somebody would be out in this godforsaken country."

Dunlap readjusted the glasses. At last he whistled slowly through his teeth. "Son of a bitch. You're right. Only two of them, best I can tell. They got a mule with a water pack. They're comin' slow and steady."

Landry impatiently retrieved the glasses and watched again. "In fact, that's my buckskin one of them's on. I'd lay even greater odds that it's that little weasel named Jenson.

And the other one's Liddicoat. He's the dangerous one, as you well know.''

''That's the son of a bitch that had us ducking?''

''That's the one.''

''Never seen nobody that could lay bullets in like he done—not from that far away.''

''But he's not so good that he'll chance a shot if we ride huddled around Morton. Morton's our trump in this little game.''

''The others might be coming in from a different direction.'' The constable looked anxiously around him.

''I don't think so,'' Landry said with measured words. ''What I'm afraid is, the others have gone after Crawford and the gold. And that worries me.''

''Nothin' to worry about. Crawford's got some good men covering him. My man Lasko ain't no bum, I can tell you. And that younger brother of Withers, he seems capable. Even your deputy, Thomas, was gettin' about good. What worries me is these two out there could hurt our treasure hunt—foul everything up.'' The constable looked determinedly at Landry. ''We're going to have to stop them. One of us will have to stay back and kill them.'' He removed his .45.

Landry studied Bull Dunlap. ''It won't be that easy. Morton's men are too desert-wise.'' He grew introspective. ''For now, we'll continue just as we are, we'll let the others know we got some bad intruders, but not Morton. We don't want to give him any such satisfaction, until he figures out what's happening. In the meanwhile, we'll just have to be careful, and hold tighter to Morton than fleas on a hound. They won't shoot into us that way. But mostly we'll have to keep our eyes open until that dust devil hits and maybe we can shake them.''

Dunlap puckered his mouth. ''You're the boss, Marshal, but I don't like it. I say we take them here and now. When that storm hits, we wait it out. Ambush them afterward. A man's senses don't work too good after a sandstorm.''

Landry kept the glasses on the outlaws as they appeared

and disappeared. "I don't stomach bushwackin' a man, no matter how worthless he is, but we may have to resort to it."

"No use to delay. It ain't worth riskin' our necks. Somehow, they might know about your nuggets." Dunlap's eyes had a peculiar, feverish glow. "Otherwise, why would them two risk their necks for Morton? There ain't no honor among thieves."

"Jenson and Liddicoat are like brothers to Morton. They've been loyal a long time." Landry looked hard at the constable. "But it's far more than that. Morton has a history of caching parts of his hauls all over the basin—it's his insurance, so to speak. You see, that way nobody back-shoots him. If Morton dies or lands a long term in prison or is hanged, they're out of luck. This, I would guess, is what brings them—a desperate bid on their part." Landry licked his dry lips thoughtfully. "It'll be up to you and me to stop them. But we don't want to get sucked into a duel with Liddicoat."

"I got a better idea—kill Morton. You and me, we're the only law out here," said Dunlap, his face alive with malice. His words came out like the clear shattering of breaking ice. "I say kill him, bury him out here and good riddance. Who's to know? Them two owl hoots ain't gonna squeal on us. The reward on Morton's carcass ain't worth the chance of a bullet in the back, and it sure ain't equal to the Breyfogle that's out there somewhere. With Morton dead, then those two would have no more concern with us."

# (15)

Earlier that day, near Desert Roost where the road serpentined down toward Silverpoint, Vallee Crawford watched with crushing defeat as her father slanted Lasko's horse through the glades toward the town ruins. "Why? Why?" she lamented. "Why is he so bullheaded?"

Both young men were still on the ground watching Crawford; Ted Withers sitting, rocking with pain; Dale Thomas leaning on one knee.

"Your pappy is proud and mad as hell," said Ted Withers. "He don't figure no man has the right to take what's his. And I shore understand. I respect him."

"But your pop ain't thinkin' square," said Thomas, his eyes still on Crawford. "He ain't trained to go up against that Morton gang."

Ted looked at the deputy, his jaw set. "Maybe you ain't givin' her pappy enough credit."

Thomas labored to his feet. "I know about Morton and his kind. Look what they done to all of us here."

Vallee listened, her eyes darting from one young man to the other. "I've got to do something to help him," she announced. "I can't let him go in there alone."

"What can you do?" Ted asked, his voice earnest and puzzled.

"I don't know. I just know I'm terribly afraid." The girl extended her hands palms up, almost hopelessly. She took a deep breath, her breasts rising, as she straightened her body with renewed determination. "Just maybe." She licked her lips; her eyes grew intense. "If I followed Papa, if I covered him with a rifle, I might protect him somehow."

"Ain't no worry, 'cause I'll go with you," Ted announced. "We'll think of something."

"Oh, I can't ask that of you. You two are so hurt. But I can go."

"And do what?" Thomas challenged.

"You might be surprised. I shoot tolerably well."

"Papa won't listen to any of us," Seth piped up. He still held the yellow dog.

Vallee's eyes flashed with anger. She regarded her brother with disgust. "We can try. Try anything. He's our father."

"Papa, he's gonna do what he sees he's gotta do," Seth retorted.

Rolling his husky body, Ted came sluggishly to his feet. "We can't let you go alone, Miss Vallee, and we can't let your pappy walk up against all of them alone."

"And how the hell you figure to stop him? Just how you gonna save him? Answer me that." The deputy's eyes hardened with resistance.

Ted squared his shoulders. "Like Vallee said, I don't know. But I aim to do something." Ted loosened his revolver from the holster.

Thomas shook his head in exasperation. "So we stumble after him, we could all get killed."

Vallee looked at Thomas with wounded eyes. "I'm not asking either one of you to risk your neck. I'm just telling you I'm going." She turned around and looked at where her father had disappeared somewhere in the rugged mountainside. "All I need now is a rifle."

"You can count on me, Miss Vallee." With difficulty Ted shuffled toward his horse, which was waiting nervously beneath the trail.

Thomas pursed his lips, took off his Stetson and ran his good hand across his thick brown hair as he sighed audibly. "First we gotta give that Lasko fellow a quick burial until we can get back here and do it proper. Ain't Christian leaving him lie out here after he come all this way to help us." He looked hard at Vallee. There was resolve in his next words. "We'll do what we can for you, Vallee, but how we go after your pop is up to me. You two must take my orders. You understand?"

Ted nodded in compliance, and Vallee expressed grateful relief. "What do you think we should do?"

"First, all of you help me." Dale Thomas removed a small shovel from his horse. He was becoming most proficient with his left hand. Beside the twisted body of the fallen lawman, both men took turns struggling to cover the body with soft dirt. Seeing their discomfort, Vallee took the shovel from Ted. She quickly heaped a mound over the dead man, shrinking back only when she approached the face, with its mouth and sightless eyes still open, frozen in stunned shock. Thomas removed the shovel from her hands, closed the dead man's features and settled the last necessary shovelfuls. "The coyotes," the girl reminded. "There're so many up here."

"The rocks around, pile some on—quick," Thomas answered.

"Time's wasting," Ted remarked. "This Lasko fellow, him and that Bull Dunlap, they was concerned more about the Breyfogle mine than helping you folks."

"Don't matter now. Get him covered some. We'll come back later. Ain't ever right that a lawman should be left for coyotes." Thomas spoke with urgency.

"I want a gun," said the girl after they'd finished. "In case we get separated. I won't go through again what I went through with that horrible man." She shuddered. "I'll never forget his eyes when he grabbed me."

"I have an extra revolver in my pack," said Thomas.

As they moved out, a heavy downpour arrowed in. Hurriedly they moved to protect themselves with ponchos. But before Vallee could cover herself, she was drenched. Despite the grievous situation, Seth looked at her straggling hair and laughed; the men tried not to, although both choked with repressed mirth.

"I must be lovely. I lost my hat someplace," said Vallee, wringing out long strands that hung below the hood of her poncho. "Enjoy yourselves. I don't care. All I care is that my father don't get hurt."

Carefully avoiding a further response, Thomas pointed at the heights hidden in the dropping clouds. "We'll get the animals, and follow the road back a ways, then cut above the town. Maybe we can see where your pop is." He looked at the girl. "But don't get your hopes up too high, Vallee. I don't think there's going to be much we can do, not against the Morton gang."

"I want to thank you for your help—any help," Vallee said simply. "I know you both are hurting bad, and that you don't have to do this."

"No, we don't have to," said Thomas. "Yet, I understand your pop's feelings—all that gold he's worked so hard for— but I ain't doing this for him. His gold don't mean nothin' to me. I'm doing this for you."

Not to be outdone, Ted interrupted. "I'm doing it for both you and your pappy, Miss Vallee."

The girl smiled sweetly at both men. Thomas and Ted retrieved the two horses and the mule which still carried the sister's and brother's gear. Vallee climbed astride the long-eared animal and laid her hand on the borrowed revolver snug in a coat pocket.

Crawford approached the town from above the old road. He left his horse behind an outbuilding and worked into the main drift. He sidled up to a small air vent, and from the protective shadows he could see that Wasatch and Tunin had removed their saddles. He watched Liddicoat and Jenson set the gold sacks in a pile. Then the two began dragging them into the storage room where they had been originally. He felt a hopeful excitement, a great relief when he realized the latter two were not staying. After they left down the old Indian trail, Tunin and Wasatch began preparing the animals for the night. Crawford checked his Colt and cocked his Winchester. A slow, satisfied smile creased his face as he

moved past abandoned ore cars, along a strip of wooden
rails, and under precariously hanging beams. Through an
alcove he stepped down the wide stairs, lit a match and proceeded along the manway. As he lit a second match and
crawled up the old ladder, he could hear the outlaws grunting
and talking while they toiled outside. With carefully probing
fingers he lifted the familiar hatch until he could reach up to
slide the worn rug so that it barely concealed the outer edge
of the lift. With a pencil from his vest he braced it open a
slit enough to permit light and to see the room. He rested the
cocked revolver in a niche under a cross beam near the top
rung and began waiting.

As covertly as possible, Landry told Billy and Jake about
the followers lurking not far behind. Billy handled it without
emotion, but Jake Withers straightened in the saddle, his eyes
wild and searching. Morton could not help but notice. The
outlaw became more withdrawn.

Although a mountain rainstorm had gutted the ravines
and watersheds below Desert Roost, the harsh desert remained sultry and parched. Gradually the thermal contrast
brewed strong winds, creating once again the hated dust
clouds that slithered sinuously and built fantastic spirals,
the edges white as sea fog. With time, the dust columns
mounted ominously.

The storm hit, a yellow-brown beast of clawing, snarling
fury that engulfed them in a smothering dark, its force slash-
ing and biting away at the overhead outcrops until sand and
rocks tumbled down, forming cones. Before the onslaught,
the men had taken refuge in the lee of an overhanging promontory. But they found little relief as the windy blasts whipped
their clothes and forced them to huddle while the animals
stomped and pulled with uneasiness. Man and beast with-
stood, however, until the upheaval had passed.

Sluggishly the men set up camp, took dry food, and
organized a three-hour watch as darkness closed. There
was no keeping the facts from Morton now. The outlaw
watched them patiently. Jake Withers reacted. "If them

bastard partners of yours out there try to take us, they better understand you're a dead man," he hollered to Morton, his voice just audible above the buffeting wind. Morton watched him impassively. Landry studied the rancher, wondering what would happen if the two shadowers did attempt something. The night crawled by miserably but uneventfully.

At dawn they watered the animals and struck north, the direction Landry had plunged that silvery night, when alone after Shoshone Joe's death. Only Jake complained of needing coffee when Landry ordered that no telltale fire be made. Fortunately, the sandstorm had covered any previous tracks. But with the numerous stretches of open space, they had little hope of escaping the scrutiny of the two who were surely somewhere behind.

The early morning wind rose steadily, humming and moaning through the scallops and hollows. Dimly Landry remembered trudging into the night, his boots growing heavier under the ooze of grated blisters, his constricting throat clenching tighter; every breath, every gasp ripping through him, his legs and thighs and arms tingling with spasms. Methodically now, they followed a fractured ridge past clumps of mesquite. Vaguely he recalled the area, recalled hearing a rattlesnake shrilling its warning and the cry of some creature in mortal anguish.

With time, they crossed a high volcanic plain. The sun rose swiftly, warmly, giving the distance a vibrant sheen that distorted images. In the next hour they worked through a winding pass. "Surprisin' to me that you are remembering so tolerably well," Temple tossed forth, "considerin' the shape you must of been in."

"So far so good," Landry said prudently.

"How much further?" Jake Withers asked, leaning forward with an anxious tilt.

"Long ways yet."

"God, no wonder Breyfogle's mine got lost forever. Nobody in his right mind would ever come into this hellish country." Bull Dunlap squirreled his head around at the steep rimrock lining each side. They continued to hold close around Morton.

The gorge opened gradually onto a boulder-strewn plateau. By the time they had crossed it, the sun beat pitilessly. The creosote boughs hung limp and seemingly lifeless in the sullen air. Steadily they descended, until forced to take refuge under a high, frowning cliff that seemed most familiar to Landry. Without talking they ate jerky and hardtack and watered the horses again.

Billy Temple studied the way they had come. His eyes narrowed. "Ain't seen no sign of them varmints yet." He ran a hand caressingly over the breech of his shotgun. While they rested from the heat, all the men kept careful watch, each assuming a sober responsibility, aware that they could be ambushed anytime, anywhere. Morton sat morosely, his eyes revealing nothing.

Dunlap motioned Landry to him, out of the hearing of others. "Them two we seen—been no sign of them. Think we lost 'em in the storm?"

"I've tried to keep us in as much cover as possible," Landry said, "but they're not going to be that easy to shake."

Dunlap's eyes hardened. "If we see 'em again, me and you better hang back. They got to be stopped."

With resignation, Landry replied quietly, "I know."

They waited for the second storm to hit, but shifting winds lost their force by midday, so that the dust clouds dissolved into smoking streamers that bounced along the horizon. After a needed rest, the men set out again in the late afternoon. The White Mountains to the northwest, so remote and austere, remained Landry's constant beacon. Their high ramparts rose in a misty veil of drooping clouds. They rode with grim but set determination, covering twice the distance Landry had managed during his ordeal on foot. He remembered fearing that he might unwittingly circle and lose his way, a certain death in the desolate land.

After several hours of plodding in the intense heat, all eyes turned to Landry. Even the tight-lipped Morton studied the lawman, watched his tense posture, a slightly forward lean with features, alert to every rise and lay of the formidable expanse. As they crossed a broken crater of hollows and rifts, the marshal drew his horse to a halt.

"What is it?" Jake Withers called anxiously.

"That hump ahead there, see where it drops down into that wash below?"

"Yes."

"I damn near broke my neck going over that. I was trying to get down it into the flats and I fell. Could have finished myself right there," Landry recalled.

"Let's go," Dunlap whooped, "Hell, you must be damn near the gold, Landry."

"Let's get on." Jake Withers stiffened upright in the saddle, his head pivoting, a wildness commencing to blaze his eyes.

"I'm not that damn sure," Landry said more to himself.

They advanced at a faster pace. The wind rose again and streamers of fine-stinging sand commenced, clouding the horizons to the east and passing on, only to twist back in tumultuous spirals. The dust devil came at them suddenly, humming and grinding, forcing them to take refuge in a nearby draw, sheltered by an escarpment of high banks. They dismounted, covered their mouths with their neckerchiefs and held the heads of their horses against their chests. The sandstorm howled around them, abrasive to both men and animals. For a few endless minutes it battered them, tore at their clothing and lifted off their hats. It flapped the coverings on the packs and made the animals shift and stomp and squeal. Then as quickly as the devil had come, it passed on. They found the lay of the land once again altered, with sand mounds and shallow little depressions spotting the nearby landscape. With the grit miserable and heavy in their clothes, and the animals wheezing, they agreed to rest out the night.

"No use pushin' it too hard," Temple advised.

"I got hit hard in this same area by a sandstorm," Landry

recalled. "Can't tell you how glad I am to have a horse, lots of water, and company."

An excitement was building as they departed in the morning. Temple, the practical man always, warned them, "You're spreading out, driftin'. Keep close to Morton. Them friends of his might be lurkin' somewhere close."

"Ain't seen no signs of 'em, not since the constable and Landry spied them," Jake said. "And not a sound from 'em at night. Maybe we lost 'em far back."

"We'd be fools to count on that." Dunlap spat tobacco juice.

Within the next hours, they angled toward a battlement of high crags. Landry's heart quickened. He had taken refuge in the area, he knew; refuge from the powerful dust devil that had threatened his life. And somewhere here, ahead, in the chaotic labyrinth of cul-de-sacs, washes, and serrations, he had found the cave and the gold. Along the wearing miles they all kept vigilance. But the hours passed without incident or even a sign of the two outlaws. The White Mountains began bulking higher, the base blue with juniper and pinyon; higher above, where Jeffrey pine took root, the poplars had begun paling in steep ravines. But now as they approached, Landry felt uncertain once more. He stopped his horse and let it yank from side to side as he contemplated the setting. The others drew close beside him.

"Problems?" Jake inquired.

Landry curled his lips in momentary disappointment. The battlement of rocks, like the towers of a castle, stretched to his left, north and south above a chain of steep bluffs. But the lay of the land seemed different somehow. The sand slanted steeply toward the bluffs. Or did it? Over and over while recovering at the Withers' ranch, while returning to Desert Roost, while on guard at night at the superintendent's building, he had thought of the spot; had tried to refresh all the landmarks embedded in his mind. There had been a deep and decided wash under a low ridge, with a moon-shaped cave below bluffs with the battlement above, all backed by

the wall of the White Mountains. At least that's how he remembered—or thought he had envisioned it. The area before
him was familiar, and yet. . . . He chewed his lips. He eyed
the jut of the mountain and worked downward to the corrugated battlement. But the landscape appeared more extensive, more encompassing, more varied, with a thousand
complex creases and folds and prongs. With the terrible
sandstorm blowing upon him, he had been obsessed by the
immediate need to survive. What the land looked like had
been the least of his concerns. He had headed toward the
nearest, most likely protection—the cave that now was nowhere to be seen.

Landry became aware of the anxious, disturbed expressions of those next to him.

"What's wrong?" Bull Dunlap pressed.

"Damn easy to get confused in this country," Temple
offered with his knowing wisdom.

"It just isn't right," Landry admitted.

"What the hell isn't right?" Dunlap growled.

"Just what I said, the lost mine—it's near here somewhere.
But it doesn't look right, somehow." Landry did not take his
eyes off the nearby ridge.

"God damn," Jake blurted, his eyes wide and his head
pivoting about. "God damn, come this far, you gotta remember. Think, Landry. Think."

Morton, sullen, tight-lipped, watched with curious interest.

"All these breaks and rises and stuff, it's a damn confusing
area," Billy Temple said. He was looking over some
mounded swells toward the scarred flank of ridges that forged
ahead. The sun was now loafing high in the west.

"Just what the hell you looking for? Maybe we can help
you?" Dunlap demanded.

"I hid out from one hell of a dust devil in those bluffs
up there," Landry explained, pointing. "I was in a cave
that was in full view from here. But I don't see it now.
God damn it, I don't see it now." Frustration exploded
from him.

"Anything else you recognize?" Temple pursued.

"Those castlelike bluffs. And, of course, the big mountains behind them. All that's familiar."

"What else?"

"The lower ridges."

"What else?"

"I don't know for sure."

"Maybe we ain't in the right place," Temple suggested. "Maybe that cave is being blocked from view."

"Let's ride closer and look. A cave ain't going to disappear. It's bound to be up there," Jake barked.

"Shut up," said Temple. "What else, Dirk? Anything else you recognize from here?"

"There was a deep wash in front. But it's not out there now. Not anywhere."

"Storms can fill places up in no time," Temple said quietly. "Let's ride ahead. Maybe you'll recognize something more. If not—we'll just have to explore the whole area."

"It's the cave. That's what we've got to find." Landry blinked his eyes and looked in bewilderment at the splintered rise.

They proceeded slowly for a good mile, paralleling the battlement. But Landry saw nothing that he recognized. "After I found the gold, I struck out into some terrible heat," Landry commenced, all ears and eyes upon him. "I didn't know which way to go to get through that rimrock up there; if I got into some dead-end, I would die, I knew. I didn't have the strength to fight my way back and start over. But somehow, luckily, I did find my way through. There was a natural draw up ahead there somewhere that took me through. After that I don't remember much of anything."

As the party angled west in the next hours, they lost sight of the White Mountains, blocked out by the raw bluffs gradually darkening in shadow; the sun tinted the eastern desert; the party came to a frustrating and confused halt. All the men sat their horses side by side and looked up, searching north and south along the blemished heights for a cave. Nowhere could they locate the natural rift that Landry had apparently followed. No place was there a shallow cave.

"We're looking too high—the cave wasn't that high up because I was able to get to it pretty easy." Landry said slowly, hesitantly. "There seems to be more dunes in here, more than I remember. It just doesn't look the same."

"God damn." Jake slapped his thigh in frustration; the snap startled his mount to snort and pull against the reins.

Landry didn't look at anyone, because now he wasn't certain if the shallow cave was someplace in the towering bluffs before him, buried by the shifting sands, or farther out in one of the many humps and folds and backdrops that strewed the tangled wasteland. Could they have ridden by it? Maybe they were standing over it.

"Best we camp here tonight," Temple suggested. "Tomorrow in the morning, when it's cooler, things may look better. I suggest, Dirk, that we retrace our route. Go back for maybe half a day. You done great so far. Go back some miles and you might see something you'll recognize," the old man said with assurance. He grinned broadly through his bush of whiskers. "Damn, it gives me the shivers to know we're right near Breyfogle's lost mine. Wish we could smell gold."

"Right now I'm going to ride along the base of these bluffs and look for that goddamned cave," Landry said. "If we can't find it, we'll move out in the desert far enough that I can get a broad view and try it again."

The sun had begun casting red lances into the sky. "Well, there's a few more hours till complete dark," Temple said, "but those dust clouds way out there don't look too friendly. And there may be a couple of Morton's partners around here that ain't too friendly, either," he reminded.

"That storm comin' might change things again," Dunlap urged. "Seems to me time is short."

Landry turned his horse to the south. "We'll swing back

a few miles along where we've come—search for as long as we can. Maybe with another look at this damned country, I'll see things better this time.''

# (16)

Finished with feeding and watering the animals, a weary Wasatch and Tunin returned to the cabin. "Damn nice take, huh?" Wasatch said, shuffling to the water pump, where he leaned over, pumped the handle and gulped thirstily, the liquid splashing over his face and down his front.

"Damn nice." Bleary-eyed, Tunin took a seat before the table and cradled his wounded arm. He examined where the bullet had sliced the flesh. Wincing, he twisted the swollen elbow and slipped the makeshift sling down. His face pinched with dismay and disgust at the mushed and drying flesh.

Wasatch lowered his britches, took a cloth Vallee had left by the sink, soaked the material and placed it soothingly over his backside. Like a luxuriating bear, he closed his eyes and sucked in air. "If I ever get the chance, I'm gonna cut that Landry's guts out for this."

"Forget Landry," Tunin scoffed, "it's them people we got the gold off, someone might try to come back for it." He looked down the old road, his face apprehensive for the moment. The road reminded him of the ambush. He laughed then through his teeth. "Liddicoat sure took care of that one tinhorn. He ain't gonna be no bother no more." The young outlaw massaged his throbbing arm. "I just wish I'd killed that bastard that tried to run me down with his horse. Would of, if someone hadn't gunned me from behind." Tunin held the arm against his side.

"Best we rest up a couple of days." With difficulty Wasatch ambled to a cupboard and opened it. "There's staples here besides what we got, good lot of grub. Looks like coffee, some flour and molasses, and beans." He pawed through a few crocks and cans. "Some corn and tomatoes. Even some sowbelly they left. And lookie here." He lifted a bottle of whiskey from a top shelf and pulled out the cork with his teeth. He took a long swig and carried the liquor to Tunin, who shared a swallow. "Maybe it ain't gonna be all that painful here."

"Don't plan on bein' here too long." Tunin rose to explore around.

"You still talkin' about cuttin' out with the gold?"

"It keeps weighin' on my mind."

"Knowin' Morton, and even Jenson and Liddicoat, that'd be damn stupid. They'd hunt us down. You know that." Wastach looked at Tunin with knowing resignation. "Country ain't big enough to shake them, least not Morton."

Restlessly Tunin wandered about the room, looking at the pictures on the walls, at the furniture. He opened kitchen drawers and dug around in one that had receipts and invoices. "Morton's on his way to prison or to a hangin'. If Jenson and Liddicoat can't bust him loose, and if they just happen to get it tryin', that gold out in that storage room, that's all ours, and so is the mine here, if we want it."

"But we wait it out for 'em like planned. Right?" Wasatch took another long swallow from the bottle and rumbled a hefty belch.

"Sure, we wait a couple of days and like you said, rest up, clean up these wounds of ours. But after that there ain't nothin' to hold us." Tunin meandered into Vallee's room. He banged around in a bureau drawer for a time and emerged sporting a white pair of lacy white bloomers over his good arm. "Wouldn't have been bad duty with that little she-cat here." He grinned. "Bet her cookin' and entertainin' would have made this arm of mine feel mighty fine real fast." He took the bottle from Wasatch, gulped a swig too fast and spat some of it out.

"Jenson told me you was funnin' with her, 'stead of stickin' to business—that's what got you near killed."

Tunin took another quick gulp and handed the container

back. "Hard to back off from a pretty little she-cat like that."

"Well, you're payin'."

Tunin glowered at the big man. "Ain't your concern."

Through the crack of the hatch door, Noah Crawford measured the distance and reached for the readied .45. The clutching desire to raise the hatch and surprise the cocky blond with two or three bullets in his middle was almost overwhelming. But the big man, Wasatch, was out of sight, near the kitchen sink. Crawford had to wait for them to move nearer each other and in front of him so that there would be no wasted motion. He had to be patient, he told himself, until everything fell in his favor—the right position, the element of surprise, the accurate shots that guaranteed the end.

Wasatch grunted across the room and stretched on his side at an angle on the couch to rest. "When I feel better, I'm gonna heat us some water so we can wash ourselves good. Don't hanker to start festerin'."

"Since when you ever used hot water?" Tunin moved to a north window and looked across at the remains of the town and up at the mines. "Best we take turns guardin'." The young outlaw's features had wizened with pain and with exhaustion. "I have a gut feelin' one or more of them will track us for the gold and they'll end right back up here."

"They ain't gonna leave them two kids unguarded, not after what happened with you."

"For the price of this gold and that mine out there, they'd leave their mother and their grandmother, too. They'd be a fool not to." Tunin tossed the bloomers onto a chair and pulled his revolver from its holster. "I'm gonna look around some. Lot's of places a man could hide up here, and we got a blind spot behind us with all them connecting buildings."

"Just how good you goin' to be, all shot up?"

"Good enough if I have to." Tunin grinned at his big partner. "You know, if Jenson and Liddicoat make it back,

it would be too bad if we mistook them for someone snoopin'
around for our gold, like them miners." He stepped out on
the porch and pressed along the building.

High above, overlooking the superintendent's building, in the sheltered mouth of a tunnel, Vallee, Ted, and
Dale Thomas scrutinized the setting, searching for signs
of Noah Crawford. Seth, holding the dog, Mono, tried
to muzzle the animal when it sniffed the wind, raised its
snout and looked toward the old mining buildings in back
of the superintendent's house. The animal began shivering with excitement. Suddenly the dog erupted in a rapid-
fire barking.

"Damn it, shut him up," Thomas hissed. The boy grasped
the snout and clenched the jaws as the yellow mongrel struggled in resistance. Ted Withers assisted, clutching the animal
until it quieted. Down behind them, where their horses were
tied, one beast whistled restlessly, sensing something. A
horse down by the superintendent's building gave an an-
swering whinny. Thomas whispered, "Get down. Down.
Quick." The four crouched behind some brittle sage that
partially shielded the entrance, and waited.

"What did Mono see?" Vallee asked, her face tense and
eager.

Thomas, studying the area that Mono had reacted to,
smiled slowly and pointed. "I see in them scrub trees back
of that little old outbuilding down there. See, Lasko's horse."
He winked at Vallee. "Your pop made it safe."

"Sure enough," Ted Withers agreed, raising his head
slightly.

Vallee gasped. "Papa, he's gone into the buildings. He's
going to try to make his way into the manway."

"I'm sure that's just exactly what he's doin'." Thomas
sighed with relief.

"Then how can we help him?" the girl asked.

"We can't right now. It's up to your pop now. All we can
do is give him support if he needs it."

"Maybe we can draw their attention to us. That would give Papa a better chance."

"Them horses soundin' off probably gave us away already. Best for now that we lay low. Otherwise, they'll get suspicious of everything. That could put your pop in danger." A thought struck Thomas, and again he winked at Vallee.

She was eyeing him. "What is it?"

"I'll give any odds he's planning to come up that hatchway. Right into the living room. From there, with luck, he could take them all out."

"Maybe I could help," Vallee suggested.

"How?" said Thomas.

"If I let them see I was here. If they thought I was alone, one or more might come out."

"Are you crazy?" Ted snapped.

"We don't know how many are in there or where they're all at," Thomas said to the girl.

"But somehow, if I could draw a couple of them out, that would split them up, and give Papa a better chance."

Ted solemnly assessed the situation. "Chances are they're all in or around that building." From their commanding position they could see some mules and horses hobbled and feeding, but it was impossible to tell how many.

Suddenly Mono turned his attention to the superintendent's building. He bristled, growling. Both Seth and Ted Withers held him tightly. "Damn it, look," said the latter, sprawling lower but still peering.

"Keep down," the deputy ordered. "It's that polecat I shot, he must have heard the horses."

Gun in hand, Tunin stepped off the porch and edged around the north side to scan the main buildings. From a north window, Wasatch stood observing him.

Ted Withers pushed his rifle in front of him. "Should I try to drop him from here? I might nail him before he could gain cover."

"It's too far," Thomas said. "Let's see what they do."

Abruptly, without warning, the yellow dog bolted so powerfully that the force swung Seth aside. With a curse, Ted made a mighty attempt to grasp the rangy animal. Writhing wildly, Mono twisted around and nipped the rancher soundly. Ted recoiled with a sharp cry as the dog burst away, bounding and barking toward the stranger in his yard. "God damn," Thomas responded.

Shouting a warning to Wasatch, Tunin stumbled up the steps and plunged into the house to fire through a window at the dog. Cowed by bullets that mushroomed dirt in front of him, Mono skidded to a stop and darted obliquely into a spur of sage. There, he crawled until he found a depression, then cowered. Wasatch hobbled to a neighboring window, his rifle cocked. Rigorously, the two outlaws looked for some movement. "Might be the dog was just comin' home," the big man said without conviction.

"No, somebody's up there. I heard a horse. And you heard one of ours talk back. The survivors have come after us and the gold."

"There's so much cover up there, buildin's and trees and stuff, that they could be anywhere." Wasatch pointed his rifle, swung it about as he squinted down the sight. "Likely they might be up in one of them mines lookin' down on us, if you're right."

"Can't tell." Tunin's eyes blinked determinedly. He swayed his revolver. "If someone's out there, they ain't goin' to come for us till dark. We're goin' to have to set up for them real good, so as to welcome them right."

"How you figure to do that?"

"At dark, we'll light a lamp. Leave it real bright in here, and then take cover outside. Whoever comes around, we'll welcome with lead."

Noah Crawford watched in anticipation. Both men, some five feet apart, had their backs to him, their attention hard on the mountain. Crawford took another step on the ladder and raised the hatch cover with his head, cushioning it on his hat. With his left hand he quietly removed the pencil and placed it in his vest. He stood straight so that his head and shoulders came above the floor. Silently he stretched forth his arm and pointed the revolver at Tunin's back, a man more agile and dangerous than the lumbering Wasatch. The two shots exploded in the room, filling it with a thick black smoke. The impact stiffened the little blond, slammed him into the windowsill, the back of his shirt and vest renting apart, erupting red as he spun loosely to roll out the window, where he collapsed on the ground and lay quivering. Stupefied, Wasatch whirled around awkwardly, his rifle discharging high over Crawford's head. The latter punched three quick rounds into the man's middle, lifting him and knocking him back against the wall, where he lurched forward in a grotesque dance of reflexive gestures before toppling like a fallen timber. He crashed into the table, upsetting it, and sent a chair spinning like a tiddledywink before he stretched lifeless.

When silence reined, Crawford emerged coughing in the smoke-filled room. He looked at the body of the big man, the blood spreading slowly, staining a throw rug. He reloaded and stepped cautiously out the front door and around the porch to view the still form of Tunin. He replaced his gun and stretched in the sun as Mono came bounding joyfully down the hill to his master. Crawford embraced the wiggling animal, cupped the wide head as the dog licked and slobbered over him. The man looked up to study the town and the mountain. "Guess nobody come but you. Guess you must have come alone, huh, old fellow? Ran away to come home to me. And you know," he said affectionately, "because of you, I was able to stop the bastards."

From the cave opening the young foursome watched in stunned silence upon hearing the blasts and then seeing Tunin roll crazily out the window. Vallee almost swooned with dread, a waxy chill spreading through her body. When Crawford emerged to look about and greet the anxious dog, Thomas placed his arm around the girl's waist as they stood up for a better view. "I think your pop has things pretty much under control."

Vallee stepped forward, wanting to call out to her father, but she restrained herself. Ted moved up beside her, his hand enclosing her elbow. "Let him be for the time," he said. "He done it all by himself." She looked up at the young Withers and around at Dale Thomas. Strange new emotions tugged inwardly at her, emotions that were exciting but troubling. She had never dealt with men her own age, and was finding herself strongly attracted to both young men at the same time, but in different and confusing ways. She liked their attention but not the conflicts within her, for she wanted to be in control, and momentarily she felt torn by new and wonderfully fearful desires.

"Do you want to go down now?" Thomas asked. He suddenly looked gaunt and tired. Both men appeared in dire need of rest and medical attention.

"You two look terrible," she said frankly. "I think we better get both of you to Silverpoint and a doctor."

"My sister-in-law at our ranch is much closer," Ted informed them, again.

Thomas looked apologetically at the girl, his eyes pale and his head slightly bowed. "I have to go down. I have to bring your father back. And you know that."

Vallee looked him firmly in the face. "Papa may well have saved our lives. Ted is right, let him be for the time being. My father is a man of his word. He said he would come back, and he will."

To the south, Landry and the posse members could see another dust devil approaching. "We should make camp and take cover before that hits," Temple warned. "Best find some protection behind a high rock someplace or in a draw."

Steadfastly, Landry nudged his mount ahead. "Just give me a little more time," he said. "I want to get an overlook once more, just to see if I can tell where in the hell I was that first time."

Withers and Dunlap drew up the rear, leading Morton. The animals moved sluggishly, their heads bobbing side to side, their tails swishing. They sensed something unnatural in backtracking the harsh route they had come. Temple moved his mule up next to the marshal. "If them two pals of Morton

are still behind, we could be moving right into their laps,"
the prospector said seriously, glancing around at the ponderous wall of bluffs and ridges to his right.

"I'm well aware of that, Billy." Landry had loosened the
rifle in his scabbard.

Within the next hour, Landry led them to an elevated flat
that afforded an ample view. The dust devil had shifted east
some, carried by the steady westerlies, but it remained
threateningly dark all along the southeastern flank. The men
lined their animals up next to him, all looking now toward
the battlement of rocks that stretched north and south. "I
remember those castlelike peaks out there," Landry insisted. He pointed to the impressive cluster of parapets,
spires, and turrets "But god damn, I don't see that cave.
And I saw it from somewhere around here. I was moving
along those cliffs, closer than we are now."

"Then let's move in. Try it like it was," Temple suggested.

For half an hour they paralleled the ridges, pushing gradually nearer. But the effort proved fruitless. Landry wavered.
Nothing else was particularly recognizable. And no indica-
tion of the shallow cave could be found. Again they swung
away from the rises, somewhat farther north. His face
strained and pale, the marshal dismounted and walked around
aimlessly. Withers followed suit, dropping stiffly from the
roan to pace beyond the cluster of animals as if he were going
to find some significant clue.

"Maybe you're just conveniently forgetting," Dunlap
said meanly. "Maybe you're seeing things that you don't
want to share." He did not see Morton behind him smile
slightly with pleasure. Landry remained impassive, except
for a slight sneer as he turned slowly and looked coolly at
the constable.

Alarmed, Temple stretched his bulky form as high as he
could. "Dirk." The threat of his tone made the others alert.
"That dust storm, it's swinging this way. I'm sure of it. In
fact, I can hear it."

All eyes centered on the tawny-brown swirl. This was not

the typical flatland devil. This was a sand blast of suffocating proportions that had been scooped up and carried many miles by winds created through a sudden and dramatic change in temperature. An additional down gust from the high reaches of the White Mountains was pouring thick clouds of earth and debris toward them. The zephyr winds had ripped free vegetation that came bouncing in sizable balls to threaten safety and frighten the horses. Soon the warming downrush would rise to suck the outer dust storm inward, where they would collide in a furious confrontation that neither man nor beast dared confront.

"Let's go." Landry signaled. "Take cover and wait this one out. Then tomorrow we'll try again."

"Best we get in them gorges down yonder," Temple shouted, pointing at a low riverlike bed that serpentined toward the bluffs.

"Down there. Down there. Got to get protection." Landry waved the men ahead. Then he saw. His heart commenced pounding. Despite his troubling confusion, he suddenly felt a light of hope, a sting of recognition, and he knew with unshakable certainty. Far ahead, north of the cliffs and the battlement, there appeared a natural rift, an opening with a gradual rise that wound onward; beyond the opening he could see another low mountain. Landry knew then that he was seeing the pass that he had found, the fabled route through the last reaches of the desert wilderness, the one he had taken to the Withers ranch in a state of madness. He knew now that he was finding his way back, that he was in the region of discovery, that he was close to the fabulous mine. But before he could share the good news, Temple cried out and punched a finger toward the earth.

"Look." In a shallow, under the curve of an embankment, spread the droppings of a horse. Quickly, impatiently, the men circled their animals around the leavings. Anxious to be moving, the creatures jerked and jangled their bits while yanking from side to side. "And over there," Temple motioned. "You can see it clear now." Embedded in the caked ground was the distinct U of a horseshoe, and farther on, the scuff of iron shoes left distinct striations. Landry nodded, keenly aware of the implications. His eyes scoured the steep wall of stone ahead.

"What the hell you saying?" Withers pressed anxiously, looking at the prospector, then back at the scuff marks and then at Temple. The wind from the mountains flapped their vests and hat rims and plumed the tails of the animals.

"Them compadres of Morton, they shortcutted us, took this low route so we wouldn't see them," Temple hollered.

"Meaning?"

"Meaning they're somewhere ahead of us," Landry answered.

"And probably waiting," Temple added.

"God damn." Withers looked anxiously at the marbling spread of dung. His roan kept swinging its head and shifting. "That's almost fresh, even in the desert. Them horses passed here not long ago."

Temple kicked his mule into a fast trot toward the shelter of low-winding canyons. "I'd say they passed by just a few hours ago, if that long."

Withers scowled fiercely at Morton, who sat emotionless, his eyes looking afar. "Why don't we shoot this son of a bitch now and leave his carcass out here. That'll get them off our backs."

"Exactly what I been tellin' you, Marshal." Dunlap grinned tightly, with obvious enjoyment. "Let's do the bastard in and we can still keep lookin' for the mine. If them owl hoots out there want him, then give them his worthless carcass. Then they won't have no need to hound us no more." With purposeful disdain, he spat a link of saliva. "Maybe Morton's got some identity on him. With that and one of them ugly ears of his, we might even collect the rewards."

A powerful blast of wind suddenly pounded them repeatedly; it howled down the draw and thrashed the sparse foliage. A humming commenced from somewhere; the frightened horses squealed, bunched, and shifted, almost falling back on their haunches. The mules brayed and low-

ered their heads in resistance. "Come on," Landry ordered.
"Head for that break in the cliff up there." He spurred the
sorrel away, and in a clamoring run of slapping leather and
wheezing beasts, the rest headed after him.

# (17)

They swung into a low rimrock and wound through some fluted narrows. When they reached a rocky bench, they rolled from their animals and pulled them toward a cut—a miniature box canyon—that promised some protection.

Already in the lead, Withers charged ahead into the chaos of stone and sought his own hideaway. "I see how you look at me." He jerked Morton from the dapple gray and slammed him to the ground. The outlaw doubled, his hard features contracting torturously. "You hate my guts, and I hate yours." Withers reached down and grasped the man's belt with one hand and the long hair under his hat with the other, "Take cover, you son of a bitch. Me and my family, we used to sweat blood with you on the loose, not knowing when you and your cutthroats might come ridin' in." He pulled Morton to his feet and hurled him ahead, but the force tumbled him so that he sprawled again, facedown. His hands bound behind, the outlaw rolled to his side, spitting sand. Dirt and grit had caked his face like some grotesque mask. Instinctively he pulled up his knees for protection, but Jake was at his side. The big man delivered a vicious kick to the lower ribs. Morton howled in agony as spasms of pain wracked his body. "Get up, I said."

Cursing under his breath, Morton struggled to rise.

"I'm gonna get the price on your head, Morton." Again Withers lifted the man and saw hate glinting in the ebony eyes. "Dead or alive, Morton. Don't matter, I get the reward. That's why I might put you out of your rotten misery now." Withers picked his prisoner up and heaved him ahead.

"Trouble is, dead, your hide would rot before I got you in."
Behind, he saw his partners veer into the box canyon. Too
late for him to join them, he dragged Morton forward toward
what appeared to be another little break. From overhead a
counterwind off the higher mountains began pouring more
dust and sand over the great bulwark of cliffs.

Billy Temple, spurring his mule, saw something ahead on
a ragged shelf above them. "Landry," he bellowed. "Up
there! A man with a rifle." A barrel appeared, leveling toward them. The sound was absorbed in the thrust of wind.
But Dunlap, still astride, toppled, to hit the dirt hard and
tumble crazily.

The storm was upon them then in a dizzying slash of sand
and dirt, embroiling, battering them with a blinding thickness that momentarily blotted out all landscape beyond a
score of feet. Landry, struggling to secure his neckerchief,
saw Dunlap hit the ground nearby. The lawman slapped his
horse into the cut where Temple was tugging the mules.
Withdrawing his Colt, he hop-skipped to Dunlap, who was
crawling forcefully on his hands and knees, cursing and
grunting as he struggled for safety. Landry caught him by
the collar and dragged him toward the canyon. He thought
he heard the racketing of more gunfire but was uncertain. As
they entered, he fired blindly in the direction he had seen the
rifleman.

They huddled then, their eyes half closed, their collars
turned up, the neckerchiefs across their mouths and noses to
wait out the biting wind. "Where you hit?" Landry shouted.

Dunlap lay holding his left side under his coat. Landry
and Temple opened the flap and saw blood squirming between compressed fingers. The bullet had passed through his
body below the ribs. "You're a lucky man," Landry assured
him. Although temporarily out of the fight, Dunlap would
heal in a short time to be as good as ever.

"I'll make it," Dunlap said, his words barely audible. But
his suppressed bravado revealed that he needed help.

"This storm is a blessing in disguise. It'll blind them,

too,'' Temple yelled. ''Wonder what happened to Withers and Morton?''

Their separation from the two concerned Landry. ''I've got to find Withers,'' he told Temple, not certain the old man could hear. ''Morton's dangerous, even if he's hog-tied.'' He pointed to himself and then in the direction where the pair had disappeared. Temple understood and tried to peer through the gloom. But the storm blotted everything. The old man turned away, his eyes smarting. ''Be careful,'' he called.

''Get Dunlap's bleeding stopped and *you* be careful.'' Landry readied his guns and plunged into the tumult.

Gravely searching for more protective covering, Withers hauled Morton to his feet, booting him ahead, tumbling him again. ''Move, you son of a bitch,'' he hissed. Pulling the gray and the roan, he forced Morton into a third cut, a cleft-like canyon strewn with boulders that overlooked a six-foot pit. He wrenched his rifle from its scabbard and pushed the outlaw roughly. Behind them the world blotted out with exploding dust. Withers began coughing, his neckerchief next to useless in protecting him. His eyes watering, he tried to see his partners, but quickly realized that he had lost contact. He was on his own with Morton.

Morton lay choking in the clotting dust that engulfed them. ''I can't breathe,'' he said, gagging.

Withers wiped his eyes. ''Choke to death, you bastard.''

Then the swirling dust passed, clearing momentarily. Overhead came the distinct sound of gunshots. Withers twisted about, his legs bowed as he pointed his rifle toward the sheer bluffs that bulked hugely. Withers aimed at what he thought was movement on a shelf directly above, but again a whiff of dust made everything indistinct and confusing.

Seeing the opportunity, Morton came to his knees and reached backward with his bound hand to extract Jake's knife from the sheath. With it free, he stood upright.

Feeling the knife leave, Withers whirled around, surprisingly agile for his bulk. Too close to fire, he swung the Win-

chester viciously. Anticipating the move, the outlaw slid to
the side in a crouch. The rifle barrel shattered over a boulder
and broke free from its stock. Momentarily shaken, Withers
hesitated. Morton kicked him high in the belly. Air erupted
from the rancher as he doubled over. Morton kicked for the
head and caught the chest, knocking the big man to the side
and almost off his feet. Withers stumbled away, the features
above the neckerchief strained white, his eyes rolling wild
like that of a cornered animal. Morton belted him in the chest
with another wicked kick, staggering him. The rancher pulled
his revolver. As dust and sand twisted about them, Morton
shrieked in rage and kicked higher, with all the force he
could muster. His boot struck Wither's forearm, dislodging
a shot that flashed in the swirling dust. Gasping from ex-
pended energy, Morton struck again and again, spinning the
gun loose to bounce once and go over into the pit.

Landry heard Morton's shriek, saw the gun flash, and
heard the horses whistle and toss in fear. Gun in hand, still
advancing, he threw a shielding arm across his blinded eyes
and stepped ahead.

Desperately Withers tried to punch Morton and missed,
but managed to clutch a leg in the next kick, lifting it high
to throw the man over backward. But the athletic outlaw
landed on a shoulder, twisted in a snappy backflip and came
to his feet, the knife still clutched behind him. Dismayed and
breathing hard, Withers reached out and lunged forward,
attempting to grapple with Morton and to strike him solidly.
But Morton connected with a perfectly timed boot in the
rancher's groin. The big man screamed, clutched himself and
reeled to the side. Morton slammed the rancher in the ribs
with a heel, and knocked him over a rocky parapet to crash
into the pit. Debris poured in after him.

Morton walked to the edge and looked down. "If my hands
was free, I'd smash your head in with one of these big rocks."

With a crablike jog, Morton found his way into the cut
where the frightened horses balked and milled. The outlaw
backed against a block of stone and twisted the knife upward
into the ropes that held his wrists. Hurriedly he ripped at the

bindings. Then he pressed his weight into the blade, but nothing gave. Once he thought the horses might break out, and he shouted at them, driving them to the rear of the cut. Landry would be looking for them, he knew. With a supreme effort his strong fingers worked the knife harder, faster, until he felt the ropes loosen, felt some strands unravel. In a matter of seconds he was free. He caught the gray's reins, steadied it, and leaped into the saddle, the knife still tight in one hand.

Vigilantly, Landry tried to see through the suffocating clouds. Then he heard the thundering clump of a horse and instinctively knew that Morton had broken free somehow. But he dared not shoot, not knowing the whereabouts of Jake Withers. His eyes smarting, his lungs clogging, Landry dropped to his belly and began crawling, swinging from elbow to elbow, his rifle cradled. He hoped to see enough for a chance shot. A horse squealed and plunged away. Vaguely he saw the dark form of an animal pivot, then rear and paw. But before he could shoot, the rider gained control and they were gone.

Abruptly, the impact of the storm lessened. The mushrooming cloud slithered to the north along the battlement. Landry saw the roan sidling, its rump to the wind. But Morton's gray was gone. The marshal crawled to the protection of a bulging rift and looked about for Withers, his eyes searching always for the ambushers. He called out the rancher's name and heard a painful moan, hardly perceptible above the passing storm. "Withers? That you?" Once more he heard a sound, less loud than the hum of wind in the rumpled stone. His eyes steadied on what looked like a sunken opening. Landry scrambled to his feet, clutching his rifle, and sprinted the best he could toward a jut of rock. He tumbled behind it and waited. A moment later he crawled to the edge of the drop, looked down into a pit and spotted Withers, flopping around on his side.

Landry worked around the jut, keeping it between him and the bluff where the rifleman had last been seen. High winds still boiled the dust around the upper regions and sifted down like massed smoke. "What the hell happened?"

Withers sat up carefully in his rocky tomb and blinked, his head resting back. "He jumped me. The son of a bitch jumped me."

"With his hands tied behind his back?"

With difficulty, Withers's glazed eyes tried to focus on Landry. "Somehow he got my knife."

"God damn. And he's gone." Although the top of the rocky columns were still obscured, Landry could now see far into the desert to the east, and there was no sign of movement anywhere. More practically, Morton had chosen the ready cover in the twists and dips and crannies that flowed from the high battlement. That surely was where he had vanished. "Can you move? I see your Colt about ten feet from you. And you can get out of there. That split in the rocks to your right goes into a kind of tube about twenty feet downslope. You might have to crawl some, but you can get out."

"Don't know if I can do anything. I hurt all over." Stiffly, Withers stretched out his arms, flicked his wrists and felt his legs.

A movement caught Landry's attention. He saw Temple approaching, low, his shotgun against his chest. The old man kept glued to cover, his head twisting constantly, looking for danger. Landry waved, and Temple waved back. Then Landry told the battered Withers, "You take care, we've got those ambushers to find."

"I'll be all right," Withers said.

It seemed logical that Morton would try to make contact with his rescuers. If he had, they would all be gone by now, Landry concluded, sitting up. Scanning the mountain bulwark, he straightened up, shook his head and wiped his eyes as if to see better, and looked again. On the far side of the lower rimrock, below the shelf where the first shots had been fired, and along what might have been an old sheep trail, a small man appeared, descending, picking his way warily. Landry recognized the twisted face of Jenson. "Stay put," he said low to Withers. "I see one of them." Crawling quickly through a funnel-shaped wash, he readied his carbine. Suddenly he saw the little outlaw signal to someone above and gesture eastward with a jabbing motion. Apparently Jenson had spied Billy. Then Landry saw the end of a barrel slide forward to project from an overhanging ridge, saw it come down to point.

Landry started to cry a warning when the wounded Bull Dunlap fired from the cut where he was covering both Billy and the marshal. Maybe I've misjudged you, Landry thought to himself. Jenson disappeared and the rifleman above ducked, swung away from Billy and snapped a bullet. The flat shot drummed into the cut and twanged about the little canyon, forcing Dunlap to retreat, his curses filling the air. Billy Temple was on all fours, crawling sluggishly but safely into a volcanic enclosure. A second bullet showered dust at the entrance of the cut and whined away, making the horses shrill. A third bullet mushroomed dirt next to the enclosure where Temple cowered. Then the rifleman withdrew. "Only Liddicoat could shoot like that," Landry told himself.

Landry scoured the area trying to see some telltale movement, but the cliffs were blackening, dull silhouettes against a flush of red sky. The marshal left the cover in an attempt to intercept the rifleman. He began climbing, when he saw Liddicoat slipping from spot to spot, saw him disappear and reappear, until he came out along a little ledge. The outlaw stopped to hug a sandstone column with which he blended in the twilight. Like Jenson, he was working his way down, apparently unaware that Morton had escaped. Landry could make out his slight form, huddled against the rise, his rifle held ready across his chest while he looked for bearings. Suddenly he looked Landry's way. What had the outlaw detected? At that moment, from the corner of his eye, the marshal saw Withers stagger into the open, distinct in the waning light, the recovered .45 hanging in a hand to his side. Landry saw Liddicoat step away from the column and slowly raise his rifle at Withers.

Immediately Landry rose to a squatting position, supporting himself against a rock. With the rifle braced snugly in his left palm, he hurriedly angled the gun for trajectory and eased the trigger. The impact stunned Liddicoat. He froze,

then lurched to the side, discharging his rifle. The bullet
careened far from Landry, who came to his feet, aiming and
levering his rifle fast and steadily, two, three, four, times.
Liddicoat tried to swing his rifle, but the slam of bullets
staggered him against the column. He came back, tried rigidly to direct his rifle, stiffened and clutched his belly. His
hat sailed off. The rifle twirled in slow motion, dropping free
from his curling fingers. His sullen features contorted with a
venomous disbelief. Landry punched in another bullet and
watched the sharpshooter pitch forward in a loose fall, hitting
hard to spin over and over in a clattering descent down a
shale slope, ending near the bottom. Sliding rocks humped
over his body and head before settling.

Withers had vanished, apparently back into the narrows.
Cautiously Landry moved toward where he had last seen
Jenson and Billy. A bullet hit near him and wailed off. The
lawman bolted across an opening, dropped to a knee and
rolled several times into a rocky hollow as another slug serrated the ground. Ahead, in the jungle of stone, he glimpsed
the shadowy form of Jenson, his black-eyed barrel searching.
Landry cracked three rapid shots, and Jenson again dropped
from sight.

Landry's eyes roamed the area ceaselessly. Nothing
moved. The evening wind had calmed and the dust had settled. Darkness would be upon them shortly. He waited, wondering what had happened to Morton. Obviously the man
had not joined his rescuers. Otherwise all of them would have
left, unless they were chancing their lives to retrieve what
remained of the Wells Fargo money. It seemed unlikely.
Morton and his men had other hauls, other vaults to blow
and more banks to hit. Of course, with his hands bound in a
dust storm, it would not have been easy for Morton to locate
his partners, Landry decided. He surmised that Morton had
not even tried, but had ridden for his life. By now the storm
would have covered his tracks, and unless Withers, when he
recovered, could shed more light on what had happened,
they had lost their prize. Sensing a movement behind him,

Landry whirled around. Withers had emerged again, looking dazed and still disoriented.

"Get down, damn it," Landry ranted.

The rancher nodded dully and sat down.

As Landry stole forward, a loud resounding blast shattered the air. The startling sound forced him to lie flat. Only Billy Temple had a shotgun that he knew of. Landry thought he heard the sliding rush of broken earth, but he was uncertain. He listened for a moment. The shadows faded in the mist of dark. A night breeze commenced, whistling about the broken columns. As he chanced another advance, he saw Temple emerge from under the bluff. Landry rose slowly. The old man faced him, grinning broadly to raise his shotgun overhead and to wave it triumphantly.

# (18)

Before dawn a day and a half later at the edge of the desert, Rattlesnake Morton hobbled the gray in thick willows along a watery meadow where the animal grazed hungrily. With Jake Withers's knife in hand, he approached the first sign of civilization since leaving Desert Roost. Like a slinking cat, he moved along a prong of low growth. He then sprinted across a corral and hurdled a gate, to halt at the back of a small barn. He didn't notice a little sorrel standing at the far end of the enclosure. It snorted and ran away. From somewhere in a field, a Hereford lowed with mild alarm. Inside the barn a half-dozen horses stirred anxiously as he entered. When they continued protesting, the outlaw progressed along the stalls. With experienced hands he moved amongst the horses, patting their flanks, massaging them, and talking low with soft utterings until they calmed. When they commenced munching hay again, he slipped to a window that fronted the sprawling ranch house. The little sorrel, curious, approached the window, looked at him and snorted again. Then a dog inside the house began barking. That worried him.

Morton had arrived outside the ranch the evening before, but had decided to rest his horse until dawn, when, with a little ingenuity and luck, he might gather food, guns, and ammunition before fleeing west. Briefly during his escape he had considered trying to locate his partners, who he assumed were Liddicoat and Jenson, but a frightened horse in a dust storm had changed matters. Besides, he was realistic. The two gang members were loyal to him, it was true. But they were more loyal to the hidden caches that only he had access to, that only he could parcel out when and if he wanted.

With an instinct for survival, and much good judgment, he had threaded the dapple gray through a maze of stone, unknowingly choosing the route that Landry had found earlier. And now if he was careful and prudent, freedom was his. With enough supplies, he could head west into the High Sierras.

The dog set to yapping again, and the door opened from a lighted room. A husky man with a broad chest walked onto the porch. The kerosene lantern he carried flooded over him to accentuate his blond hair. A heavy bandage encircled his left shoulder and wound around his neck. He looked into the dark. Morton's eyes narrowed, his body tense. Apparently satisfied that nothing was wrong, the young man returned to the house, reprimanding the dog that had remained inside. But after the man slammed the door, the animal continued an urgent, disturbed yapping, sometimes drifting into a frightened growl. Morton pulled the knife from a boot and ran a finger across the blade in vague anticipation.

The man appeared again. "Anybody out there?"

Morton eyed the space around him, eyed it for a heavier weapon, for anything to better combat the man whom he sensed would search the premises. Then, in the pale light, he saw a hatchet lodged in a stump outside the back entrance where someone had split kindling, the sticks piled neatly along a wall.

As he slid the hatchet inside his belt, he heard the dog bolt, barking with fury, heard the thump of padding feet. Momentarily confused, the animal stopped midway in the yard, circled some, whining and sniffing erratically before arrowing toward the barn.

While the dog circled, Morton climbed a ladder, knife in hand, and swung himself feet first into the hayloft. He peered between the winged doors of the hayloft and saw the young Withers leave the house with the lantern and a revolver in hand.

A tall stately woman in a long, high-necked dress appeared, her hair pulled tightly. "What is it?" she asked with concern.

"Probably them damn coyotes again," the young man answered. "Get back here, you stupid mongrel."

The dog, picking up an alien scent, and encouraged by his master's presence, began growling deeply. It prowled into the barn, its eyes catching some faint light. It sniffed and fumed about with growing excitement. The horses stirred and began pawing, their heads tossing. Catching Morton's scent, the dog barked uncontrollably, announcing its discovery to the world as it traced the direction the outlaw had taken to the hatchet and back. But when it reached the ladder, it faltered. For a time it whined, looking up at last.

Crouching, Morton had watched the animal, judging the distance in the dim light. As the dog looked up, he pounced with the ease of a great cat. Cushioning his landing in the hay, he held the sharp knife poised at his side. The dog yelped once with surprise and bobbed to the side; but in a poetry of motion, the outlaw caught the animal by the scruff of its neck with one hand and plunged the slicing blade into the throat with the other. The one terrified yelp gurgled away in a spirting gush of blood that painted the plank floor. The writhing creature stiffened as involuntary shudders wrenched through its body.

Morton wiped the blood from his knife in the fur and returned it to his boot. He then removed the hatchet from his belt. With the limp dog still in his clutch, he backpedaled into the darker shadows, for dawn was silvering the outside.

Midway across the yard, Ted cocked his head, not sure what he had heard but feeling something was amiss.

Melba stood at the kitchen door. "What's the matter?"

"Heard something. Dog must have got some animal cornered."

"Don't worry. He'll come back."

"Yeah." Ted decided to return, but then he heard the horses, restless and complaining.

His alarmed stance alerted Melba. "What is it?"

"I don't know."

"Let me get the deputy."

"Don't need the deputy. I can take care of whatever it is."

"Don't be foolish." Her voice had a tender but motherly firmness. "Let the two of you look together."

While Ted waited like an impatient little boy, Morton hauled the dog's carcass away, flung it into a pile of hay and covered it, then tossed hay over the splots of blood. When he was through, he exited the way he had come.

Dale Thomas came out of the house carrying a rifle and a revolver turned backward on his left hip, his right arm still in a sling. He moved quite well. Both men looked rested and healthier. The young Withers led the way into the barn, holding the lantern aloft to see better. "A skunk, or maybe a snake," he told the deputy. They walked to the stables, where the rancher soft-talked the animals. "Ain't nothin', I guess, except our imagination."

"God, I just wish I knew about Landry and all." There was exasperation in the deputy's voice. "All them out there with Morton. I keep suspecting the worst."

"They'll be comin' in. Probably found the Breyfogle by now."

"They should have taken Morton in first, then gone lookin' for gold. Bein' with him out there, that's like carrying a rattlesnake in your saddlebag. Why do you think people gave him that name?"

Ted was unconvinced. "They was all so anxious to get after that gold, even Landry, especially while his memory was fresh. Believe me, they know what they're doing."

As the two men continued looking, Morton skirted some outer buildings. From his position, he could see the glow of Ted's lantern blinking and flashing throughout the interior of the barn. Judging himself safe, he darted behind the house and cautiously peeked in a window. Inside, Seth and Vallee sat at a table, eating without enthusiasm, their eyes straying toward the woman. He saw the crippled boy look to the girl with uneasiness, saw him mouth a question, and saw her look again to the woman, who raised her hand in a gesture of assurance.

Seeing Vallee aroused dormant stirrings in Morton that he'd long kept under control. He recalled clutching her body, soft, full, his arm tight around the small waist, pushing up under her breasts, her struggling against him, the sweet scent of feminine hair and flesh, accentuated by her fear. He understood Tunin's captivation. His men, while drifting in their scavenging, had indulged with the ladies of a town, but not Morton. Seldom did he allow himself. Women were trouble. But the memory of the frightened girl resisting at first, until submitting helplessly in his arms—the taste lingered.

His eyes still fixed on the girl, Morton checked the hatchet in his belt, and pointed the knife ahead of him in readiness. With the flowing smoothness of a stalking panther, he crept around to the front of the house, stepped silently onto the porch and glided to Melba, who was looking back, discussing something with the girl. Morton struck her, his hand open. With a stifled outcry she fell inside, to look up aghast, her shocked features whitening with terror. Vallee screamed and ran toward a rifle and a revolver above the hearth. Seth came awkwardly to his feet. Morton stalked past the prostrate woman and, like the predator that instinctively seeks the weakest prey, he sought the boy, caught him around the chest and pressed the knife to his throat. "Do as I say or the boy is dead."

Vallee withdrew her hands. She twirled about, her eyes brimming with fury and contempt. Melba rose slowly from the floor and squared her shoulders with dignity. But she was holding the side of her face where it smarted. "Turn out the light. Now," Morton ordered. With composure, the woman reached for the overhead lantern, pulled it toward her and turned down the oil wick.

Hearing Vallee scream, both young men rushed from the barn as fast as their abused bodies would permit. Before the light went out, they saw the figure of Morton with the boy. "Scatter, take cover," Thomas barked. Ted set down his lantern, and both hurriedly took positions behind two outer buildings some fifty feet apart.

Morton saw the two young men find cover. The pearl-white of dawn had exposed the features of the land and the small ranch. It gave sufficient light now in the kitchen. He looked earnestly at Vallee. "Girl, slide them guns from above the mantel to me. And slowly."

Trembling, Vallee lifted the rifle and the revolver down. "Oh God, please tell us, where's the marshal and Billy? What did you do to them?" She brought the guns and slid them along the floor to the outlaw, who forced Seth down with him as he reached for the revolver, checked that it was loaded and slid it into his holster. The rifle he drew next to him with a probing toe. With anguished pity, her heart rending, Vallee looked at her hapless brother and saw his eyes water and his lips drain blue. "Where's the marshal and Billy?" she pursued, trying without success to control the desolation she felt for the boy.

Morton was looking out at the yard. "Landry will probably be on my tail shortly, girl. So both you ladies play it smart and do as I say."

"But what do you want?" Melba said fearfully, almost as if afraid to ask. "What do you want of us? We have no money."

"I want out of here, free and safe, and you all are my ticket." Morton turned his attention to the men. "You out there. You two, throw out your guns," he ordered, "or I'll slit the boy's throat and toss out his little carcass. And then it will be the women—the girl last. And maybe I'll take longer with her."

"You son of a bitch," one of the young men raged.

After a moment's silence Thomas called. "Let them go, Morton. Exchange them for me."

"I ain't no fool, deputy boy. I ain't playin' no games. We

do it my way 'cause there ain't no other choice. Throw out them guns, God damn it. *Now.*'' Morton pressed the knife to form a white indentation in Seth's throat, almost splitting the skin. The boy wailed.

"Please," Vallee begged.

"You beast." Melba stood with her back against a near wall; her bosom rose and fell with flooding emotions.

Outside, both men listened; their eyes hunted one another. Thomas sucked in his lips and tried another ploy. "What happened to Landry?" he called.

"I buried him."

"You're lying."

"You're right. I didn't bury him, I left him and the others to rot for the buzzards. Now, I want to see that rifle come out first."

"Why are you here and what do you want?" Thomas continued.

"Just do as I say." Morton eyed Melba. "You, lady—I want ammunition and grub in a sack. And hurry. And if you got a spare gun someplace, don't try nothin' if you want this boy alive."

Moving woodenly in the faint light, Melba took several handfuls of bullets from a box in the cupboard and dropped them in a flour sack.

Insistent, Thomas shouted, "If we knew what you wanted, maybe we can bargain. But we have no money."

"Ain't lookin' for money."

"Just let the boy and the women go, we'll not bother you." Thomas tried to get a bead with his .45 by bracing it against the building. A good shot to the head would end it all. But with his left hand he felt totally unsure of himself. Besides, Morton had anticipated such an attempt. He was holding Seth to the side with the door ajar, making an accurate shot almost impossible. Thwarted, Thomas motioned to Ted Withers: circle to the right and come in from the side.

But Morton, ever alert, saw Ted start to leave. A gleam of amusement, of cold assessment, filled his dark eyes. He jabbed the knife. Seth cried out. Vallee screamed and Ted froze. The boy kept gasping for breath, the sound diminishing into garbled sobs. Morton's voice was icy. "Fools. Try something again and the boy's dead. Don't be bullheaded like your old man, Thomas. Give any more orders again to your partner out there, and you'll regret it. That's my last warning."

"Please, Mr. Deputy." Seth's voice quavered.

"Hear that? The boy's pleading to you," Morton called.

"Why should we trust you? How do we know you won't hurt or kill everybody?"

"I ain't gonna kill nobody if you cooperate. But if I have to, I ain't got no qualms. And you got no other choice. Now, the guns."

Both young men searched each other's faces and after an extended silence, begrudgingly threw the rifle and their sidearms into the open.

"Now, any knives?"

"Don't have any," Ted Withers said.

Thomas flipped his Bowie toward the guns; it stuck in the powdered earth.

"Now, come out, slow like, hands high." Gingerly, both young men stepped into the gray morning. "Come this way." Their hands above their shoulders, they trudged forward.

"Now move close to each other." They obliged. Melba brought the sacks of ammunition and food to the outlaw and lay them near his feet. With cool confidence he took up the sacks and held them, the rifle, and Seth while keeping aware of the women and the men. To Vallee he said, "Come here." Her large eyes regarded him with loathing. "Come here, I need you to do something for me." He held onto Seth, but replaced the knife and withdrew the revolver as the girl edged reluctantly to him. "You see that big haystack yonder?"

"Yes."

"Behind that in them willows is my horse. Bring him to me. Now go. I'll give you about five minutes. No longer."

"Let my brother go," Vallee blustered.

Morton appraised the girl with approval. She was a fighter, and he respected that. "Sorry, this young man is my guarantee out of here." Seth, trembling, his face drained, stretched as high as possible to breathe against Morton's clamplike grip. Blood trickled down his neck into his collar from the fresh cut.

With a sense of hope, Vallee walked into the yard. She tried not to look at the young men, but inevitably their eyes met. Both appeared frustrated and apologetic. Ted looked more baffled and apprehensive than did Dale Thomas, who held no illusions, only resentment and a seething anger. Morton watched her go and then turned toward Melba, who stood tall with attempted dignity. But a quiver in her lower lip betrayed her. "You, lady," he said, his voice less menacing. "You get out there with them two." Relieved, Melba brushed by and joined the men.

The five minutes seemed interminable. Withers and Thomas stood at bay, with Melba between them, her fingers entwined in front of her. Imposing, his face unemotional, Morton held the boy loosely now, the .45 on the prisoners, his black eyes moving only to assess Vallee's progress.

Vallee circled the corral and approached the animal with confidence, releasing its hobble. But before she climbed into the saddle, something arrested her attention. At the edge of the desert, far to the southeast, under the last of a windworn mesa, she saw movement—dotlike forms. Riders? Vallee shielded her eyes from the new brightness that was casting long, changing shadows. Was it her imagination? The distance was too great, even for her young eyes.

Despite the play of shadows, Vallee knew that the desert was deceptive. One sometimes imagined things that weren't there, or hoped were there. Her head pounded with weariness. The nerves in her stomach contracted. She considered racing the horse toward what was out there. But that would ensure Morton's wrath and most likely cost lives. She hesitated. There was movement for certain. It could be a small herd of roving mustangs, she reminded herself. They were common in the area. The dots were coming on slowly.

Vallee climbed on the horse, hiking her skirt up around her thighs. She forced herself to swing the animal toward the ranch house where the figures stood, waxen and pitiful in surrender. Morton ogled the girl's white legs as she dropped from the mount.

Then, without comment, Morton marched Seth before him and took the reins, plunged the carbine in the scabbard, the ammunition and food into a saddlebag, and swung aloft, pulling the boy up in front of him while still keeping the .45 on his prisoners. The animal began prancing. "We cooperated with you. You don't need to take the boy," Thomas protested, his eyes sliding toward the tossed guns.

But Morton caught the glance. "The boy is my safeguard, I'll let him go somewhere out there a ways. Now you, lady," he said to Melba. "You bring the rifle and pistols to me, real careful like. You lift 'em by the barrels and hand 'em backward to me."

As the woman retrieved the discarded armament, Vallee addressed the outlaw. She pointed to an alert animal flicking its ears toward them, its head over the top rail. "Please, Mr. Morton, let me saddle that little sorrel in the corral for my brother. Please. I won't be out of your sight. There's that saddle on the fence. That way he can ride back no matter where you leave him, and if he gets lost, the horse will find its way. Besides, you can travel faster with two horses." She looked him square in the eyes.

Morton studied the girl with interest, relaxing momentarily. His thick mouth curved in pleased agreement. "Hurry. I ain't got much time."

Both Thomas and Ted Withers stared at the girl with perplexed expressions as she headed to the corral. With the utmost care Melba handed the two revolvers and the rifle, one by one, to Morton, who dropped the handguns in a saddlebag and tied the rifle to a saddle string along with the hatchet from his belt.

The gray shifted and backed, anxious to be moving. Morton held the wet-eyed boy and watched Vallee halter the sorrel, place a blanket on its back, and remove a small saddle from the fence. "Hurry, girl." As she began to cinch the saddle, Morton's age-old instincts filled him with a sudden restlessness. He squirmed in the saddle and then sat straight, his eyes shifting here, there, his nostrils extending as if sniffing for some threatening scent. His eyes gravitated toward the desert mesa. He squinted. His dish face hardened in total concentration. After a moment his eyes rounded and his jaw dropped. His head snapped toward the girl. "You little bitch, you're trying to stall me—trick me."

The deputy, in desperation, started toward Morton, who leveled his .45. "Killing your old man, Thomas, is enough for me—for now. So I'll just put you out of business." He fired twice. The bullets crushed Thomas's left knee and Withers's right. Ted howled with agony and collapsed. Thomas pitched forward onto his face. Melba screamed a long, shattering shriek of horror as she clasped both hands to her mouth and sank to her knees.

Thomas started crawling toward the knife, still angled in the dirt. Torturously, he dragged himself, foot by foot, cursing Morton, who had whirled the horse away, riding quickly westward toward the old wagon road that curved under the White Mountains and ultimately south to Desert Roost. Beyond the buildings, Morton untied the extra rifle that was flailing dangerously and heaved it. Vallee saw. As he spurred the gray on, Morton knotted several saddle strings around Seth's belt, his hands rough and fumbling in securing them.

Vallee ran to Ted, who was rocking on his back, grimacing, his eyes closed. He held his shattered leg—the knee bones, flesh, and tendons all red and mushed. Then she turned to Thomas, who had left a trail of blood. In despair, he lay with his forehead on the earth, his knife ahead of him, too far out of reach, and useless even if he could get to it. Melba, still in shock, managed to reach Ted. "Oh, God," the woman exclaimed. "I'll get water—cloths." Vallee made a dazed pivot toward Ted and back to Thomas. She suddenly rushed back to the waiting sorrel. "Where are you going?" a distraught Melba called as the seventeen-year-old sprang into the saddle, to race past on the little horse, its mane and tail flowing. Beyond the buildings, out of everyone's sight, the girl retrieved the discarded rifle and rode on after Morton.

# (19)

Burdened now, with the pack animal and the extra horses, the posse dropped slowly from the mesa toward the green meadows and the watery flats that mirrored the sky. They all rode in silence, a heaviness of fatigue and failure hanging over them. Jake Withers drifted last, in a kind of self-imposed exile, although he perked up at sight of the distant ranch, inviting in the cool shade, a few of the cottonwoods and poplars already tinting an early gold. Bull Dunlap's horse had pulled up with the animals led by Temple. The constable had given free rein to his mount. His figure curved forward in an arc of exhaustion and misery. Some three lengths ahead, Landry pointed the way.

Rolling across the distance came the distinct explosion of two shots. All four men jolted alert from the sleepy rhythm of their plodding animals. They looked at each other, anxious and alarmed. Withers cocked his head to hear better. Landry stood tall in the stirrups, confident on his buckskin again. None could see anything but a tranquil space with fat, sluggish cattle. Landry removed his field glasses and picked out a wake of dust spearheaded by a big horse and rider. Then, from behind the house, appeared another rider—a slender form dressed in what looked like a skirt. The rider dismounted and picked up something, then rode on.

"Has to be Melba. Come on," Landry urged. "Trouble, I think. Let's get down there." The tired men stirred their beasts into action, all somehow tapping hidden reserves. Landry and Withers, on their stronger mounts, soon outdistanced the other two. But Temple, with the packs and the horses, and the hurting Dunlap, set to cantering in a steady hold.

Melba Withers kept looking up anxiously, waiting for them as she leaned over Dale Thomas, bandaging his knee, a basin of water and strips of shredded clothing at her side. He was assisting her by holding a pad in place while she wrapped it tight. Ted Withers sat dejected, blood staining a cloth around his knee.

In a swirl of dust a perplexed Landry drummed the buckskin up to them, with Jake right behind. "What the hell happened? I thought I just saw you riding off."

"That was Vallee. She went after him and Seth."

"Vallee? Vallee went after who?"

"Rattlesnake Morton—he was here," the woman blurted. "Morton? Jesus!"

"He was here, and God—he shot the boys, deliberately shot them in the knees."

"Will they walk again?"

"They'll be on crutches for a time. I'll hitch a team and take them to Silverpoint and the doc," she said anxiously. "I'm going there as it is."

"Then take care," Landry whirled his horse, spinning more dust. "They're in your hands."

"The bastard admitted—bragged—that he'd killed my father," Dale exploded with indignation.

Melba interrupted, almost babbling, "He took food and guns and Seth as a hostage." Jake Withers sat his horse while listening intently. Temple and Dunlap were reining in.

"Seth," Landry hissed the name through gritted teeth. Hardly containing himself, he looked along the old road that Morton and the girl had taken. "Damn." The buckskin steadied but kept pawing restlessly. "And Vallee went after them! Least now I know where Morton is."

"How'd he get away?" Thomas asked.

"Constable Dunlap can fill you in. He'll go back with you, to escort the lady and get patched up." Anxious to be moving, his face mottled with pressure, Landry did not offer any other explanation, but tossed the Wells Fargo bag to Dunlap.

"See that this gets back. You can explain what happened to the missing amount."

Dunlap managed to catch it, his reflexes slow. "Much obliged, Landry, glad you understand that I wouldn't be of much use to you."

"I can't stay any longer. Who's with me for the sake of a boy and a brave little fool of a girl?"

"What do you think?" said Temple. "Just give me time to get the pack mule and horses in the corral."

"Better get a fresh horse, Billy, that mule of yours has about had it. Question is, my friend, can you make it?"

"Hell, yes, I can." He turned the animals toward the corral.

"There's some fresh ones in the barn," Melba called.

"Don't understand why you are still here." Landry addressed Thomas while staring at Ted in the shoulder bandage.

"Long story," Thomas said, looking embarrassed.

"Well, I don't have time to hear. Where's Crawford?"

"After we left you, part of the gang members ambushed us and killed Lasko." Thomas could not look the marshal in the eyes.

"Killed Lasko?" Dunlap echoed.

"Crawford followed them back to Desert Roost for his gold and killed two of the gang. We seen it from a distance after we buried Lasko."

"And Vallee claimed her father would be a man of his word, that he'd give himself up." Landry cleared his throat. He turned around. "You, Jake? You with me?" The big rancher hesitated. "Seems you should have a real interest now—in stopping Morton." Landry swung his horse.

Thomas hollered after him, "Bring back that spunky little girl and her brother. Wish to hell I could be with you, but I guess I ain't much good anymore."

"Get well, Deputy," Landry shouted back. "You'll be with me in some way or another." Landry wheeled the buckskin away down the road.

An observant Melba had been watching her husband as Landry challenged him. She saw Jake's eyes avert, his squar-

ish face harden with resistance and defensiveness, a look she
had encountered often and recognized immediately. Giving
him a superior, knowing smile, she rose to her feet. "Go
with him, Jake," she said. "I've kept your place in order—
fed and watered all your livestock. Go with the marshal,
because I'm not coming back. I'm going for good. My things
are packed in the bedroom."

"What the hell are you saying?"

"I was waiting until you returned. I wanted to face you.
And I couldn't leave the animals unattended. But now that
you're here, I'll get my things."

Jake climbed stiffly down. "You just leaving me?"

"Yes."

"You can't. You're my wife."

"And I'm leaving too, Jake," Ted announced. "I'm goin'
with Melba. And I'm gonna get a job up north. I ain't lifting
a hand, not one more finger on this place."

"You too?"

"Like me, he's had it with you," Melba added. "He's a
man and he's your brother. But you treat him like a common
ranch hand." She bristled and added, "No, more like a
slave."

"What the hell? He owes me everything. I gave him a
job," Jake stormed. "He owes me everything, and so do
you. You're my wife. You owe me for all you have here. It
ain't been that bad." The muscles in his face constricted.
The veins knotted, dark and purplish.

"And what all do I have here?"

"You can't do this to me."

"I've never been more than a possession, Jake, no different from your horses and your cattle. As I said, now that
you're back, why delay?" Melba stalked toward the house
with Jake behind her.

Saddled on a fresh horse, Billy Temple rode by, indifferent
to the domestic tiff.

Inside the building the couple exchanged stronger lan-
guage. Melba returned, slamming out the door, lugging two
oversized pieces of baggage. Jake lumbered out behind her.

She hoisted the bags up onto a wagon near the barn, and headed toward the house again. "I'm taking these men to Silverpoint now. I'll get their gear." She entered the front door with Jake still raving and ranting behind her. She came out quickly with some belongings and saddlebags, which she tossed onto the wagon. Then she marched with long determined steps into the barn. Her husband did not follow this time. He stood subdued for the moment.

Those remaining watched Melba bring out two horses. With experienced movements she harnessed and hitched them to the wagon. Then she led out two horses and tied them to the tailgate. "You gonna help me get them men on the wagon?" she asked Jake.

"Hell, no."

"Fine." She assisted Ted into the wagon bed, where he squirmed to the front. Dunlap dismounted and, with difficulty, helped her get Thomas aboard. Then he too tied the reins of his horse to the wagon along with the others. Slowly he climbed in beside the two men, to let his horse pace behind as Melba took her place on the seat like a statuesque queen. She clicked her tongue, slapped the reins and started the team toward Silverpoint.

Jake began stumbling along beside his wife. "You'll pay for this."

"I'm sorry, Jake, to do this in front of everybody, but it's been coming a long time and you know it."

"You'll never make it without me."

"You'll be surprised," Melba said.

"What're you talking about? A woman's job is to serve her husband. What are you gonna do? Starve? Scrub floors again? You ain't that young no more. And you're too old to walk the streets."

"Lay off her, Jake." Ted glowered at his brother.

"Oh, mister lady's man." Jake pointed an accusing finger at Ted. "You owe me everything, too. You'd be a saddle tramp or in jail if I hadn't taken you in when you come cryin' for work."

Melba whipped the horses into a gallop, thundering away,

the spinning wheels kicking a shower of dust over Jake. Coughing, he yelled, "Both of you. You're both Judases. Go to hell then." Shaking a big fist, he stared after them. "You, Melba, you too little brother, you'll both come crawling back. You'll come back begging me. And I'll never take you in. Not now. Not ever."

Tired, his body throbbing for rest, Landry plunged the buckskin along the road. But when he saw Billy Temple behind on a fresh horse, a hefty brown, he slowed until the two were beside one another. Landry noticed how incredibly old the prospector appeared, his face puffy, the eyes sunken, the cross grains of his forehead deeply creased. The lawman knew that eventually he would have to go it alone.

"Withers is mad enough to chew nails," the old man announced. "His woman packed up and left him—she's takin' the boys to Silverpoint; told him she wouldn't be comin' back." Temple looked at Landry for a reaction, his eyes red with exhaustion. "Even his brother said he wasn't comin' back."

"I'm not surprised," Landry said, his mind reflecting on the night the woman had asked his help.

A half-mile from the ranch they saw Jake on the roan, following them. The road, more a trail now with two ruts and sage growing between, had been an old stage and shipping route when the area boomed. On this road Jake Withers had first spied the land that he wanted to homestead. Some miles west it connected to the road between Silverpoint and Desert Roost, the one between the White Mountain and the central desert plateau. Landry wondered what Morton's intent was. When he reached that thoroughfare with its intermittent springs, would he choose to use it, or would he continue on westward, maybe pushing around the north end of the White Mountains, into the Owens Valley and on up into the Sierras? With his gang members dead, he might try a new beginning in California. But Morton's world was western Nevada, where he knew practically every pass, every hideaway, every trail. Landry guessed that the infamous outlaw would find refuge somewhere in the Golden State, but with time he would return to the land he knew best.

The tiring days of heat and dust had tapped Landry's strength and energy. The failure to locate the Breyfogle had shaken his self-confidence, despite his assertions that it would not be easy. Mostly, the escape of Morton had devastated him. All the years it had taken to capture the man again. And then Jake's blunder. Landry blamed himself, however. He, like the others, had been blinded by greed. Instead of splitting forces, they should have stayed with Crawford, Thomas, and the kids. They should have taken Morton to justice and then, after a rest, returned to the desert and retraced his steps. The fear that time might blur his memory had motivated the immediate search. But, disappointingly, their haste had not helped stimulate his memory. And moreover, Landry censured himself for allowing Jake to break away ahead of them with their prisoner. It was little excuse that it had happened so fast in a nasty, blinding storm.

En route to the Withers ranch, his only thoughts had been on a soapy bath, a clean shave, a few shots of Jake's whiskey, and a hot meal. He had not been surprised to find her there still, dedicated and faithful to the ranch, remaining to confront her husband in person. She would deliver the wounded men and find proper care for them, he knew.

But now, with the realization that Morton was but a few miles ahead, that he carried Seth as a hostage, and that Vallee was after him, against impossible odds, Landry was revitalized, filling with a rebirth of determination, so that he dismissed any remorse. From ahead he heard shots echo. He pushed the buckskin faster.

To the southwest, from below the rim of a dry wash, rose a sheet of drifting dust. Landry pointed and Temple swung his horse closer. They reined up where the road curved over a rise. Landry took his field glasses. "Ain't no dust devil," Temple said, "them puffs is made by animals, running." Landry peered into the trailing streamer and waited, adjusting the lens. Suddenly he sat straighter in the saddle and peered with intensity.

"What is it?"

"Just a minute, they're coming up an embankment." Landry dismounted because the buckskin was shifting and whickering. The lawman squatted slightly, leaning back to brace his elbows on his hips while holding the glasses. He watched. "My God—it's somebody leading a pack train." He observed the animals clambering out and humping over the rim. "And they look like mules."

"Could it possibly be Crawford?"

"I can't tell. Want to look?" He offered the glasses.

"Ain't got eyes that see that good no more," said Temple.

Landry studied the situation again. Clearly, someone was leading the train toward the western flank of the windworn mesa from which the posse had just descended. Landry's next words rang with the slow clarity of a bell. "Billy, I swear there's two people on that lead animal."

"Jesus Christ. Morton? You see Vallee anywhere?"

"No. But we're going to find out." Landry hiked into the saddle. His dirt-streaked features hardened with purpose. "One thing. No way can a pack train outrun us. Come on." As they set off, Jake Withers reached them and continued a few lengths behind.

As the pack train moved at an angle, the three men cut directly, quickly shortening the distance, despite the soft alkali surface that crushed in, sinking the animals to their fetlocks. They skirted the rim of the wash. Then, below in a shallow curve, they spied four horses standing with heads lowered. Landry motioned that way. In the shade of a big bitter brush, a person of slight build was kneeling, hunching over a prostrate form. Landry directed them down the side, the horses jangling their bits, the leather slapping as they dropped stiff-legged, scraping their hocks.

They came upon Vallee, her tousled brown hair flowing outward in a warm breeze; a man lay stretched on the ground, his upper torso resting in her lap. The girl, her face contorted with grief, raised tearful eyes, showing alarm at first, until recognizing them. She began sobbing uncontrollably with relief. Both Landry and Billy spun from their saddles and rushed to her. They saw a slow blood-flow saturating the dry ground beside her and the man. Then they recognized Noah Crawford, eyes closed, his body sunken in repose as the girl swayed back and forth, holding him.

Landry squatted next to her and touched a shoulder as he picked up her fallen rifle. "What happened, Vallee? What happened, honey?"

Her mouth worked, bubbly with saliva as she attempted to answer. At last she said, "Papa was coming back with the gold, Marshal."

"And Rattlesnake Morton. He did this."

"When Morton saw him, he just went straight at Papa. Just rode right at him like a madman. Papa tried to stop him, but probably was afraid of hitting Seth. Instead, he shot Papa first. Just shot him away." She turned her face aside and broke into tearful convulsions.

Landry took her shoulders in his big hands and held tightly. "Take her and Noah and the horses back to the ranch," he said to Temple. The prospector nodded with gravity. Jake had come up to see, remaining back some on his horse. Gently, Landry unfolded the girl's arms from her father's head and brought her to her feet. "You must go with Billy now. I'm going to finish it with Morton," he said simply.

As Landry and Jake Withers closed in, Morton whipped the mules, cursing them to greater speed. But the soft desert surface and the weight of gold made them more resistant and balky. The two men could hear the animals hawing and squealing. From his horse, one hand free, Morton flung a rifle shot toward them. But with the distance and the erratic movement, accuracy was impossible; the slug hummed harmlessly overhead. Determinedly, without breaking their beat, the two trotted their animals, galloping them when they reached some hardpan.

Leaving the flats and moving up an alluvial fan, Morton reached the base of the mesa, the beginnings of the central desert plateau that had been the harrowing setting for all of them in the past days. But Morton had no intentions of entering that hell, knowing that he could not outrun his pursuers. Instead, he forced the pack train into a cut—a round cul-de-sac where the mules milled and slowed and finally quit. Then, on his feet, he led the gray with Seth tied on to a narrow ramplike shelf and forced the horse upward. They climbed swiftly, Morton taking long spiderlike steps, the horse lathering with effort as it tossed its head, its eyes bulging with uncertainty. Seth hung onto the saddle horn and gazed hopefully back at the two riders who came steadily on. Sweat rivered down Morton's face and neck, soaking his shirt so that it muddied in the caked dust. He cursed the animal, jerked the reins, sending the gray jockeying ahead, almost slipping once on a section of slick rock. The hooves clacked and scrunched until the horse found its balance, snorting in protest. A gasp of horror escaped the stricken boy. Morton went behind the gray and slapped its rump, forcing the reluctant creature beyond the cut where the mules stood waiting.

Purposely, he left Seth in full view. He had a good command of the flats and could see the riders still coming. He crouched, checked his rifle and readied himself. There was no way the two could storm his little citadel, he knew, except to come up the rocky ramp to the shelf. In front of him, below the promontory, the perpendicular wall dropped to a volcanic pit, an ancient fumarole some eighty to a hundred feet below.

Spotting Seth placed prominently where Morton had topped the rise, Landry signaled Withers to join him. He left the buckskin and dove into the skimpy brush next to the first outer covering of rocks. Seeing the maneuver, Morton sent a shot, high again, strewing the earth beyond Landry. They were not within effective range yet. Landry saw that Jake Withers, although cowering behind a large tooth of rock, had not released his mount. "Let it go," he snapped.

Jake Withers shook his head slowly, like a bear might, warding off a swarm of bees. "No," he said softly. "No," he said louder. "No," he roared defiantly. Landry twisted around on his back to see if the man had lost his senses. "No," said Jake firmly. "My wife, she deserts me. My brother, he leaves me. And you can't find the mine."

"What the hell you saying?"

"We may be partners still, but we ain't partners enough for me to risk my life. Not against the likes of Morton. I don't owe that much to anybody."

"Didn't say you had to," Landry answered with calculating judgment. "But seems to me you had some responsibility in his escape."

"It don't matter. Right now the only thing certain is my ranch. It's the only thing I got left." Jake eased his hand to his sidearm and backed away. Landry didn't flex a muscle as the rancher mounted his horse and kicked it into a breaking run back toward the ranch.

Above, Morton watched with great pleasure, his thick lips parting. For an instant he was tempted to try and drop the rider, like a hunter might try a chance shot on a faraway buck or a high honker. But watching Landry abandoned and left on his own was more than enough gratification.

Alone, Landry broke closer to a low barrier. Morton stood up and discharged a slug, ducked, stood up and cat-footed to his right past the horse and punched a shot from another angle. Both bullets slivered rock and twanged away, close, but with no danger to Landry, who crawled ahead on one hand and his knees, the rifle held aloft in his right hand. Landry could see Seth on the gray in full view where the cliff topped. Then he caught sight of Morton stepping back and taking cover in front of the boy, making it impossible to return a shot. So Landry continued advancing. He saw Morton bob up looking for him, the face reflecting sunlight, the body shielded between two rocky wedges, roughly in front of Seth's thigh as the horse kept shifting. Landry wondered if Seth would think of drumming the horse away, but Morton had probably tethered it somehow.

"Hear me, Landry." The outlaw's voice floated clear and strong in the morning quiet. Landry pressed flat, not wanting to reveal his whereabouts, his one advantage over Morton, who needed to locate him. Landry took his time. The red-hot sun rose up over the mesa. Landry felt the trickles of sweat beginning. Soon the air would be furnace dry. He could feel it in his mouth and throat. But Morton had to initiate the first move. Now it would be a waiting game.

Morton's horse whinnied, and Landry's buckskin answered it. Morton broke the silence at last. "Damn it, Landry. Hear me. We've played our game long enough. The boy here, he ain't for long unless you come out." The click of a revolver cocking, played ominously across the corrugated mesa. "You come out and I'll let the boy go. You or the boy, Landry. No other choice." Morton eyed the broken rocks below him, trying desperately to find his hated adversary. "You got one minute, Landry. One minute."

From his concealed position, Landry raised himself. He could barely see the top of Morton's hat, rotating as the outlaw looked about, knowing the marshal's proximity, but having to locate his exact position to ensure deadly perfection when he fired. "Less than than one minute, Landry. Stand up slow. I'll let the boy go. You got my word. Just you and me, at last. You and me can finish our differences here."

A heaviness of primal gloom filled Landry. His bone-tiredness, the unabating tension of the eternal days in the desert, had drained him to near collapse. And now it had come down to this, the boy in mortal danger, and Morton in command.

With cold resolve Landry decided he had no alternative, he had to chance Seth's life in one desperate effort. Once he exposed himself, the moment he stood up, Morton would gun him down, and probably do in Seth afterward. Therefore, he would pretend surrender, he decided. As he rose, he would shout for Seth to duck over the horse, to offer the smallest target possible. In the same instant he would flip up the rifle and lever as fast and as accurately as he could. He would be vulnerable, naked to Morton's firepower. But it was his only chance.

Above him Morton called, his voice gloating. "Now, Landry. Now." The outlaw rose slightly, his rifle up, readied, his attention on where Landry might come out. Behind him Seth worked furiously on a saddle string, loosening it. The boy heard Morton say under his breath, "I've got you, Landry. At last, I've got you."

Landry took a deep breath and prepared to bound up, hoping for an element of surprise, that Morton would not realize how close he had gotten. He would come up and step to the left as he yelled to Seth and as he blasted away. Morton, a right-hander, would tend to shoot to his left or over Landry's right shoulder. If the outlaw missed, Landry would have an extra instant.

As Landry sprang into view, Seth sank the hatchet through the hat into the outlaw's skull with a sickening crunch. Morton pivoted mechanically around, his eyes hollow and glazed. He tried to react as Seth swung again to graze the man's forehead but instead knocked the hat loose and saw the hair, a mush of red. Frantically he heeled the horse away. Below, with Seth clear, Landry pumped shots at the broad back, aiming between the shoulder blades. The slugs rent the flesh, splattering blood as they tore inside the cavity of the man's enormous chest. Morton fell backward over the parapet, spun along the promontory, arms flailing, and went over to scream his way down. The scream was heard until the outlaw hit a stone outcrop, bounced off and plunged end over end, hitting deep within the pit, a crumpled, indistinguishable blob of what moments before had been a human form.

Landry stood transfixed, his legs spread, rifle held aloft, still pointing. He had not seen Morton's end, but he had heard the cry, and it still lingered, tingling his spine.

Seth had loosened himself by the time Landry reached him. The boy stood by the gray, vomiting, pale and shaking. He had wet himself. When he saw Landry, he broke into big tears. Landry held him, assured him, called him brave and told him that he had saved both their lives. He soaked his neckerchief from Morton's canteen and washed the boy's face. "It may help to know that you didn't kill him," he said gently. "I did. You just gave me the opportunity." Landry then peered cautiously over the parapet and saw the broken remains of Morton far below. There would be no retrieving the body for now, he knew—eventually, perhaps with a posse and special equipment in the fall.

Landry and the boy, pulling the mule train still laden with gold, rode side by side up to the porch of the ranch house. For the past miles Seth, his knuckles white, had gripped one of the pink nuggets that the marshal had given him. They passed Jake forking hay in a field. He looked up, surprised, even stopping work to gawk. But he did not leave to greet them.

Vallee burst from the house, her arms outstretched, her skirt swooping over the ground. As her brother sank from the dapple-gray, she took him in her arms and they both cried and hugged one another.

Billy waddled out behind her, on his face a cavernous grin. "How in the hell did you do it, Dirk? Frankly, I was afraid we wouldn't see either of you again. I didn't want to leave the girl here alone, but I was readying to come after you. Especially after Jake come back with his tail between his legs. Don't much respect a man who won't back another in need, especially after it was him who let Morton escape."

Smiling happily over the reunited brother and sister, Landry dismounted. "Everything got to Jake, I guess—his wife and all. But it was the boy who saved me," he told the prospector when they had moseyed out of hearing. "Seth put a hatchet in Morton's brain."

"Christ, he did?"

"Not the final blow, but enough to give me a chance to finish him."

"Dead?"

"Dead. Went over a cliff into a deep pit. His remains won't be easy to get."

Temple pulled out his pipe and began filling it. "End of an era."

"Long time in coming, but finally."

Temple pressed the tobacco level. "I'll fill you in on what happened to 'em all on the mountain and here. Lucky that only Lasko got killed."

"How's Vallee holding up?"

"Not too good, but she's strong. Her papa's body is laid out in the main bedroom. Jake Withers gave me some lumber for a coffin. Best we bury him here."

"It is. I've got to talk to her now—won't be easy, but I've got to."

"She wants to go on to Silverpoint," said Temple. "I think them two young men kind of caught her fancy. Claims she wants to nurse them. She wants to look up Withers's wife there, that way she won't be so alone in a man's world."

"I'll help her get started," said Landry, pulling out nuggets from his coat, which he had just recently transferred from the saddlebags. He handed some of them to Temple. "Here, I want you to have these. I'll keep the biggest ones for memory's sake."

"The dream ain't over," said Temple, resisting them but then accepting. "Next time you might get your bearings." He looked at his lawman friend with warmth, his face wise and serene. "Remember—you can be sure: what the sands uncover one day, they will cover the next. And what they cover, they will also uncover again—someday."

"For now, I'll be satisfied in grubstaking you. You go after it. We're partners still, remember? Besides, I've told you all I know and can remember."

With gratitude, Temple beamed. "Just might take you up on that, when I've rested a spell and after it cools a little. And you, Dirk?"

Landry looked west toward the high mountains. "I've got too much desert burned in me for now, maybe forever. I want to clean up—cut the smell of horses and dust and dried sweat. I want a long sleep in a real bed. Mark my words, Billy, my next assignment is going to be somewhere in the High Sierras. There, I can sit around an icy lake and look at lots of green meadows and snow.''

The marshal headed toward a thankful Vallee, who smiled adoringly at him.

# About the Author

Kenn Sherwood Roe, a community college instructor at Shasta College in Redding, California, has been an administrator, a rancher, park ranger, navy reservist, public relations man, and the author of several novels and more than two hundred articles and short stories. He once worked at CBS Television City, Hollywood, in production.

He and his wife, Doris, have three children and an apricot toy poodle, Andre Phillipe, who enjoys the seashore as much as does his master, Kenn.